YOU ARE LOVED

Their encounters at Games were businesslike and professional. But she sensed a watchfulness in Matthew. For what, she had no idea. Sometimes she wanted to scream at him to tell her what he wanted. Instead she kept her mouth shut. As long as he never touched her or mentioned what happened that night, she felt strong enough to maintain the thin façade that passed for professionalism.

To complicate everything, each day her love for Matthew grew stronger. The prospect of being in his arms, close to him, caused a spark of excitement to flare within her each time they met. She loved him and found him in her thoughts constantly. His remark about a love affair had been closer to the truth then he realized.

Lisa took a giant leap of faith when she made love with him. By morning light she had almost convinced herself they could make a relationship.

BOOK YOUR PLACE ON OUR WEBSITE AND MAKE THE ARABESQUE ROMANCE CONNECTION!

We've created a customized website just for our very special Arabesque readers, where you can get the inside scoop on everything that's going on with Arabesque romance novels.

When you come online, you'll have the exciting opportunity to:

- View covers of upcoming books
- Learn about our future publishing schedule (listed by publication month and author)
- Find out when your favorite authors will be visiting a city near you
- Search for and order backlist books
- Check out author bios and background information
- Send e-mail to your favorite authors
- Join us in weekly chats with authors, readers and other guests
- Get writing guidelines
- AND MUCH MORE!

Visit our website at
http://www.arabesquebooks.com

YOU ARE LOVED

Karen White-Owens

BET Publications, LLC
http://www.bet.com
http://www.arabesquebooks.com

ARABESQUE BOOKS are published by

BET Publications, LLC
c/o BET BOOKS
One BET Plaza
1900 W Place NE
Washington, D.C. 20018-1211

All Kensington Titles, Imprints, and Distributed Lines are available at special quantity discounts for bulk purchases for sales promotion, premiums, fund-raising, and educational or institutional use. Special book excerpts or customized printings can also be created to fit specific needs. For details, write or phone the office of the Kensington special sales manager: Kensington Publishing Corp., 850 Third Avenue, New York, NY 10022, attn: Special Sales Department, Phone: 1-800-221-2647.

First Printing: May 2003
10 9 8 7 6 5 4 3 2 1

Printed in the United States of America

This book is dedicated to my aunt, Hythia Minefield.
Thank you for your support.

ACKNOWLEDGMENTS

Thanks to my editor, Chandra Sparks Taylor, and my critique group, Natalie Dunbar, Kimberly White, and Angela Patrick Wynn.

A special thanks to John Ray, the computer technician at Best Buy, for his quick response to my computer concerns.

One

"My badge. Where is it?" Frustrated, Lisa Daniels halted in the center of the busy hospital corridor, tearing through the dark recesses of her red Coach bag. "I can't get into the nursery without it." Good Samaritan Hospital required volunteers and hospital staff to wear photo ID. Someone bumped into her, sending the contents of her purse spilling onto the marble floor.

She resisted the urge to stomp her foot. Mentally retracing her steps, an image of her bedroom dresser flashed inside her head. "Great. That's where I left it," Lisa mumbled, scooping up her comb and lipstick from the floor.

Quickly recovering, Lisa set off with determined steps for the elevator. Her name should be included on the roster of volunteers for the nursery, she reasoned. The staff knew her and her driver's license should suffice in lieu of that AWOL piece of plastic. Lisa checked the time and picked up her pace. It was after six, time to get a move on if she planned to get to work by nine.

At the personnel-only entrance, Lisa took a deep breath, fluffed the edges of her dark shoulder-length hair, then knocked on the door. She refused to allow one misplaced badge to spoil the best part of her day. Caring for the abandoned babies fulfilled a part of that mothering instinct and brought her such joy that today wasn't going to be any different. Lisa squared her shoulders, put on a big smile, and shifted into persuasive mode.

The door opened a crack and half of a long, golden-brown face regarded her quizzically for a moment. "Yes?" he inquired in a wickedly husky voice.

"Hi. I'm Lisa Daniels. And I"—she placed her hands on her chest, speaking in an eager and persuasive voice—"volunteer in the nursery."

One toffee-colored eye slid over her petite frame. "Where's your badge?"

Her heart jolted and her pulse pounded as his deep, sexy utterance swept through her. The man's voice did wonderful things to her. No time for that, Lisa decided, pushing those sensations aside and focusing on her task.

Lisa offered her most engaging smile while her insides quivered in response to him. "I left my badge at home, but I've got my driver's license." She dug in her purse and produced her ID. "See. And if you check the volunteer roster, you'll probably find my name."

"No can do," he stated and began to close the door.

"Wait." She laid the flat part of her hand on the door, feeling panic rise within her. "This is my day to work here. Come on, give a little. Check the roster. Lisa Daniels. I'm sure you'll find my name on the list. If that doesn't work, ask one of the nurses. I've worked with all of them."

His forehead wrinkled. "Look, lady. I don't have time for this. We've got a room full of hungry babies. If you don't have a badge, you don't get in." And with that said, he shut the door.

No, he didn't. Lisa fumed, knocked a second time, harder. She sucked in her cheeks, folded her arms against her chest and waited. The door opened a crack and the harsh, demanding cries of infants poured from the nursery and practically broke her heart.

The wrinkled forehead of a moment ago morphed from bored curiosity into a frown. That one eye flashed with annoyance when he saw her. "Lady, we're busy. I told you, I can't let you in. Hospital policy. Come back when you've got a badge." She flinched away from his inconsiderate words and retreated a fraction from the cold, exacting tone of his voice.

The man started to close the door. *You're not going to close that door in my face a second time*. Lisa blocked the door with her foot and asked in a firm voice, "Is Judy here? Ellen? Rebecca? How about Sidney? They all know me and if you would take a minute to ask someone, perhaps you'd get the help you claim is needed so desperately."

That one eye narrowed to a dangerous slit. He puffed up like a balloon; ready to explode at the same time his voice took on a sharper, colder edge. If Lisa hadn't been so intent on her own goal, she would have responded to the warning. "Look woman, I don't have time for this crap. No badge." He unclipped his badge from his blue hospital gown and wiggled it under her nose. A puff of baby powder made her nose twitch, feeling the urge to sneeze. "Go away."

Again the door shut and Lisa fought the urge to kick it. "That arrogant ass." She cursed. Calm down. Get a grip. Irked by his cold, authoritarian manner, she knocked a third time, ready to kill the idiot guarding the door.

Ellen opened the door and glanced around the small, honey-gold waiting area. "Lisa?" She brushed an ash-blond lock away from her gray eyes, glanced around the small waiting area before opening the door wide. "How long have you been out here? Come on in. We're shorthanded today. If I'd known you were here, I'd have put you to work." She gave Lisa a little shove toward the locker room. "Go change. When you come back, I'll introduce you to our new volunteer. He's almost as good as you with the babies."

"Really?" That was hard to believe, if Ellen was referring to the idiot guarding the door. Her gaze focused on him, tending to an irate infant. She bit her bottom lip, fighting the urge to laugh out loud. He looked like a giant surrounded by tiny babies, nurses, and other volunteers.

"If you're talking about that jerk that refused to let me in," she jabbed a finger in his direction and rolled her eyes at his tall, broad-shouldered back, "no thank you."

"Now, now." Ellen patted Lisa's shoulder. "You know the rules. Matthew was doing what we trained him to do. Security is a priority in the nursery. Besides, can't we all get along?" she asked, tongue-placed-firmly-in-cheek.

"Cute, Ellen. Real cute," Lisa answered, before returning to her previous topic. "It really bugged me that he refused to let me in. All he had to do was ask somebody. Ask you. He acted as if he was too good to do that. What a joker," she ranted loud enough for him to hear over the demanding cries of hungry babies. "If he had listened to me, I could have been working instead of standing in the hallway twiddling my thumbs. It wouldn't have hurt him to look at the roster."

"Don't judge him too harshly. Keep an open mind," Ellen advised. "He's a good guy. After a while, you'll see that for yourself."

"Maybe," Lisa muttered doubtfully.

"Go change, Lisa."

"Okay. Okay." She raised a surrendering hand. "I'm on my way. Give me a minute."

"Hurry back. We need you today," Ellen said.

"Hurry back," the giant parroted.

Lisa stopped, turned, and scowled at him before continuing to the locker room. She shoved her purse in her locker, pulled a gown over her purple jogging suit, washed and dried her hands with antibacterial soap, and returned to the nursery.

"Before you start, let me introduce you to our newest volunteer." Ellen cupped Lisa's elbow and guided her across the room. Her voice carried a note of admiration. "He's so wonderful with the babies. It's a pleasure to watch him."

Maybe the giant had some redeeming qualities after all. Rarely did the hospital find someone to take an interest in the abandoned babies or anyone who felt comfortable enough to hold those fragile bundles of love.

Lisa followed Ellen to where the giant sat stuffed in a rocker, holding a newborn in his arms. He looked up and put a finger to his lips.

"Sh-ssh." He stood, cradled the infant against the wall of

his broad chest, placed the empty bottle on the table, and laid the sleeping baby in his crib. With a deliberately casual movement, the giant turned and faced Lisa.

Her eyes slid over him as she got her first good look at all six foot plus of male glory. His broad shoulders were covered by an ill-fitting blue gown that revealed more of his powerful build than it hid. Long runner's legs were visible under the knee-length gown. Short, dark brown hair framed a long, narrow face. Their gazes locked and she gasped. This man had the most beautiful eyes she'd ever seen, one toffee, and the other hazel. What were the chances of that? One in a million, maybe? Stunned, Lisa stood, totally captivated by the contrast.

Ellen sandwiched herself between the pair. She placed an encouraging hand on the shoulders of each volunteer and smiled broadly, first at Lisa, then the giant.

"You two are my best volunteers and I'm happy to have you. Matthew James, this is Lisa Daniels. She works in the nursery a couple of mornings a week and on Saturdays when time permits. Matthew started four days ago. His gentle manner has made him a hit with our little ones and our staff."

Matthew drew closer and the clean, male scent of him wafted under her nose. "Lisa," he greeted in a husky rumble, then reached for her hand. With the first touch of his flesh against hers, a wave of heat swept through her. Shocked, her mouth dropped open, forming a perfect "O." She stared back at him, only to find he seemed as shocked as she was. Those unique eyes widened with a stunned expression.

Okay, what just happened here? she wondered. Confused, Lisa pulled away and stared at her hand, searching for an answer to what caused her reaction.

"Matthew, right?" Lisa made a big production of considering him, nibbling on the tip of her fingernail as she strolled between the cribs, checking on a baby here and there. "Hmmm." She knew someone named Matthew. Her eyes slid over him and she turned aside, hiding a slight smile. That Matthew was a far cry from the one standing before her. "Let me think. Matthew. Matthew James. That's interesting," she mumbled more to herself. "You know, the new CEO of the company I work for is named Matthew James."

One dark eyebrow arched above Matthew's hazel eye. "Really? Who do you work for?"

"Scorpion Games Software."

A big grin spread across Matthew's face, and Lisa began to shake as a tiny bud of suspicion took shape. A dimple winked at her from his left cheek. "I just acquired that company."

No way, her mind screamed. This was just too coincidental for her taste. This must be one of those bizarre situations that happened to other people. Not to her. Not today.

"I beg your pardon," she mumbled, afraid to consider how her earlier comments might effectively destroy her career.

He folded his arms across his broad chest, eyed her with a dangerous hint of amusement, and chuckled. "You heard me. I own Scorpion Games Software."

Lisa's mouth dropped open. Amazed, she stood, her gaze darted up and down his tall frame, searching for the truth, hoping for a lie.

Could this be true? She shook her head, rejecting the idea. How many CEOs of million-dollar companies spent their free time in a nursery feeding babies?

"Ohmigosh!" Lisa's hand flew to her throat, twisting the gold chain at her neck around her finger. All the nasty cracks she'd made came back to her in a flash. A lump of misery made it impossible to swallow. "I don't believe you."

A sardonic grin spread across his face. "What you believe makes little difference to me." The outraged whine of a newborn drew their attention. "Duty calls." Matthew turned his back and picked up a crying baby. "Hey, little man. What's ailing you? It's all right. It's all right," he cooed, stopping Lisa in her tracks with a fierce gleam in his eyes. He said, "See you at the office."

How was I supposed to know he was that Matthew James? Lisa reasoned silently as she hurried through the revolving doors of the Sears Tower and marched to the bank of elevators. Who would have thought a CEO of a major company would spend his spare time feeding abandoned babies? "Who indeed?" She mumbled aloud.

Okay, I was wrong. But she was big enough to admit it. Would he admit to his share of the blame? Probably not. One thing she'd learned while working in corporate America: no one took responsibility for his or her mistakes. *So why should Matthew James be any different?* a voice in her head reasoned. Matthew James had been different from the moment she'd met him. Spending time and feeding the abandoned infants, that alone made him different.

Lisa whipped the sunglasses from her nose, stuffed them inside her purse, stepped into the elevator, and pressed the button for the twenty-eighth floor. When the doors opened, she slipped through them. Autopilot guided her through the office layout to her cubicle, while she mentally considered the problem of Matthew James.

The unmistakable aroma of fresh popped popcorn filled the corridors and caused her stomach to grumble as she strolled through the maze of cubicles. Plants, flowers, and framed photographs added distinction to the otherwise identical putty-colored cubicles and workstations. A makeshift coffee stand was next to the administrative assistant's desk. Mugs and boxes of herbal tea lined the tabletop. Lisa stopped, filled her cup with coffee, then continued to her desk.

She placed her briefcase on the corner of her desk, turned on the computer, and sank into the chair. Cupping the mug between her hands, she blew on the dark liquid while she waited for the computer's operating system to load. A few minutes later, a little mailbox icon appeared in the lower right-hand corner and she clicked on it, then groaned. "Good morning to you, too." She saluted her computer.

"Oh man," Lisa whined, frowning at her computer monitor. "Twelve e-mails and another message from Cynthia. Will that girl ever quit?" *No,* whispered the voice in her head. *Never.* Family meant the world to her friend. Each workday for the last three weeks, Cynthia had written Lisa regarding what she coined as Lisa's inexcusable absence from her parents' home.

Lisa's eyes slid across her desk and fastened on the photograph of her parents at their thirty-eighth wedding anniversary party. Biting her bottom lip, she looked away as guilt wagged its finger at her. She hadn't been to her parents' house for dinner since Jenn announced her pregnancy.

She loved her sister-in-law and wished Jenn and Eddie the best. She just wasn't ready to put on a brave face and cope with their happiness. At the same time, their marriage amplified how hollow Lisa's life felt. With a shiver of vivid recollection, she thought of how her own happiness had been snatched away in an unexpected and most painful way.

Lisa shut her eyes, gritted her teeth, and willed the anguish that rose from the pit of her belly to quiet, be still. It didn't happen. The pain felt so intense, so fresh, she felt its power choke the life out of her.

Soon, one of her brothers, probably David, would show up on her doorstep and demand to know the real deal. Why had she missed Sunday dinners with the family? She and David had always been close, and Lisa found it difficult to keep anything from him. His sharp eyes would study her for a beat and realize the truth. Once David understood the situation, he'd agree to run interference between her and the family and smooth the way so that explanation wouldn't be necessary.

Pensively, she stared at the monitor. Lisa double clicked on the e-mail icon, opened the first e-mail, and groaned. "Human Resources," she muttered and read the body of the note: Mandatory staff meeting, ten o'clock. Be there. No excuses.

Would Matthew James be there? Oh yeah. That's probably what the meeting was about. Matthew James would probably be introduced to the staff and the transition of power would be discussed.

There was still the disagreement to resolve. There was no

way they could maintain a professional relationship with this situation between them. The proper thing to do would be to take the initiative and apologize. Lisa needed to explain the situation and hope for the best. Whatever the circumstances, she must attend the meeting. There must be a way to work out their misunderstanding, if she didn't screw that up, too.

Two

Disheartened, Lisa dragged herself to the boardroom at 9:45. With a determined lift of her head and heart pounding in her chest, she entered the room and locked gazes with Matthew. He rose and started toward her. Alarmed, sweat beaded across her forehead. Someone called his name and he changed direction. Lisa let out a shaky breath and brushed away the moisture on her brow. A face-to-face confrontation was the last thing she needed.

Lisa sank into a chair at the rear of the room and settled down to watch her coworkers. Seconds later, Red Door perfume filled her nostrils as her best friend, Cynthia, slid into the chair next to her.

"Hey, hey, now," Cynthia greeted. Her head tilted to the left as she ran an appraising eye over the giant. "So, that's the new boss."

"You've got it."

Gone were the T-shirt and running shorts Matthew had worn at the hospital, replaced by an impeccable Ralph Lauren suit of corporate navy blue. Razor-sharp creases in each pants leg emphasized Matthew's long runner's legs, a pair of polished wingtips peeped from under his trousers, and a crisp crème silk shirt completed his business attire.

At total odds with his professional image, Matthew wore a midnight blue tie with Mickey Mouse's smiling face plastered in the center. This prosperous-looking executive seemed light-years from the giant she'd encountered that morning at Good Samaritan Hospital.

"What do you think of him?" Cynthia asked, searching for a clean sheet of paper in her portfolio. "Do you think our days are numbered?"

"I hope not." Lisa also ran an appreciative eye over Matthew. "The stuff I read on the Internet indicates he doesn't buy companies to dismantle them. He adds them to his conglomerate."

"We can't forget there's always corporate restructuring when a company is bought out." Cynthia smoothed her stray strands of hair into its customary ponytail. "We might get caught in the middle of it."

Noncommittal, Lisa shrugged, "It's a possibility. But I hope not."

Cynthia studied him with clear, intelligent eyes. "You run our intranet, our Web sites, plus all the in-house system stuff. I think your job is safe."

"No more than yours. You're the best game programmer on this side of the state." Lisa jabbed her thumb in Matthew's direction. "This guy would be a fool to let you go."

They watched as Lisa's ex-fiancé, Stephen Brock, approached the giant and they shook hands. Matthew's broad shoulders and superior height towered over Stephen, who suddenly looked like a ninety-five-pound weakling.

A rush of emotions hit her, and Lisa blinked repeatedly, feeling the biting edge of tears. Sometimes Stephen's presence brought back all the agonizing times between them, and she found it impossible to control her emotions.

Cynthia glanced in Lisa's direction. Worried, her forehead crinkled above clay-brown eyes as she snuggled deeper into her chair. "You okay?"

"Yeah," Lisa's voice quivered. If Cynthia knew what caused her tears, she'd be in for another lecture. "I'm fine. Just thinking. Losing a job at this point is not on my agenda." Lisa brushed away a renegade tear. "I don't plan to work for someone else for the rest of my life. This is where I want to stay until I start my own business."

Cynthia gave her a conspiratorial wink and said, "You won't. Five years from now you'll be ruling the world."

Lisa's gentle laugh rippled through the air. When she looked up, Matthew's warm gaze was on her, and something intense flared between them. Heat settled in her cheeks. "I-I-I," she stammered, "like that idea. But, I'll settle for my own piece of the American pie."

"It's coming. Until that day, let's enjoy the show. Ooh-h-h, baby," she cooed. "Now that I've got a good look at the new boss, I can safely say, he is fine. Whip me, beat me, teach me love."

A second string of laughter floated through the air. "You are ridiculous. Lower your voice, he might hear you."

Here we go again, Lisa thought. Cynthia always admired handsome men. She made no pretense about it.

Surprised, Cynthia lifted her glasses and resettled them on her nose. "Am I seeing right? One brown and one green eye?"

"You've got it."

"I've never seen that before. Sweet."

"Definitely unusual," Lisa agreed.

"You know what?" Cynthia nudged her.

"What?"

"He's still fine."

"Stop! You are so bad," Lisa said.

Cynthia's eyes sparkled with mischief behind her narrow-rimmed frames. "And speaking of fine. How's that brother of yours?"

Lisa knew exactly who Cynthia was talking about, but decided to play dumb. "Which brother? JD, Eddie, or David?"

Cynthia's face turned serious and her eyes narrowed dangerously. "You know which brother."

"You tell me."

Oh girlfriend, look at you, Lisa thought, watching the play of emotions on her friend's face. *Your feelings are so transparent. It's written all over your face, I hear it in the tone of your voice each time you mention my brother, and I see it in your body language. Brother man has really got you going.*

"David," Cynthia replied through stiff lips.

"Oh, him." Lisa cleared her throat, shifting around in her chair. "I haven't seen him for a couple of weeks." Now, it was her turn to feel uncomfortable.

Cynthia knew her better than anyone and understood the dynamics of her family. Her eyes narrowed as she watched Lisa fidget with her jewelry. "What's going on? You still haven't settled things with your family?"

She shrugged and answered a bit sheepishly. "Not really."

"Oh, Little Bit. That's why I kept e-mailing you. Don't close your family out. You're too close to them to let this situation separate you guys." Cynthia turned to Lisa, an understanding expression in her eyes.

"I know," Lisa whispered. "It's hard for me."

"You have a lot of life ahead of you. Be happy for Jennifer and let the pain come and the healing will follow. If you try to suppress them, you'll cause yourself more grief."

"I know," Lisa lied. Her sense of loss went beyond tears. "It's the Stephen thing and how everyone treats me since then that bugs me. Like I'm such a reject that they need to pet and reassure me each and every time something good happens to the people in my family. I hate that. It hurts." Her voice broke and she bit the inside of her lip to stop the flow of tears threatening to fall. "I don't know how to make it stop. It's like a big fat wave that washes over me and there's no life jacket around to save me."

"Don't let it drown you. Get a grip and think about your future. Remember, Stephen Brock is not your future, he's your past." A mischievous note entered Cynthia's voice and a glint of devilment sparkled in her eyes. "And maybe Mister Matthew James can be your future. After all, he is fine."

Lisa's head snapped back as if she'd been hit, and her voice carried a note of surprise. "Don't start," Lisa warned. Cynthia always felt it was her duty to play matchmaker.

"Oh come on. It's time you start checking out the scenery

again. Go on, jump on it." She wiggled a bit in her chair and her silky voice held a challenge that dared Lisa to prove her wrong. "That crap you called an engagement is good and dead. Move on. Live. Enjoy."

Feeling love for her dear friend, Lisa grinned and squeezed Cynthia's hand. "You are too wild for me. What makes you think the new boss is interested in me? And for that matter, why would you think I'd be interested in a man like him?"

"Well." Cynthia paused dramatically, "I've been sitting here about, mmm"—she glanced at her watch and pursed her lips—"five, maybe ten minutes, and he hasn't taken his eyes off you. You're being checked out, girlfriend."

"Stop. That's enough." Lisa felt heat burning her cheeks. "You're embarrassing me. Besides, it looks as if the meeting is about to start."

Watching John Mitchell, Cynthia muttered out of one side of her mouth, "The old man is in the house."

"Hush," Lisa chastened. "Leave Mister Mitchell alone. He's a good guy."

The room hummed with sudden tension when John Mitchell reached the podium and brought the meeting to order. "Good morning. Let's get this meeting started. As everyone already knows, I've decided to retire." His voice broke and it took several minutes for him to get control over himself. "Scorpion Games Software has been in negotiations with Games People Play for months." He waited as the hum of chatter rose then died from the hundred-odd employees. "Matthew James, creator of Tech Squad One, Star Strike, and Demon Invasion game software has added this company to his network of businesses. We signed the paperwork last week."

All eyes went to the man sitting at Mitchell's right. The giant sat quietly. His eyes stared intently on the older man, an impassive expression on his face.

"Here's a little background info on your new CEO. He has a bachelor's degree in computer science and a master's and a Ph.D. in business management. We should probably address him as Doctor James. I'll let you in on a secret: he doesn't believe in that much formality and would prefer to be called by his given name. Matthew originates from California. Join me in welcoming the new CEO of what will be known from this point on as Games People Play, Matthew James." Mitchell turned and held out his hand to the younger man.

Matthew rose, took Mitchell's hand and shook it.

"Welcome. We're delighted to have you." Mitchell pumped Matthew's hand. "Why don't you take a moment to address your staff and give them a heads-up on your plans for the future?"

Matthew stepped to the podium at the head of the table with hands thrust deep into the pockets of his trousers. His deep voice captured everyone's attention as he spoke with cool authority.

"Thank you. I've really appreciated the warm welcome I've received so far." His eyes moved across the audience and settled on Lisa. Heat crept up her neck and filled her cheeks as she remembered all the things she had said that morning. This was the third time in one day this man had made her blush.

"First, let me put your minds at ease. It's not in my plan to eliminate any jobs. This company will be the sister company to the one in California. The financial and marketing end will remain in California, while development and game packaging will stay here."

A collective sigh spread throughout the staff.

He lifted a finger, silencing the room's occupants. Matthew prowled the room like a coach giving his football team the granddaddy of pep talks before the championship game. "I believe in hard work and expect the same from my employees. Do your job, do it well, and I promise you'll be rewarded. I also believe in sharing the wealth. If you have an idea or product that could help streamline our business, come to me. I'd be proud to say that the next generation of millionaires started with me.

"My door is always open. If you feel a little shy about stopping by, I'm going to set up an intranet chat room exclusively for employees to talk to me. You'll have more than one way to contact me. Well, enough about the future. It's time to concentrate on the present. Again, thank you for welcoming me." He stepped away and Mitchell concluded the meeting.

Cynthia nudged Lisa in the side. "Come on. It's time to meet Mr. Fine."

"Stop!" Lisa rolled her eyes and swatted a hand at Cynthia. "If you don't stop, I'm not going to be able to keep a straight face when I meet our new boss."

Pfff! Cynthia dismissed with a wave of her hand.

Matthew stood at the door, talking to the staff as they filed out of the boardroom. Accepting the inevitable, Lisa waited in line to add her words of welcome. When her turn came she extended her hand and he enfolded it in both of his. For the second time, a tingling sensation shot through her system.

"Welcome aboard," she muttered, confused by her feelings. *Boy, I wish he'd let go of my hand,* she thought. *I can't concentrate when he's close.*

"Thank you. I wondered if you would come over," Matthew answered in the husky voice that touched everything in her.

"Why wouldn't I?" She covered her reaction with false bravery. "I want to wish my new boss every success."

His brows rose high above his eyes. "Every success?'

"Of course," she answered, absently tugging at her necklace.

"That didn't seem to be the case the other day," he reminded, releasing her hand. "You acted as if you wanted me dead."

"Not quite," Lisa admitted, then realized her mistake. Embarrassed, she lowered her lashes and gathered her thoughts. "I'm sorry. I wasn't thinking. There is something I need to discuss with you." Her eyes darted to the left then the right, relieved to find most of her coworkers were gone from the room. *Good. Nobody will hear me.* "I know this isn't the best time, but I'd like to talk privately with you. It'll only take a moment."

Lisa took a step closer as her belly cramped. She opened her mouth to apologize, but shut it when the words stuck in her throat. To cover her attack of nerves she moistened her lips with the tip of her tongue, and brushed away a bit of moisture forming across her forehead. "I want to clear up our earlier misunderstanding. I don't want you to believe I make a habit of being rude." Matthew's different-colored eyes stared at her, sending her skittish heart into a gallop.

"Excuse me, Mr. James." Georgia stepped between them, shot Lisa a quick glance, then studied Matthew before saying, "I have a long-distance call from Jacob Summers on hold."

"Thanks, Georgia. Tell him I'll be right there." Matthew turned back to Lisa. "Let's finish this another time."

"Ohh, I-I-I," she stammered.

He turned away and tossed over his shoulder, "Next time."

"How about tomorrow? Can we meet for a few minutes?" Lisa touched his arm. The muscles hardened beneath her hand and she jerked away. Matthew rubbed his arm where her hand had been. "I'd really like to clear things up as soon as possible."

"It'll keep." A slightly puzzled expression was in his eyes.

An awkward silence followed. Suddenly, Lisa felt anxious to escape his disturbing presence. Each time they touched she felt wild sensations that confused and frightened her. Nodding silently, Lisa fought to steady her rapidly beating heart.

She slipped out of the boardroom without another word. Her opportunity to charm and dazzle the boss had slipped away with his secretary's arrival. Plus, Matthew's lackluster interest in what she had to say made the situation more difficult. Today had been one from hell, filled with mistakes and problems, but well within her ability to repair. If, and that was a big if, Matthew gave her a chance to explain.

She snatched one additional glance in his direction. Matthew sure cleaned up well. No one would have guessed that he was the owner of a major player in the software industry. His business attire created quite a different character from the giant she had met at Good Samaritan Hospital.

Heading for the stairwell, Lisa's head swirled with the information she'd just received. When she had stepped into the boardroom, her plan was perfectly arranged in her head: smooth over the hospital incident with Matthew. At least, that was the plan. Unfortunately, that idea went bust. Now, she was no closer to her goal than she'd been when she'd strolled into the boardroom.

At the twenty-eighth floor, she pushed open the door and hurried to her desk. Cynthia's voice carried over the row of cubicles and her earlier uncensored comment about Matthew took center stage in Lisa's mind. "Whip me, beat me, teach me love" was so outrageous, only Cynthia could get away with it. Her friend was quite a character, but Lisa's greatest supporter.

And those comments brought her back to her own reaction to Matthew. The rush of sensations worried her each time she and the giant got close. She couldn't be attracted to him, could she?

No. She had no plans to get involved with another employee of the company. Certainly not the boss. None whatsoever. Her breakup with Stephen had been quite public and embarrassing. No. She refused to put herself in the same situation. She'd learned her lesson.

Was Matthew the type of person to use his position as her boss to score points? If Stephen had the chance, he would, and had in the past. Her instincts told her a different story. His speech hinted at a fair and equitable man. Unless he showed her a different side of himself, she planned to hold out for a quick and easy resolution to their misunderstanding.

Still, she needed to apologize to Matthew at the first opportunity. Once that was done, she'd steer clear of the great man at work and at Good Samaritan Hospital.

Three

The aroma of freshly brewed coffee penetrated the room as the last drops filled the pot. Jacob Summers stuck his head around the door after a quick rap, spied Matthew, and asked, "Are you ready for me?"

"Man, where've you been?" From the bar, Matthew glanced at his watch, then waved the other man into the office. "It's after five. I expected you around three."

Strolling into the room, Jacob answered, "Out chasing down leads." His brows shifted into a frown as he settled his designer sunglasses in his hair. "Unsuccessfully, I might add."

Matthew's multicolored eyes pierced the distance between them as he studied his former college roommate. He gathered his mug of freshly brewed coffee, crossed the room to the conference table, and hugged his friend. "It's good to see you, man."

Jacob was six feet tall and as skinny as a yellow pencil. The blond mane of shoulder-length hair was gone, replaced by a neat conservative cut, peppered with lighter blond highlights. His deeply tanned skin was leathery from too many hours in the hot California sun.

Matthew believed there were things about Jacob that remained comfortable and the same. Like the way his bud methodically went about solving a problem. That calm, precise attitude made him a computer genius and a sought-after private investigator.

"How's San Diego?" Matthew asked.

"Same."

"Zoe? What's up with that?" Matthew drew away, eyeing his friend.

Jacob shrugged. "She moved out a month ago. No big."

"No big?" Matthew questioned. "What about marriage? I thought you two were talking about it?"

"We were. It didn't happen for us." Jacob ran an agitated hand through his hair. "That's one of the reasons this job is perfect for me. Away from San Diego. Gives me time to clear my head."

"You sure everything is okay?" Matthew added, a touch of concern in his voice.

"Oh yeah." A sad smile came and went on Jacob's lips. "I'm just glad I didn't marry her. Think of the mess that would have created after the wedding."

"True."

"Let's get back to why I'm here. I forgot to ask while we were on the phone, but you're a businessman, so forgive me if I'm asking the obvious. While you're working on software, you do copyright it, correct?"

"Of course. But"—Matthew shrugged—"if someone steals the software before it hits the market and makes enough changes it's almost impossible to sue someone for copyright infringement. That's why we have to plug up the source."

"Fair enough. Before we proceed, I want to make sure of that. So, what's been going on with our Ms. Daniels?" Jacob asked in a deceptively calm voice while he unpacked his laptop from his black leather backpack, placed it on the conference table, and dumped his blue-jean jacket next to it. With the power cord in his hand, Jacob searched the baseboards until he found an electrical outlet and plugged in his computer. "Have you learned anything?"

Matthew let out a frustrated sigh, hunched his shoulders and said, "Not about Lisa Daniels. I hate to think she'd let herself get roped into something that could land her in jail. But,

I can't ignore the possibility." Strolling to his desk, he sank into his chair and tented his fingertips together.

Jacob watched Matthew for a beat. "Did you get any indication that she's mixed up in this?"

"I've only talked with her a couple of times. It's hard to say what she knows. But, that could be because we had that run-in at the hospital," Matthew said between sips of coffee.

"What run-in?" Jacob returned to his laptop. "How did you meet?"

"I had a run-in with her at Good Samaritan."

Jacob dropped into a black leather chair. "What was she doing there?"

"Same as me." Matthew tapped his chest and focused on the floor, hiding his face from his friend and confidante. The sparks that passed between him and Lisa had been explosive. He'd never felt anything like that before in his life. His whole system seemed to catch on fire and burn the moment their fingers met.

His buddy would tear into him if he read anything on his face. Jacob's instincts were the best and he picked up on every detail, no matter how minor. "She's a volunteer in the nursery."

"Hmmm," Jacob's eyes narrowed a fraction, then he stated in a warning tone, "Don't let it sway you. Nice people do bad things just like anyone else."

"I understand. You've made your point." Matthew dismissed with a wave of his hand. "I'm not going soft. Everyone involved in this case is going to jail. And I mean *everyone.*" An image of Lisa Daniels popped into his head. Her round face full of life, skin the color of smooth peanut butter, auburn hair, and brown eyes that sparkled with wit made it difficult to see her as a thief. For a moment his resolve weakened, then his smile turned dark and threatening. "If Ms. Lisa Daniels has any part in this, that pretty face won't save her."

Without comment, Jacob rose from his chair and headed to the bar. He removed a mug from the cupboard, blew in it, and poured a hearty quantity of Martell. "Each year white-collar crime costs companies millions of dollars. Business revenues and production are affected by it."

"I get it." Matthew raised a halting hand and added in a low, smooth voice, "I don't need you to preach to me."

"I'm not going to. My point is I see no reason to let those involved in what's going on at Games get away with a slap on the wrist. No matter who it is. You saved old man Mitchell's ass when you bought Games. The business was on the verge of going under when you took over." Returning to his chair with the mug in his hand, Jacob sipped the cognac. "Until you find out who's selling the test versions of your game software, you won't be able to pull this company out of the financial fire."

"I know." Matthew drummed his fingers on the desktop. "I know. What kind of businessman would I be if I let this go? I'm no fool. Nobody plays me. That's where you come in. We need to find out quickly what's going on at Games People Play."

"Then we're going for the gusto," Jacob quizzed, swirling the Martell in his cup. "You want me to search for the person or persons on this end and every contact. Once I've plugged your leak, it's time to go after the buyers. Right?"

"Correct." Matthew nodded, swiveled the chair toward the floor-to-ceiling window, and stared at the crowds of workers headed home for the day. "We're on the same page."

Jacob drained his mug, gave it a little shove toward the center of the table, then switched on his laptop.

"What did your research turn up?" Matthew asked.

"Mmm," Jacob answered, typing away on his laptop. "I'm trying to narrow the range of suspects."

"Have you had any luck?"

A look of frustration flashed across Jacob's face. "No. What about you? What's the skinny on Ms. Daniels?"

Matthew pursed his lips in thoughtful refrain. "Didn't find out anything."

Jacob scratched his head with the blue cap of his white pen. "Which means what?"

"I haven't learned anything more about Lisa than I knew before I came to the company. She keeps her business real low key."

Jacob pointed the pen at Matthew. "Remedy that."

"What do you mean?"

"Get to know her, man. Take her to lunch, talk about business, then slip in some personal stuff. Find out what's going on in her head." Jacob tapped the pen's cap against the conference table.

Matthew rubbed a finger back and forth across his chin, "That's not going to be easy. She's no fool."

"I didn't say she was. But she's one of my top suspects."

"That's another question I have. Why Lisa? What makes her such a strong candidate?"

"She has the security clearance and opportunity. But I haven't found a motive or been able to trace any money. If she's behind this, the woman is very clever."

"She is clever," Matthew confirmed. "But not in the way you're thinking."

"We'll see. That's why you and I have to either eliminate her from the mix or move her up a notch on the list of suspects."

"Maybe you're right." Matthew stepped over to his desk, opened his Franklin Planner, and jotted down some notes. "I'll send her an e-mail."

"No." Jacob shook his head and added in a voice that was crisp and clear. "Don't do that. Drop by her office one day. Surprise her."

Matthew shoved his hands inside his trouser pockets while considering Jacob's suggestion. "I think I will. That way she won't have an opportunity to hide anything. Or put on her game face. I'll show up at her desk one afternoon and try to get her talking."

"Now your brain's working." Jacob's voice held a note of

approval. "So stop by her office and have her show you some of the security stuff."

"What are you going to do in the meantime?"

"Check the employee files." Jacob guided the mouse over the conference room table, double clicked on an icon, leaned closer to the table, and opened a file on his laptop. "I'm looking for anyone who seems to be living beyond their means or has made a substantial upward change in their lifestyle. Bought a home well beyond what they can afford, without some valid reason for it. That's the type of employees the buyer targets." He reached for his jacket, pulled an energy bar from the pocket, tore off the wrapper, and bit into it. "Someone who can be manipulated by the promise of large sums of easy money. Once I'm done with that I want to surf through the office e-mails. See if I can pick up a trail. Some small connection that links someone here to a buyer."

"Sounds like you're on the right track."

"Hope so. But about Ms. Daniels," Jacob said, "remember we need to either eliminate her as a suspect or find out where her loyalties stand."

That glimpse of sadness Lisa wasn't able to hide tore at Matthew's heart, and for a moment he hesitated about continuing the investigation. Matthew didn't add that he wanted to know more and find out why the sadness in her eyes never faded. Until Lisa Daniels was removed from the list of suspects, he couldn't let any feelings develop between them.

Frowning, Matthew ran a finger back and forth across his chin. "What if we're wrong and she's not involved in any way? She'll be upset."

"But Games People Play can't afford to worry about her feelings. With time, Ms. Daniels will get over it. She's a professional. She'll understand." Tilting his chair on its back legs, a speculative gleam entered Jacob's gray eyes. "You're not going sweet on her, are you?"

"No can do. This is about my business." Matthew stopped

his pacing, shoved his hands deep into his pockets, and said, "But I do like her and would hate to be the cause of a lot of trouble for her."

"Think of it this way. If she is involved, you can't afford to let her continue. She must be stopped ASAP." Jacob popped the final bite of the energy bar into his mouth, balled the wrapper into a knot, and tossed it on the conference room table near his empty mug. "If she's not involved, we'll eliminate her as a suspect and move on to the next candidate."

"I know you're right. I'm responsible for more than a hundred employees, and they deserve my loyalty." Matthew grimaced, remembering the feelings that swept between Lisa and him when their hands touched. He couldn't let his emotions supercede what was really important. "My company comes first. So tell me, do you have other suspects? Any leads that point to anyone else?"

Jacob tapped away on his laptop. He glanced at Matthew with a faraway gleam in his eyes. "A couple of names have cropped up. And I'm on them right now."

"Who are they?"

"Dale Smith had a super grudge against John Mitchell. Mitchell demoted him from manager to little more than a clerk."

"Strong motive. What did Smith do to get demoted?"

"Screwed up a major project that cost the company millions. But he's not the only one. Mitchell made a lot of enemies during his tenure. I have to find all the pieces and put the puzzle together."

"I feel better about things. We have a plan."

"That we do. Let me add this. You can take your investigation one step further," Jacob suggested.

Matthew's heart rate tripled as he returned to his chair. "What do you mean?"

"Instead of going to her office right away, ease into that. Bring her to your office and discuss her future role at Games. Win her trust, then get close. She'll let down her guard. That's when we'll find out the details."

"Define close?"

"You know exactly what I mean. There's no harm in it. Close. Get to know her. Have a meal with the woman." Jacob pointed his pen in Matthew's direction. "Use that charm you're famous for and dazzle her. That way, if she slips up, you'll be right there."

Matthew frowned and answered in a skeptical tone, "I'm not sure about this."

"Sure you are," Jacob said. "Help me out. I need you on board with this."

Matthew ran a hand over his head and scratched the side of his face. "Your idea has merit. I'll give you that. But, I don't like to get involved with my employees."

"I didn't say marry her. Just get to know her. Find out what makes her tick. See if you can find a motive to explain why she might do a thing like this."

Matthew sat at the conference table long after Jacob returned to his hotel room. The sun went down and the moon shined through the windows. Standing, he stepped to the door and flipped on the overhead light, then strolled across the room to the bar, running a hand over his hair.

I need a drink, he thought. Unlike Jacob, he removed a tumbler from the shelf, rinsed it, opened the refrigerator door, and added enough ice cubes to cover the bottom of the glass. Martell wasn't Matthew's drink, and he shoved that particular bottle aside in favor of whiskey. He reached for the Johnny Walker Red bottle and filled the glass.

Returning to the conference table, he sank into his leather chair, leaned back, and sipped the contents of his glass. Man, it was good to see Jacob. Seven years had passed since they'd spent time together. Matthew wished it hadn't been so long and they were meeting under different circumstances. But Jacob was back and ready for action.

If anyone could figure out the truth, it was Jacob. He was a bulldog when it came to computer crimes. Matthew felt confident that his buddy would find the culprit. Then it would be up to Matthew to prosecute.

But what if it was Lisa? He shut his eyes against the rising tide of panic as he mentally coached himself. Her image, smile, and scent filled his senses. She couldn't be treated any differently from other suspects.

He smiled, remembering how Lisa refused to give up that morning at Good Samaritan. She was a feisty little thing, so determined to get into the nursery, and he wasn't going to stop her. That woman had a way about her. Already he found himself intrigued by the little he'd learned.

It might be fun to get to know Lisa better if she allowed him to get past the brick wall she kept firmly in place. If she were involved in the sale of game software, sticking close would be the perfect way to learn all of her secrets. That woman had plenty of secrets to tell. Matthew wanted to know everything.

Jacob's right, Matthew admitted silently. He'd bought Scorpion Games Software believing he had the skills and knowledge to turn it around, and under ordinary circumstances there wouldn't be a problem. But this was an extraordinary situation and he questioned whether he would come out on top.

Four

Outside Matthew's office, the warm April morning sun caressed Lisa's face. *What did he want?* she wondered, absently fingering the gold chain at her neck. Although it had been weeks since he took over the company, she hadn't been able to make her apology.

Finally, after more than a month, the window of opportunity had again swung open her way and she planned to take advantage of it. For whatever reason he'd asked her here, she intended to get her apology off her chest *today.*

Repeatedly, she had tried to talk to him. Employees, telephones, pagers—everything possible had come between her and her apology.

Georgia, Matthew's secretary, stepped through the door to his office, sped past her, stopping long enough to explain that she had to get a package down to the mailroom. "Knock on the door and announce yourself," she advised. "Matthew won't mind." Now that the moment had arrived, the pound of twisted flesh called her stomach quivered with anxiety. What did he want?

Lisa drew air deep into her lungs and raised her hand to tap on the door. Before she made contact with the wood surface, the door swung open and Matthew plowed into her. Surprise flashed across both their faces. A sensual current of heat coursed through Lisa as Matthew's muscular arms enfolded her.

"Oops. Sorry about that." His husky tone danced along her

sensitive skin and goose bumps began to form. "Are you all right?"

"I'm fine," she answered in a breathless whisper.

"Did you see Georgia?" He glanced over her head. "I need to speak with her before our meeting."

Stepping from his imprisoning hands, Lisa answered, "Georgia was headed to the mailroom when I got here. She had a package under her arm."

"Good, that's what I needed to know. Now that that's settled, why don't you come in?" Matthew held open his office door, took her arm with gentle authority, and ushered her inside.

"This is one time I didn't watch my step." Matthew followed her into the office. "Are you sure you're all right?"

"I'm fine." Fresh brewed coffee tickled Lisa's nostrils and she sniffed appreciatively. "Is that happy I smell in here?"

"There's coffee? Is that what you call happy?"

"Yes. You've got it." She gave him a big smile. "It makes me feel good and gives me energy when I get up. It makes me happy."

His pleasant chuckle touched a cord in Lisa as she watched a dimple come and go. "I've heard it called plenty of names, but that's a new one. Come over here, Ms. Daniels. Your cup of happy awaits you."

Lisa crossed the room and checked out the enormous black lacquered conference table that seated twenty black leather chairs. A TV, VCR, and DVD audio-video equipment waited in one corner. She spied the elaborate bar. This setup rivaled any bar on Wacker Street. Bottles lined every possible space on the surface. On the Formica counter, a coffeemaker warmed her happy. Mathew poured coffee into a mug, then opened a portable refrigerator located under the bar.

"Do you take cream in your happy?" He lifted the carton from the refrigerator shelf.

"Black." Lisa retrieved the steaming cup from Matthew's

hand, careful not to let her fingers touch his. "Thanks." She drew the lush aroma into her lungs and smiled. "So, how do you like Chicago?"

"I'm still adjusting to the cooler temperatures. I'm sure you're aware of that," Matthew replied. "But, Chicago is more comfortable, stable. I was tired of California's fast pace," he explained as he cupped Lisa's elbow and guided her across the floor. As usual, his touch made her feel warm.

"I'd love to visit California. It appeals to my sense of adventure. But just for a visit." Lisa scrunched up her face, shaking her head a bit. "I'm a Chicago girl at heart. I don't think I'd like to settle anywhere else. Besides, my family is here. I don't want to be that far away from them."

"Have you always lived in Chicago?"

"All my life." Lisa stopped at the conference table.

"Let's finish our coffee before we get started." Matthew pulled out a high-backed leather chair and sank into the one opposite hers. She followed his lead, sat, sipped her coffee, and sighed with pleasure.

"There's a lot of information I'd like to go over with you—" Matthew announced, setting his empty mug on the table as the insistent ring of the telephone cut off his next words. "Excuse me." Using the tip of his foot, he gave a little shove and the chair rolled to the opposite end of the conference table and he picked up the receiver. "Yes? Tell her I'll call her back." His features hardened and a muscle jerked at his temple. "Okay." He sighed. "Put her on."

Something was up. Lisa sat as still as a stone, pretending she was invisible.

"Hello, Mother," Matthew's flat, steel-edged voice offered little warmth. "I'm fine. Thank you." There was a pause, then, "No. This isn't a good time." Another pause. "No can do! Maybe this summer you can visit for a few days. How about a long weekend in July?"

Matthew's voice changed from clear and firm to a husky,

persuasive mutter, "Wait until I'm settled. I haven't found a house yet."

Mother problems. Lisa jumped up and prowled the room. She didn't want to be accused of eavesdropping. From the beige, brown, and blue decorated room to the walls peppered with degrees, awards, and trophies, Matthew's personality was stamped all over this room. He had made good use of his short time in Chicago.

The back of a framed picture caught her eye. She glanced at him, saw that he was occupied, and stepped around his desk to take a look at the photo. Perhaps this was a girlfriend or wife?

"Nice." She picked up the frame and took a closer look, stroking the wood grain. Bright, multicolored eyes with a hint of wonder and devilment gazed back at her from the picture frame. A pair of handsome adults framed Matthew. His parents, perhaps?

"Those are my parents." The man in question's velvet-edged voice intruded into her thoughts.

Caught, Lisa jumped, whirled around, and faced him. "Oh-h. You scared the heck out of me." She shrugged. "You move around like a cat. Why don't you make some noise, clear your throat, announce yourself? Don't creep up on people that way."

"Sorry," he said without an ounce of remorse. He removed the frame from her hands and stood somber, examining the three faces in the photo. "I'll remember that next time. This is my favorite picture of the three of us. It was taken just before my dad died."

"I'm sorry," Lisa said.

Matthew shrugged and gave her a sad little smile. "You know, I still miss him after all these years."

Unsure what he wanted her to say, Lisa switched topics. "Your mother looks familiar. Does she live in Chicago?"

He chuckled. "She should look familiar. You've probably seen her on TV."

"TV?"

"Yeah. Mother does Fabulous You commercials."

"Your mother works for Fabulous You Cosmetics?" Lisa took a closer look at the dark-haired woman in the photo.

"No. My mother owns the company. When I was a kid, she talked incessantly about starting her own business." He returned the picture to his desk. "She always wanted to offer cosmetics to women of color. Once my dad died, she got her chance and, as they say, the rest is history."

Lisa tilted her head in a curious study of him. "Wow! I'm impressed." Her admiration rang clear. "I bet you're proud of her."

"Mmm." His brows rose but the sadness lingered in his eyes. Something about his expression made her want to throw her arms around him and hold him close. "Mother has a knack for getting what she wants." *Mother? Boy, that seemed so cold and removed. There is more to this story,* Lisa thought, watching the brooding expression dull the light in his beautiful eyes.

"Sorry for the interruption." Matthew shrugged and steered her back to the conference table. "Come on. Let's get back to Games People Play and your role as network administrator." With a tilt of his head, he motioned her to take the chair across from him.

"Before we do, I'd like to talk about the day we met at Good Samaritan," Lisa half-pleaded, half-asked. Uneasiness settled into her stomach and it began to cramp. Perched on the edge of the table, Matthew stretched his long legs in front of him and waited.

Her body tensed and she fingered the necklace at her neck. This was a delicate matter. No way would she tell him that she believed he behaved like an idiot that morning. If she told him that, her apology and her job would be gone.

"Well," Lisa stopped, cleared her throat and placed her hand over her heart. "I want to say I'm sorry for the way I behaved at the nursery."

"You're not the only one who needs to apologize," he answered, his words austere and to the point. "I'm sorry, as well. I came off sounding overbearing and, in plain terms, like a jerk. I'm sorry."

His words surprised her. He had the upper hand and she'd expected him to use it to his advantage, but he hadn't. Lisa examined his features for some hidden agenda and found sincere regret.

"Matthew, you need to know that I have a bit of a temper, and your refusal to listen to me sent me over the edge. Sorry." She drew her hand across her forehead in a mock display of relief and sank into the deep, leather cushions. "Finally, that's done."

"You've got a point. I felt that I had a duty to make sure those babies were safe, and Ellen had warned me to watch out for people masquerading as hospital staff." He sat, tented his fingers, and said, "I'm sorry. That's not the way I want my employees to see me. Now," Matthew let out an audible sigh of relief, "enough said on that topic. We're done with apologies."

"Yes, sir." Her cramps subsided and she studied Matthew with new eyes. That was a lot easier than she expected. Maybe there was a chance that they could work together.

"Good." Matthew turned serious. "Now, let's get back to Games. Can you give me the details of what you do here?" He opened his portfolio and removed a gold Cross pen from his jacket pocket. "Tell me about your background, education. The types of things you've done since you came to the company. Where do you see yourself going? Speak now or forever hold your peace." His open smile defused the heat from his rapid-fire interrogation.

Dazzled, Lisa almost drooled. That smile was a knockout. *Come on girlfriend, get your brain in gear.*

"I'll start with my education. I've chipped away at about twenty credits toward my MBA at Loyola University." She played with the gold chain at her throat. "I've been with this company since I finished my undergrad degree and that's about three years ago. Given a choice, I'd like to try my hand at creating some video game software."

"And your job here?" he asked between sips of coffee. She watched his fingers, tapered and long, hug the mug. "Tell me more about your duties as system administrator."

"I handle our intranet's postings, applications, and all material related to new hires. Update the Web pages," she explained, restlessly stroking the cool, smooth arm of the leather chair. "I assign access codes to the company's employees, set up passwords, and change the level of privileges and/or delete them when they get promoted, demoted, or leave the company."

Lisa watched Matthew's expressions as she spoke. He sat very still, his eyes narrowed, with a faraway expression. It reminded her of a computer processing information. Every word moved through his brain for systemic analysis.

"Let's talk about that for a minute," he suggested, leaning back in his chair, relaxed and in charge. "How do you choose passwords? Where do you keep them?"

"Passwords and the choice of them are not my responsibility. End users do that. I provide the access codes and set up the computer to prompt the user to create new passwords four times a year. The system gives them a prompt and at that point they change it. Then the system sends me a message with that new password. I enter it into my computer master file and destroy any paper copies if any are available."

"How are they destroyed?"

"Shredded. That's done once I've completed the access code process."

"Who else has access to this info?"

Lisa explained, "I have an assistant who I give permission to enter info on a shadow file when I'm out of the office or on vacation."

"Does it show the current user's info?"

"No." She shook her head decisively. "It's a shadow file that creates new records. That's all. None of the other users are available. I realize how important this information is to the company and I take the proper precautions."

"It sounds as if you do." He nodded and leaned back in his chair. "That's good to know because security is an important issue in any business and specifically this one."

Confused by the number and variety of questions Matthew had thrown at her, Lisa pursed her lips. What was going on? Why had he asked her so many questions about passwords? She'd never had any problems before. Did his questions stem from concern about the way she did her job? Well, she knew a way to put an end to his questions.

She rubbed the palms of her hands across her skirt. "I've got an idea. You haven't received an access code yet." A thoughtful smile curved her mouth. "Why don't we take a walk down to my office and I'll show you how things are done. Then you can see it for yourself."

Matthew's lip formed an expressionless line. "That's not necessary. I get it."

"Good."

"I'm sure you're curious about why I asked so many questions. In a word, security." He tapped the tip of his pen on the table and added matter-of-factly, "I want to make sure that we have the highest level of security in place. The last thing I want is for this company to become breached by a good hacker."

"That shouldn't be a problem." Lisa brushed away his concerns with a flip of her hand. "Anything is possible. I can't deny that. But I take every precaution."

"I appreciate your candor. It's imperative that our software be protected until it goes into production."

"I understand. Feel free to stop by my office anytime for a demonstration on how I do things."

"Good. One of the reasons I called you in was to discuss additional security measures and your part in implementing them." He swung out of his chair and headed to his desk. "For the next couple of months I'd like to meet with you on a regular basis to discuss alternative security measures." Matthew opened his Franklin Planner and asked, "What day next week will work for you?"

Lisa swallowed hard and answered, "Wednesday."

Lisa left Matthew's office in a state of confusion. *What's up with that?* she wondered, stopping at the administrative assistant's desk to pick up her messages. Entering her cubicle, she slipped into her chair and stared at her monitor, unseeingly. Computer security was a big issue and she knew how important her job was to the company. Matthew seemed almost anal about the hows and whys of the access code process.

She understood Matthew was new to the company and needed to know how everything worked. That she could see. But she felt as if she'd just survived a prosecutor's interrogation, remembering how his eyes glittered when she was describing her job. He turned over every stone, questioned every aspect. Freaky, that's what it was. Downright freaky.

Twirling a pencil between her fingers, Lisa considered the motivation behind so many questions. She hoped there wasn't anything wrong with the way she did her job. She didn't want to stir up any trouble because she wanted to stay at the company until she felt confident about venturing out on her own.

No one had questioned her about access codes the way he had. She sensed there was more to this story than Matthew wanted to tell her.

From now on, she planned to be extra careful about her job. No mistakes. Every part of her work would be checked and rechecked. Hopefully that would keep him out of her office and let her do her job the best way she knew how.

There was one additional problem to consider. The man's personality made her hackles rise. He was the boss and she couldn't get around that. After their dispute at the hospital, the best she could come up with was to keep him informed of her work and ask if he had any suggestions.

She must remain cool in his presence. That way he'd learn to respect her skills and talent. Treat her like the professional she was. *It will be fine,* she promised herself silently, trying to abate her growing uneasiness.

Five

Matthew emerged from the stairwell to the blazing morning sunlight. The mixed aromas of popcorn, toasted bread, and coffee hung overhead like clouds. Blinking repeatedly, he made his way through the maze to Lisa Daniels's cubicle. A check of the time told him it was a little after eight. He should be back in his office no later than nine.

Anticipation soared within him as he neared Lisa's cubicle. At their last meeting, Jacob had suggested Matthew get to know Lisa, try to determine a motive for the computer theft. That was his professional reason for this visit. On a personal level, he liked the idea of spending a little quality time with her in close quarters.

Lisa stealing from Games was hard to swallow. But the businessman in him refused to ignore the fact that her position as network administrator made her a prime suspect. While he searched for the real thief, it wouldn't hurt to learn more about this intriguing and sometimes very maddening woman. One thing he knew for certain, somehow the thief was taking extra care to make sure that all paths led to Lisa.

Lips curved into a smile, Matthew stood at the opening of Lisa's cubicle and said, "I'm taking you up on your offer." Surprised, his lips snapped into a straight line and he took a step back.

Stephen Brock. What in the hell was he doing here? He fumed silently, feeling the combination of disappointment and suspicion rise to the surface.

He glanced at Lisa, then Stephen, and back again. Had they been arguing? The tension was thick in her little cubicle. It almost suffocated him.

Lisa's eyes widened in alarm, then her lids slid down over her eyes to shield her expression. With a quick gesture she flipped a blue folder shut, opened her desk drawer, and slipped the folder inside. Matthew's hard, burning gaze traveled over her face, searching for an explanation.

Matthew's gaze bored into Stephen, noting the trace of red at the collar of the other man's shirt before he stood and stepped away from the desk. Satisfaction bloomed inside Matthew. He wanted Stephen to feel uncomfortable.

"Sorry." Heavy with sarcasm, Matthew drawled, "I didn't realize you were in a meeting."

"How you doing, Matt?" Stephen extended a hand.

Taking his hand in a firm grip, Matthew proceeded to pump it unmercifully. "Fine, thank you." *I'm fine all right,* he thought, *as soon as I get rid of you, I'll be just fine.*

"There's no meeting. Stephen's on his way out. You said something about my offer. What can I do for you?" Lisa tried to smile, but failed. "What offer?"

Annoyed, Matthew's lips tightened into a frown. Had Stephen said something to upset her?

"Did I catch you at a bad time?" Mathew asked, folding his arms across his chest. "I can come back another day."

"No. No. Not at all," she answered firmly, moving items around to make a clean place for him. "What do you need?"

Well, that was a loaded question if he'd ever heard one, but Matthew put the provocative request aside. "At our first meeting, you offered to show me the process for creating new users' access codes and passwords. I thought about it and decided I wanted the nickel tour."

"Sure." She patted the chair next to her desk. "Why don't you come sit over here."

Stephen cleared his throat and slapped Matthew on the back. "I'm done here. It's time I get back to my office. Matt . . ."

He spun on his heels to face Brock as the edge of anger and distrust hardened his features. "It's Matthew."

Caught off guard, Stephen's eyes opened wide. "Sorry. Didn't mean to offend, Matthew. We really haven't had a chance to talk. Get to know each other. I thought we could do so over a round of golf."

"No can do." He shrugged. "Thanks, but I have my hands full with Games. Once the company gets into a normal routine we can set a date." *And I can learn what's going on inside your head.* "Maybe in a month or so."

"Sure. Sure. No problem. I'll check again in a few weeks." Brock turned to Lisa. "Talk to you soon."

"Have a good day," she answered in a quiet voice that told Matthew nothing about what she felt or thought.

"Yeah. Have a good day." Matthew watched Brock stroll from the cubicle like a man full of himself.

A charged silence followed Brock's departure. Matthew moved into the room, sat in the empty chair next to Lisa's desk, and waited for an explanation. As he drew near her, her delicate fragrance awakened his senses and jolted his heart into a gallop.

"Let me get into the right program." She reached for the mouse.

Disappointment almost drowned him. He'd expected a different answer. "Whatever you have time to show me."

Lisa's head dipped. "All right." She moved the mouse around on the mouse pad. He chuckled, the mouse pad had a colored picture of Calvin and Hobbes on it, with the words "I'll rule the world" printed above Calvin's head. Returning his attention to the monitor, an Access table appeared. "Human Resources sends me e-mails or interdepartmental memos like this one with a list of new hires or terminations." She opened her desk drawer and handed him the memo.

Matthew glanced at it and placed it on her desk. "It'll have the hiring date and any other pertinent info. Once the new hire's employment is confirmed by the department, I add the person to the system and send the new hire a welcome package that explains how to log on the first time and his or her access code."

Matthew studied the monitor as Lisa walked through a series of screens. "Wait." His hand curved around hers and guided the mouse across the mouse pad. "I want to check something." Moving closer to her, he clicked the button, opened another window, and studied it.

Acutely aware of their closeness, Matthew's hand was warm and caressing over Lisa's. The very air around them seemed electrified. Caught by her heat and tantalizing fragrance, his breath quickened as his eyes slid over her profile. Each time they met, the pull grew stronger.

A gentle cough from the doorway startled them both. Hastily, Lisa withdrew her hand and placed it in her lap. Matthew cleared his throat and slowly moved away. A woman strolled inside the cube and handed Lisa a sheet of paper. "Excuse me. Hi, Mister James."

"Hi Denise." Lisa took the sheet of paper and asked, "New hires?"

"Yes. They need all the standard access codes."

"Sure," Lisa responded, glancing at the sheet.

The distraction gave them both a moment to recover. Matthew slid away and rubbed a hand across his chin. Lisa was a temptation that he could not afford. There were too many unanswered questions.

While Lisa talked with the woman, he perused her cubicle. It was pretty bland. A half-dead plant sat on top of her file cabinet supported by a few technical manuals. The only personal items were two photos on her desk. Matthew lifted one of the frames and gazed at the figures in the photo.

"Thanks Denise," Lisa said.

"Welcome," she said over her shoulder as she left the cubicle.

Lisa tapped the edge of the frame. "That's my family."

"So, I see." He nodded, gazing intently at the photo. "This picture looks recent. Is it?"

"Last June for my parents' thirty-eighth anniversary. My brothers, sister, and I got together and threw a party for them."

"Nice. Are your parents retired?"

"Ohmigosh no." Lisa rolled her eyes. "My mother's a high school principal and Dad teaches kindergarten."

He chuckled. "That's different."

"You would have to know my parents." She gave him a wry smile, pointing at the older couple in the photo. "When we were little, Dad did all the discipline until we became teens, then my mother took over. Ma knew the skinny on teenagers and she never let us get away with anything."

Touched by the love and pride in her voice, Matthew peered at the photo a second time, then pointed at one particular face. "All of you look alike except for this one. Who is she?"

"Good eye," Lisa complimented and tapped the glass. "That's my sister-in-law, Jennifer. She's carrying the next generation of the Daniels dynasty."

"Congratulations."

"Thanks. Everyone is excited about the baby."

There was an odd note to her voice that made him examine her more closely. *Not everyone,* he thought, watching a deep sadness spread across her delicate features. "It must be nice to be close to your family."

She nodded. "Sometimes. My brothers were quite the protectors while we were growing up. Believe me, that's hard on a teenage girl trying to date. What about you? Any siblings?"

"No." He shook his head. "Just Mother and me."

"That's too bad. I admit there were days I could have sold my brood for a dime. Now, I wouldn't trade them for anything."

I like talking to you when your guard is down and you feel comfortable, Matthew thought. *It feels right, like this is where I should be.*

She beamed when she spoke of her family. It felt good to be here with her, although a part of him felt lowdown and dirty for spying on her. The good news was that the more he learned about her, the less he believed her capable of stealing.

From the entranceway someone cleared her throat. Glancing in the direction of the noise, Matthew found an older black woman standing there. "Excuse me." She stared at him as if he'd stripped butt naked in front of her.

Lisa smiled broadly at the woman. "Hi, Helen. Have you met Mister James?"

"Yeah. At the meeting."

He stood and shook her hand. "Hi Helen."

"Hello," she greeted a little shyly.

"How was your vacation?" Lisa asked, as Matthew settled to his position beside her.

"Great." Helen stepped farther into the cube as her features turned sheepish, putting a hand to her cheek. "But, I've got a problem. Maybe I've had too much vacation because I can't remember my access code or my password. Can you help me?"

"Sure." Lisa clicked on the mouse, brought up a screen, and flew her fingers across the keyboard. "I'm going to reset your password to new. Then, you can log on and change it." She opened her desk drawer, pulled out a yellow sticky pad, and wrote out her code. "Here."

Looking at the scrap of paper, Helen said, "Oh by the way, I brought you a trinket from Hawaii. I'll drop it off later today."

"That's sweet." Lisa's voice and features softened. "You didn't have to do that."

"I know that." Helen turned and started out of the cubicle, saluting Lisa with the yellow sticky. "I wanted to. Thanks, Lisa."

"No problem. Whatever you need."

As soon as Helen left, Matthew asked, "Does this go on all day?"

She opened her mouth to answer, but the phone rang. "Excuse me," she reached for the telephone and her eyes sparkled with amusement. "Hello? Okay. Okay." Lisa reached for a pen and jotted a note on a yellow notepad. "Give me an hour and I'll get back with you. Thanks. Bye." Dropping the phone in its cradle, she answered his earlier question, "Yes. This is a pretty good example of my day."

"And you deal with all of these interruptions as well as do your other work?" He waved a hand around the desk. "Right?"

"Correct."

He shook his head. A drop of admiration filled his question. "How do you keep it all together?"

"I do what I can."

"It looks as if you do a whole lot more."

"You should be here when I have Web stuff to do," Lisa explained, leaning comfortably into her chair. "Then you'd get a taste of the real deal. Passwords, access codes, that's easy."

Matthew replaced the photo, picked up the other one, and glanced from the picture to Lisa, then back again. It was a great photo. Lisa and the girl with her looked ten and eight, respectively. Each girl's arm was wrapped around the other's shoulders. Tapping the glass, he said, "I know that's you."

Surprised, her brows shot up and eyes widened. "How did you know?"

"You have a mole on the back of your left hand." He touched the same spot on her hand. An electric current of heat passed between them. Matthew drew away. His fingertips tingled where their flesh touched. Shaken, he ran a hand over his face. "So, who's this?"

"Vanessa, my baby sister," Lisa chatted. "After three boys, my parents wanted a baby girl and they were so happy when I came along. But a year and a half later Vanessa showed up on the scene stirring up all kinds of trouble."

"You mean you didn't stir up enough trouble on your own? Your parents still wanted more?"

She laughed out loud. The sound of it rippled through the air and caressed his heart. Seeing her smile so freely warmed his heart.

"I'll have you know, I was a good kid."

"Sure you were," he agreed in his most skeptical tone.

Lisa tossed a hand in the air. "Fine. Don't believe me." She pointed at an item on the monitor. "Do you want to see more?"

The clock on the computer monitor read 9:30. Pulling his chair closer, Matthew couldn't resist the temptation of being with her. "As much as you want to show me."

Matthew pushed the door open that led to the stairwell after spending a good portion of his morning in Lisa's office. *I got what I came for,* he thought, climbing the steps back to his office. *Time alone with Lisa. Well, almost alone,* he conceded. The number of interruptions made revealing conversation almost impossible. But not quite.

They had shared a few special moments. Like when he placed his hand on hers and guided the mouse. The closeness, her scent, and the heat from her body almost did him in. This wasn't the time to get involved with her. He needed to concentrate on finding the thief, then he'd see where this attraction between them led. One thing he silently promised: he wouldn't let it go until he'd learned all of her secrets.

He smiled, feeling warm as he remembered how her face beamed when she talked about her family. Judging from the photo on her desk, he acknowledged they were a good-looking and loving group.

And that led him to his present problem. Although he'd spent time with her, he was no closer to knowing and understanding what made a model employee steal.

He laughed out loud remembering how anxious he'd been to get to her. All his plans to be cautious and take things slow until after the mystery at Games was resolved went out the window the minute he saw Stephen Brock in Lisa's cubicle.

This was the third time he'd found Lisa with Stephen. Last week he'd watched them leave the building together at the end of the day. Now Matthew found him in Lisa's cubicle. The gossip flying around the office indicated they had once been engaged.

Each time he found Stephen with Lisa, no matter how innocent, his logical mind shut down. All he wanted to do was get her away from him. That really bugged him. Something was going on there. The tension in the cubicle had been strong enough for a comatose patient to feel. What had Stephen been doing?

Lisa and Brock being together added to Matthew's suspicions. And what was in that blue folder she tucked away so discreetly? There was a new wrinkle to the mystery, and Matthew planned to find out everything.

The best part of the morning had been learning about Lisa and her family. She blossomed when she talked about her siblings. He loved the photo of her as a child with her younger sister. They were cute kids.

Still, there was a part of her that she kept hidden. A part that made her eyes fill with sadness. That's the part he needed to know, wanted to know. Once he knew what caused that sadness, he hoped he could replace it with happiness.

Six

"Mister James, Good Samaritan appreciates your giving up your Saturday morning to tour our facility," the hospital administrator, Aaron Persins, gushed as he dodged an empty wheelchair being negotiated through the hallway at breakneck speed by staff from the Transportation Department. "As you can see"—he waved a hand around the hallway—"we're a full-service facility with state-of-the art equipment and a well-trained staff."

Matthew stifled the yawn that quivered on his lips as his eyes drifted discreetly downward to his wristwatch. It was 12:22 P.M., eight minutes since the last time he had checked. He'd been at the hospital since nine and he'd learned many things, but now he'd seen enough and wanted to leave.

Good Samaritan's exemplary reputation was well documented, which was why he offered the facility some of his money. He'd thoroughly investigated the hospital before he'd made his donation. Persins didn't have to beat it into his head that his donation was well spent. Matthew knew this. Above all else, he was a businessman and he never failed to check before investing.

"I thought we'd stop by the nursery," Persins explained in a nasal tone, pausing to glance at the illuminated face of his pager. He tapped a button and the light disappeared; he offered Matthew an apologetic smile. "Sorry about that. Now, I understand that's where you volunteer. I'm quite impressed.

There aren't many businessmen willing to give up their precious time as well as their money."

The elevator doors opened and Persins used his clipboard to hold the doors for Matthew. Dressed in a black suit, white shirt, and black tie, Persins looked like a penguin ready to serve dinner to his guests.

"Radiology to the Emergency Room," buzzed overhead from the paging system. Matthew rubbed his nose with his handkerchief against the strong odor of disinfectant.

Leaving the elevator, they headed down the hallway. Matthew looked down his nose at the talkative administrator when the penguin-cum-administor began his eleventh commentary of the morning. As they approached the nursery's observation window, the man's voice faded to nothingness while Matthew zeroed in on a small woman with spiked auburn hair. "Lisa," he mumbled seconds before she strolled out of sight. Matthew moved closer to the window, searching the room until he found her again, sitting in a rocking chair at the back of the room.

Engrossed in the care of the tiny bundle in her arms, Lisa failed to notice anything in her immediate surroundings, least of all him. The baby's dark hair poked from between the folds of the blue blanket as he sucked the milk from his bottle.

Lucky baby. Love oozed from her and Matthew almost drooled with envy.

She must have sensed his presence because without warning she stiffened, took her eyes from the baby, checked the room, and spotted Matthew at the observation window. For a moment, she stared straight through him, her beautiful mouth sealed in an uncompromising line. Unruffled, she lowered her head.

"Well, I'll be damned!" he muttered, miffed by her blatant slight. "That little wench snubbed me!"

Frowning, Persins asked, "I'm sorry?"

Matthew waved away the penguin's question with a flick of his wrist. He said, "Nothing."

The administrator led Matthew away from the nursery,

through the neonatal unit, pediatrics, and surgery before he deposited Matthew at the front entrance.

Persins extended his pale, white hand and winced at Matthew's grip. "Thank you for giving me and Good Samaritan an opportunity to show you our facility. I hope I've explained our operation and what your generous donation will bring to our organization. Should you have any questions"—Persins reached inside the breast pocket of his jacket, produced a business card, and handed it to Matthew—"don't hesitate to call me."

"It's been an informative visit," Matthew responded, *and certainly thorough,* he added silently.

Turning away, Aaron Persins called over his shoulder, "Enjoy your day."

Matthew planned to. Soon after the penguin walked away, he retraced his steps to the elevator. A plan rapidly took shape in his mind. Jacob said he should spend time with Lisa. Here was a perfect opportunity. He didn't intend to let this call go unanswered. Maybe this time he'd be able to slip underneath her cool exterior and find the real woman.

Selecting a spot across from the nursery employee entrance, Matthew checked the time. 12:49, he noted as he lounged against the wall. From his volunteer orientation he knew Saturday volunteers worked four-hour shifts that began each morning at nine. Lisa Daniels should step through the doors in less than fifteen minutes.

Besides, he rationalized, if Lisa represented the key to solving the problems at Games, then that's where he needed to be. Until he plugged all the leaks, he planned to stick close to her.

Old man Mitchell had let his financial problems ride far too long before selling. Still, Matthew believed the company to be viable. Otherwise he would never have bought it.

His thoughts returned to Lisa and their first business meeting. When he'd scheduled the meeting with Lisa, Matthew believed she was the one behind the problems at the company. He expected to find a slick, self-centered manipulator. Instead, he found an intelligent and caring woman. Within days, he'd reevaluated his position and found himself trying to find reasons to clear her of any connection to the thefts.

Not only did he find her attractive, but he also believed her feelings were mutual. The bonus points came when he realized how much they had in common, like volunteering in the nursery.

His pager vibrated. Matthew unclipped it from his belt and flipped through his messages until the nursery's door swung open. Looking up, a smile of satisfaction spread across his face when Lisa emerged, preoccupied with zipping her purse. She looked up, and when she saw him both brows shot up in surprise and her steps faltered. Her gaze swept past him and settled on the elevator doors, fingering the jewelry at her neck. He'd bet money she was calculating the distance from where she stood to her escape route.

The controlled expression on Lisa's face gave him a moment of hesitation. She halted outside the nursery entrance, and rearranged her features into a pleasant mask before slowly resuming her steps toward him.

Matthew pushed away from the wall and met her in the center of the corridor. He came close, looking down at her intently. "Hey. I saw you in the nursery and decided to wait."

Lisa's personal scent, mingled with White Diamonds perfume, clung to her; it reached him before she did and lured him closer. "Hello." She nodded in his direction, although she dodged eye contact and slipped the purse strap over her shoulder. A lemon-yellow T-shirt fit smoothly over the enticing curve of her breasts and into her neatly pressed jeans.

Frowning, Lisa's eyes slid over him, searching his face, reaching for an answer to why he waited for her. Matthew hid a smile. The wheels were turning in her head. She was trying hard to figure out why he had waited for her, what he wanted, and how best to get rid of him.

She asked, coolly and disapprovingly, "What brings you here on a Saturday afternoon?"

Ah-h, he thought, she had decided on the direct approach. Good for her. Unconsciously, his eyes followed the tip of her tongue as it snaked out and moistened her lips.

"I toured the hospital." Matthew looked into her upturned face and decided against offering her the details surrounding his trip to the hospital or his donation. "What about you? Are you here every weekend?" He already knew the answer to this question, but he wanted to draw her out, make her talk to him, and possibly let down her guard.

"As many as I can manage."

"What about school?" he asked.

"School is during the week," she answered in a logical, even tone. "I've got time on the weekends."

"I'm impressed." His smoky toffee and hazel gaze sparkled with admiration.

"Why? I'm not doing anything particularly special. The babies need me and I enjoy being with them. I'm sure you feel the same. Otherwise, you'd be doing something different." She turned back to the nursery as a delighted smile spread across her face.

Captivated by the transformation, a new and unexpected warmth surged through Matthew. Lisa's smile was absolutely criminal. He wanted more. Did Lisa know how beautiful she was like this? Yearning to touch her, caress her warm, silky flesh, his hands twitched and he shoved them deep inside the pockets of his trousers to prevent any possibility he'd do something embarrassing.

"Your schedule is packed with school, work, and volunteering." His lips revealed clean even teeth when he smiled down at her. "How do you make your life look so carefree?"

"It's a no-brainer," she replied. The remnants of her smile still lingered on her lips. "I'm giving up a little time at the hospital. It makes me feel good when my little ones respond to my voice and their little bodies begin to fill out and they pick up weight. It's the best reward I could ever have. It's better than chocolate."

Matthew returned his pager to its holder and stared down at this exquisite creature. *What about sex? Is it better than that? No, correction. Is it better than making love?* Matthew wondered silently. Watching the lingering suspicious expression on her face, he realized, she was not ready for that question, but there would come a day when Lisa would be ready.

Glancing at her watch, Lisa started to walk around Matthew and wave farewell. She said, "Well, I need to get going. Enjoy your day."

Not ready to let her go, he reached for her. His fingers took her arm with gentle authority. "Wait." A fusion of excitement swept through them and Matthew held on. "Where are you headed now?"

"Home."

"A hardworking woman like you needs nourishment." Matthew encouraged in a smooth but insistent tone. "Let me take you to lunch."

She frowned, then scrunched up her face. "Nah. I've got a lot to do today. Thanks, anyway."

"You sure? A meal on me," he persuaded. His fingers slid sensuously over the soft skin of Lisa's bare arm. "I don't know much about this part of Chicago. Why don't you choose a place?"

Shaking her head, Lisa looked pointedly at his hand on her arm.

I'm not letting you go that easily, he decided. "Well, if I can't buy you lunch"—his hand slid up her arm and cupped her elbow—"the least I can do is walk you to your car." With a deliberate casual movement, he turned her toward the elevator and fell into step beside her, determined to extend his time with her.

"There's no need. I'm fine."

Oh there's plenty of need, Matthew acknowledged silently, feeling his lower anatomy tighten painfully when he glanced into her enticing brown eyes. *I want to know what's in your head and the only way I'm going to do that is to stick close.*

"No can do. How would that look? You can't be too careful these days. It's only fair for a gentleman to escort a lady to her car." Matthew almost laughed out loud when he saw her lips pucker as if she'd just swallowed an ounce of vinegar. It was clear she didn't think he was gentleman.

For several minutes, they moved through the corridors in silence. Jacob's speech about getting closer to Lisa reverberated throughout his head. Time to get back to business. Over a meal he could learn more about her. "What about that lunch? You sure you won't reconsider? I don't mean to push, but I hate eating alone."

She hesitated and Matthew pounced, taking advantage of her moment of uncertainty. "I found this restaurant called Shaw's Crab House. It's wonderful." Matthew shut his eyes, mentally savoring the taste and smells of his favorite restaurant. "It'll be my treat. That way you can go home with a full stomach and do your chores."

"I-I, ahh." Lisa stammered, clearly flustered by his suggestion. She recovered, then shook her head. "I'm sorry. This is not a good day for lunch."

If he pushed too much, she'd never let down her guard. Defeated for the moment, he said, "I understand." He wanted to keep her talking and the best way seemed to be through the babies. "How long have you been volunteering?"

"With the babies, about a year. I've been volunteering at the hospital since high school. At that time I worked with the seniors. But the babies have always been my greatest love." Her eyes turned dreamy and her voice softened with warmth and love. "Mr. Persins would find me at the nursery observation window after I'd finish my shift. When they started this program, I was one of the first volunteers management recruited."

"You sure love babies, I bet you're planning to have a baseball team of your own."

Lisa's smile disappeared. Without warning, all five feet two inches of her grew before his eyes. She gathered her invisible armor and shielded herself from him. "No time for that."

What did I do? Where did she go? He studied Lisa, wondering how to get back the beautiful, vibrant woman he was speaking to moments before. She had just shut down.

"Have you settled in?" Lisa switched topics. "Found a place to live yet?"

Ohh, lady, you don't what me to get close, do you? Matthew watched the cool, professional mask fall into place.

"I've got a couple of appointments set up for next week." He grunted. "I dislike apartment living. Listening to my neighbor's music at three in the morning is not my idea of fun."

Lisa's delightful laughter filled the air. When Matthew glanced into her eyes, he saw the sadness and felt it as keenly as if it were his own pain. That sadness always seemed to be lurking below the surface of everything. What caused it? What caused such pain? He wanted to make it go away forever. The instinct to draw her into his arms and reassure her was difficult to resist but he did, barely.

They made their way through the hospital to the attached parking structure. The elevator jolted and groaned, but finally made it to the third floor. Gas fumes ran up his nose and it took him a minute to adjust his eyesight to the low lighting. The shriek of an auto alarm made him glad that he had refused to take no for an answer and insisted on escorting her to her car.

"This one's mine." She stopped next to a strawberry-red Mercury Sable and fished in her purse for her keys. "Thanks for the personal escort. I appreciate it."

"No problem." He answered in a neutral tone, fighting the disappointment that weighed him down. "No problem at all," he repeated and stepped away from the car.

"You have a good day." Lisa called, turning the key in the lock, then opening her door.

Frustrated, Matthew mumbled, "Damn!" He watched Lisa's brake lights as she slowly backed out of her parking space. He'd envisioned a completely different ending for the day. They had things to discuss and he planned to create the time.

His tour of the hospital had taken a different route from what he expected. Seeing Lisa had been an added bonus. Although what he'd hoped to accomplish hadn't happened.

Lisa was as slippery as an eel, but he refused to believe she was going to stop him. So far, he hadn't found anything to link her with the computer crimes. Lunch would have offered time to learn more about her. Hopefully, she'd reveal something that would either eliminate her from the list of suspects or catapult her to the top. Either way, he wanted to know more about her and what caused the constant glimmer of sadness in her eyes. It only went away when she spoke of the babies in the nursery.

Still thinking of Lisa, Matthew moved through the parking structure to his car. Her armor felt invincible. Each time he got the slightest bit closer, she shut him out.

Ms. Daniels, he silently warned, *you better look out. This game is far from over. And I plan to win.*

Seven

Lisa slipped through the black wrought iron gates of Chicago's Institute of Arts and scanned the cavernous lobby. Cynthia promised to meet her at noon and the gold hands on the antique clock read 12:20 P.M.

I should have known, Lisa lamented. *Cynthia complied too easily, way to easily.* Normally, she begged off such outings. And that thought now ate at Lisa. Had her friend reneged? Or found something more entertaining to do and left Lisa on her own? Lisa wanted someone to share her time with at the museum.

Waiting in the museum's large, airy lobby, she felt a light tap on her shoulder that brought a smile of relief to her lips. *Good! Cynthia made it.*

Lisa turned, expecting to find a pair of dancing brown eyes gazing back at her. Instead, her gaze collided with one toffee and one hazel eye. Stunned, her heart rate quickened while a myriad of emotions surged through her. "What are you doing here?"

"Cynthia invited me," Matthew answered in that husky tone that made her weak at the knees.

An admiring lunge of excitement gripped her as her gaze caressed his muscular torso clad in a crème silk shirt, legs encased in mud-colored denims, and feet covered by dark woven leather sandals. He looked good enough to kidnap and hold hostage for a week. Or maybe longer.

Matthew's gaze slid over her blue-jean jumper, lacy white

sleeveless camisole, and running shoes with white-lace-trimmed blue socks. His easy, sensuous smile crept into her heart and held firm.

"You look nice," he complimented, although that heat in his admiring gaze told her that she looked better than nice.

Momentarily captivated by his expression, Lisa recovered long enough to say, "Thanks."

Looking around the lobby, he purred, "Where's your friend?"

Lisa sighed; she was weary of Cynthia's game. Where indeed? "Good question. I'd like to know the answer to that one. My girl works on her own time schedule."

"If she doesn't show up, do you want to hook up and see the museum together?" He rubbed a finger across his chin. "I hate doing things like this alone. It's more fun to explore with a friend."

"I don't know. Maybe." Lisa shrugged, gnawed on her bottom lip. She didn't want to get too close to Matthew. Since the day they met, there had been a special something between them. There were feelings ready to explode into much more, if they let it. An office romance was the last thing she wanted.

Red Door perfume wafted under Lisa's nose. Cynthia draped a casual arm over Lisa's shoulders. "Hey, hey now. Sorry I'm late. I couldn't get myself together this morning."

"Hey." Matthew said.

"Oh, Matthew, I'm so glad you made it," Cynthia cooed, practically jumping up and down.

He grinned, shoving his hands inside the back pockets of his denims. "Thanks for the invite. I need some fun and games. Work is all I've done since I moved to Chicago. It feels good to take a break and let my brain rest."

Cynthia bowed her head. "My pleasure."

Lisa swung around to face her friend. *I'm going to kill you as soon as I get you alone,* her gaze promised. Cynthia laughed at the threat in Lisa's eyes.

"Matthew, excuse us. We'll be back in a minute." In a

lightning-fast motion, she grabbed Cynthia by the arm, dragging her friend to the restroom.

The second the door shut behind them, Lisa jumped on her friend. "What are you doing?"

Eyes wide and clear, Cynthia shrugged. "Doing?"

"Come on, girl. Is stupid printed across my forehead?" Lisa brushed hair from her eyes and ran a finger across her forehead. "I'm talking about Matthew. And you know it."

"Lisa, be nice." She folded Lisa's hand within both of hers and explained in her most persuasive tone. "He looked so lost and lonely when I ran into him yesterday. I felt sorry for the man. You know the museum is not my thing. But it sounds like Matthew's. So stop trippin' over the little stuff and enjoy the afternoon. Remember, I was alone until your family welcomed me into your lives."

"Yeah. But you were a kid with no parents," Lisa pointed out. "Matthew is a grown man."

"I think he needs friendship, family, a connection to someone. Please, try to understand and give the man a chance." Cynthia gave her that begging-puppy-dog expression that Lisa found hard to resist. "For me?"

Cynthia knows how to pull my heartstrings, Lisa thought, feeling herself waver. Living in foster care had made Cynthia hard and distrustful until the day she latched on to Lisa and they became best friends. Lisa's parents had been very concerned over the developing friendship between the girls who were so obviously different. Once her parents recognized Cynthia's need for a little TLC, the Daniels clan drew her into their fold and practically raised her as their own.

Lisa drew in a deep breath and said, "You should have warned me. A phone call would have been a good thing."

"No way." Cynthia dismissed her with a flip of her hand. "You'd have run like a chicken."

"I would not," Lisa denied heatedly, embarrassed by Cynthia's accurate description of her behavior.

Strolling to the mirror, Cynthia smoothed the loose tendrils that escaped her ponytail. “Tell yourself another one. But I know better. Besides, what’s the big deal? We’re all here and we’re going to have a good time.”

“I’m not sure about Matthew. I get weird vibes when I’m around him. There’s always this feeling that he has more going on behind the scenes than we’re aware of and it makes me feel uncomfortable around him.”

“Or is it something more, say, for instance, the vibes I keep picking up between you two?” Cynthia asked in that know-it-all tone that grated on Lisa’s nerves. “Could that be why you’re feeling uncomfortable?”

“I won’t deny that he’s cute. But, you’re wrong about the vibes. We both know that he’s not my kind of guy.”

“How do you know?”

Lisa’s brows rose above her troubled eyes. “I know.”

That was part of the problem, but not everything. Matthew drew her. Made her feel things that she promised she’d never feel again. The more time she spent with him, the harder it became to resist him. His smile. His sense of humor. Matthew.

Cynthia grabbed her by the arms and shook her. “Come on, loosen up and enjoy the day. You love artsy stuff. Besides, you’re always looking for someone to drag along with you. And he’s definitely someone to hang on to.” She did a saucy twist with her shoulders. “Have fun.”

“I don’t want to be here.”

“Then leave. Right now. Bye.” Cynthia sighed, placed her hands on her hips. “You’ll look like a fool.”

Lisa’s lips pursed and she rubbed a finger back and forth across her upper lip. Cynthia was right. If she left now, she would look like a fool.

“Okay, my friend. We’re going to go out there, get Matthew, and do the museum. After that, I’m going to make an excuse and go home,” Lisa wagged a finger at her friend. “If you value your life, this better not happen again. Got that?”

"Yeah. Yeah. Yeah." Cynthia dismissed Lisa's threat with a wave of her hand. "You fuss way too much."

All things considered, Lisa enjoyed her afternoon. Matthew's humorous and sometimes outrageous comments made the excursion fun and exciting. The trio strolled from one exhibit to the next, critiquing the artists and their work. They debated their preferences and expressed their opinion whenever the mood struck them.

"Wanna stop at the Andy Warhol exhibit?" Lisa asked, glancing at Cynthia then Matthew. "It'll be gone in a few weeks."

He shrugged. "Sure."

Cynthia scrunched up her face. "I guess so."

"Oh, come on." Lisa led the way up the stairs. "It'll be fun." At the top of the stairs, Lisa turned to her friends before entering the room. A frown marred her features as she looked beyond Matthew. "Where's Cynthia?"

"She said she wanted to hit the gift shop before it closed. She said to tell you she'd catch up with us."

Lisa nodded, swallowing her irritation. The skunk slipped away. Well, she planned to enjoy the rest of the afternoon, with or without Cynthia.

With his hands in his pockets, Matthew strolled around the room, inspecting each canvas. "So, this is pop art?"

"This is it." She stopped in front of a silk screen filled with red and white.

"What's that?" Matthew asked, moving closer.

Mmmm, Lisa inhaled, enjoying his unique scent. It clung to him and tickled her nerve endings.

"Yuck!" he exclaimed.

Lisa giggled. "Oh, come on. It's not that bad. I like Campbell's soup cans."

"I can't believe anyone would give up their hard-earned cash for this." His eyes sparkled with mischief and he waved a hand around the room. "It doesn't do a thing for me."

"Warhol's work is one of a kind."

His brows lifted. "It's one of a kind all right," was

Matthew's skeptical response. "And I think I'll keep my change in my pocket."

Lisa laughed softly, "Cute, Matthew. Real cute." Leaving him, she disappeared into the next room. Within seconds he appeared and stopped in front of a beautiful, gold-framed watercolor reminiscent of Cézanne's work. The painting dominated the wall. A mother, father, and small boy picnicked on a vast green landscape. The child cuddled close to his mother. Love cocooned them in its adoring embrace, captivating its audience.

"How does this hit you?" Turning to Matthew, her words died in her throat when she saw the hunger on his face.

The smug expression he wore so often was gone, replaced by a sort of yearning. Caught off guard by this side of him, Lisa watched, wondering, *what is going on in that head of yours?*

"It's beautiful." He breathed with quiet reverence.

"Attention patrons, the Chicago Institute of Art will close in fifteen minutes," the disembodied voice droned on for several seconds, gently destroying the mood between them.

Dazed, Matthew pulled his gaze away from the canvas and checked his watch. "Wow!" His eyes grew large. "We've been here all afternoon."

"That we have. Is everything okay?" She placed a hand on his arm and felt the muscle leap to life.

"It just—" He ran a hand over his face and hesitated in a way that Lisa found oddly in conflict with the smooth professional she'd seen so far. "It reminds me of a time in my life. It took me to a different place."

"Where?" Lisa asked without thinking.

Shrugging, he ignored her question and said, "It's time for us to find Cynthia and get out of Dodge." He linked his fingers with hers, glanced into her face with a smile that didn't quite reach his eyes, and led her through the museum.

For a moment, Lisa couldn't breathe. Everything came to a shrieking halt, then the world continued on its axis. His touch ignited a series of new emotions, sending her heart palpitating as they walked hand-in-hand from the room.

They split at the lobby; Matthew excused himself while Lisa went in search of Cynthia. She found her at the reception desk, flirting with a hunky-looking guard.

"Hey." Lisa walked up to the pair.

Cynthia responded, "Hey you."

Lisa stated, "We lost you."

"No, you didn't. You two didn't need me tagging along."

Lisa looked pointedly at the guard standing next to Cynthia. "Hi."

"Lisa, this is Bruno," Cynthia introduced. Her dark eyes gleamed with mischief from behind her glasses. "He's the head of security here at the museum. Lisa Daniels"—she waved a hand at her friend—"Bruno Jones."

"Nice to meet you." Bruno stepped forward with an outstretched hand.

Lisa shook it, noting his smooth, manicured fingers. *Oh Cynthia, what are you doing?* she wondered.

Matthew returned and stopped beside them. "Are you ladies ready to go?"

"Yes." Lisa nodded. "It's time."

"Bye, Bruno," Cynthia said.

He smiled slyly at her. "I'll call you."

"Do that."

Lisa stared hard at Cynthia. She knew for a fact that Cynthia loved Lisa's brother David. What was Cynthia really trying to do?

"Good." Matthew rubbed his hands together. "How about dinner?"

"No can do," Lisa answered, using Matthew's phrase.

Matthew grinned. "I see I'm rubbing off on you."

"Little bit," Lisa answered. "I should get home."

"Why?" Cynthia whined.

"Come on." Matthew added his objection. "You can't end the day without a meal."

"Yeah," Cynthia insisted. "At least have dinner before you head home."

Gazing from Cynthia to Matthew, Lisa stated, "I've got a lot to do this weekend."

"It's Saturday and you've got to eat." Ignoring her comments, he took her arm and led her through the lobby with Cynthia on the opposite side. "Besides, you'll have all day Sunday to do things."

"We'll go someplace close. Then you can head home." His tone and manner made it clear that no wasn't an answer he'd accept.

For the second time that day Lisa found herself trapped. If she refused, she'd look petty, unsociable. But if she played her cards right, Cynthia's presence might act as the buffer she needed. Or maybe her treacherous friend would again do a disappearing act.

"You don't have a date tonight, do you?" Cynthia asked with that fake innocent expression that made Lisa ready to strangle her.

"No." Cynthia knew Lisa didn't have a date. She hadn't dated in months.

"Good." She grinned like a kid on Christmas morning. "Let's go."

"What do you feel like eating?" Matthew asked.

"Chinese?" Cynthia suggested. "I know a place that has the best shrimp in lobster sauce."

The dynamic duo escorted Lisa from the museum.

"Sounds good to me." Matthew cupped each woman's arm. "Lead the way. I'll walk you ladies to your cars, then follow you to the restaurant."

I had fun today, Lisa admitted as she followed Cynthia and Matthew from the museum. It wasn't the day she had planned, but it hadn't turned into the disaster she expected.

Initially, Cynthia's matchmaking had angered Lisa, but the results had been good. First, she learned a little more about

Matthew and got a chance to explore the museum with friends. That made it worthwhile.

Lisa giggled when she remembered Matthew's first impression of Campbell's soup cans. It didn't thrill him. What had intrigued him was the painting of the family enjoying a picnic. His sense of yearning was so strong that Lisa felt like an intruder when she touched Matthew's arm.

Secrets. That man had plenty of secrets.

The dynamic duo had outmaneuvered her at every opportunity. First they maneuvered Lisa into a day at the museum, and now dinner. She felt like a lab rat trapped in an endless maze. Each way she turned, an obstacle presented itself.

All she had to do was get through the meal. Dinner, then home. That was the plan.

Eight

The trip to the restaurant happened way too fast. Lisa dreaded this encounter as she tried to readjust her thinking and prepare to spend more time in Matthew's disturbing presence. She slid into a parking space next to her friend and waited.

Cynthia was playing matchmaker. But Matthew wasn't the right person for her. Nobody was.

The person in question strolled from his BMW SUV and first opened Cynthia's door, then moved to Lisa's. With a light touch, he cupped each woman's elbow and ushered them inside Wong's Eatery. Once they were inside the restaurant, his hand fell away. Oddly, Lisa felt a keen sense of lost. A round-faced Asian gentleman led the trio into the nonsmoking section of the restaurant.

Oriental fans with white backgrounds and multicolored designs draped the walls and colorful hanging paper lanterns peppered the ceiling. As they strolled across the dining room, the faint sound of clanging pots and pans from the kitchen caught Lisa's attention and a hint of ginger and sautéed onions lingered in the air.

Japanese koi made their home in the artificial pond displayed in the center of the room. Lisa smiled at the oversize goldfish wading through the water.

The waiter paused beside a crescent-shaped booth. Its high-backed, crimson-colored wall offered privacy. Lisa started to slide across the firm, leather cushion and Cynthia touched her arm, detaining her. Confused, Lisa complied as her friend nudged her aside and slithered into the booth. She gestured for Matthew to follow, which forced Lisa to slide into the seat beside him. Cynthia's quick maneuver placed Matthew between the women.

Golden flames flickered in the crème glass-covered candleholder that sat on top of a burgundy tablecloth. It provided the booth's only lighting. Quiet cocooned them while they studied the menu and selected drinks.

Once they'd ordered, the waiter returned with a tray of appetizers. "Try this," Matthew suggested, offering a toasted bread square coated with garlic butter and sprinkled with sesame seeds. "It's called shrimp toast." The aroma of butter and garlic was heavenly. She accepted a golden wedge and bit into a pink shrimp.

"Mmm, this is excellent." Lisa munched on the toast. "I've seen shrimp toast on the menu but never been adventurous enough to try it." She popped the last bite into her mouth.

"All kinds of wonderful adventures await you, if you're willing to take the plunge." Matthew smiled, and his eyes sparkled, enticing her. Lisa stared back at him, unable to tear her gaze away. Her hand hovered over the tray and she felt herself being drawn into his dynamic presence, forgetting everything and everyone. In her head Lisa heard "come into my parlor, said the spider to the fly." *And I'm the fly,* she thought, feeling completely helpless against Matthew's pull.

Coughing loudly, Cynthia disturbed the moment and brought Lisa back to the real world. Smirking, she sipped her tea as she watched the pair. When Lisa focused on her friend, Cynthia's brows lifted suggestively.

"Here comes the next course," Matthew said in that husky, sensual voice that sent goose bumps spreading up her arms. "Let's see what other adventures await us."

Lisa massaged her temples. Her head ached with tension.

What is it about this man that makes me quiver like Jell-O? she wondered, studying Matthew.

"Chicken egg-drop soup." The waiter replaced the now empty tray with bowls of streaming soup. Lisa's mouth watered as the tantalizing aroma of chicken wafted through the air.

The small group feasted on lemon chicken, sautéed broccoli sprinkled with almonds, and shrimp lo mein. Conversation was kept to a minimum as they concentrated on their meals. Lisa felt relieved to have something other than Matthew to focus on. His sensuality disturbed her.

"So, how much of the city have you seen?" Cynthia asked between mouthfuls of lo mein.

"I've checked out a few places. A couple of jazz clubs and some of the restaurants in the downtown area."

"Is that all?" Cynthia pointed her fork at Matthew. "I'm glad we got you out today. You need the time away from the office."

"Ain't that the truth," he agreed, refolding his napkin in his lap. "I haven't had time to do anything. Games has kept me very busy."

"Transitioning is very difficult," Lisa jumped in. "In a month or two everything will smooth out and you'll be able to spend more time exploring."

"That's what I keep telling myself." Matthew pushed his near empty plate aside and sighed with satisfaction. "That was a good meal. This is a nice restaurant." He readjusted his large frame inside the cushions. "How did you find it?"

"This was where we used to celebrate at the end of the school term." Cynthia lifted her cup of jasmine tea to her lips.

"You knew each other before you came to Games?" Matthew asked.

Both women nodded and Lisa turned and grinned at her friend. "We went to high school together."

"Yeah, and Lisa's family practically adopted me."

Turning to Lisa, Matthew asked, "So you have three brothers and one sister?"

"That's right." Lisa answered proudly.

He whistled. "Large family."

"But a lot of fun," Cynthia supplied. "I love them dearly."

"Cynthia, didn't you go to the University of Michigan?"

"Actually, I went to the U my freshman year," she explained. "I came back to Chicago sophomore year and finished at Loyola University."

Lisa snapped her fingers and turned to Cynthia. "Hey. I forgot to tell you, Ma wants you to call her. David is coming home for Memorial Day."

Cynthia's animated features stilled and grew serious. "David's back?" she questioned in a soft whisper.

"He will be in another week. His letter said the third of May."

"Where's he staying?" She asked in a casual, offhand manner, yet her brown eyes glowed.

"At home."

"Thanks," she said. "I'll give Ma a call tomorrow." The teacup clattered against her saucer when Cynthia placed it back in its niche. "I love Lisa's mother," she chatted. Her nervous fingers rearranged her silverware from the left to the right then back again. "Mrs. Daniels is the most warm, nurturing person. Matthew, what about you?" Cynthia asked. "Do you have children?"

"No can do. I need to get married first."

"True. But it's not always the prerequisite," she teased.

"It is for me. There's a special woman out there for me and I plan to find her." Matthew's gaze flirted with Lisa.

Don't look at me, Lisa turned away and stared at the tabletop. Matthew was a temptation that she could not afford. *I'm not the woman for you. I'm not the woman for anyone.*

"Can you guys do me a favor?" Matthew asked.

The odd note in his voice piqued Lisa's curiosity. If she hoped to gain anything from his expression, she was wrong.

Matthew's features revealed nothing as she watched him from the corner of her eye.

"Sure," Cynthia answered.

"What's up?" Lisa questioned, hoping she hadn't said yes to something that she may not want to do. "What can we do for you?"

"I'm looking for a house. Before I talk to a realtor I want to do some investigating of my own." He folded his arms across his chest. "There are a couple of areas that people have suggested. If I give you the names can you give me the four-eleven on them?"

Relieved, Lisa sighed. *If that was all he needed, she could handle it.*

"Sure. What areas?"

"Winnetka is one," Matthew said. "And John Mitchell suggested along Lakeshore Drive. I've checked out Lakeshore Drive; all I've seen are apartment buildings. Are there any homes in that area?"

"Oh-h baby," Cynthia muttered. "Yes, there are some homes. There's some exclusive property in both of those areas. I'll tell you the truth, I'd love to live on Lakeshore Drive. It's gorgeous."

Lisa lifted a finger and said, "I suggest you do some legwork. Get out one afternoon and check around."

"I plan to. My job has had me glued to the desk since I bought Games. But I plan to take next Saturday off and do a look-see."

"I believe that's the best way to find what you're looking for," Lisa suggested, absently fingering her gold chain. "Nobody can tell you. When you see it, you'll know."

"I've got an idea," Cynthia's eyes opened wide with false innocence before she piped in.

Lisa's heart did a flip in her chest. Cynthia was up to no good and her ideas tended to get Lisa in trouble. She could see it in her face.

"What's that?" Matthew asked.

"Lisa was searching for a house last year. She knows those

areas pretty well. I think she even found a house that she liked. Why don't you two hook up and let her be your guide? That way, when you contact a realtor you would be the one in control, not them."

Lisa felt her blood pressure shoot up over two hundred. The last thing she wanted to do was be alone in Matthew's company for an afternoon.

"Lisa, I'd really appreciate it. It would really help me out."

Frazzled from Cynthia's matchmaking, Lisa bit her lip and her hands clenched into fists in her lap. *How did I get into this situation?* Lisa knew the answer. Cynthia had done it to her again. And after she specifically told her to leave things alone. She was stuck and there was no way she could get out of this without looking like a fool.

"When do you want to do this?" Lisa asked.

"This Saturday coming up. Is that okay with you?"

"Sure. It's fine," Lisa responded in a resigned voice. *Big problem,* her mind shouted.

"Great!" Matthew smiled and that dimple winked approvingly at her. "I'll pick you up at your place."

"That'll work."

"Could I repay you with dinner?"

Surprised, Lisa's heart flip-flopped in her chest. "You don't have to do that."

"I know. But I'd like to. We'll talk more about it Saturday," he said. "Noon okay with you?"

"Perfect." *Yeah, just perfect,* she thought as she mentally cut Cynthia into a bite-size morsel.

The waiter whisked away serving trays and plates, and replaced them with a plate of golden fortune cookies. A white scrap of paper winked from the corner of one of the diamond-shaped cookies. Lisa took a cookie from the tray and with the slightest pressure broke the shell. It shattered into several pieces.

Lisa read her fortune out loud. "A tall, dark stranger will change your life."

"Uh-oh, you better watch out." Matthew warned. "Tall, dark strangers could signal trouble."

"Don't worry about me. I can handle myself," she challenged. "What about your fortune? What does it say?"

"Look closer. What you believe is not always the truth," Matthew read. "This must be a mistake. I'm always right," he joked. "How could anything I believe be untrue?"

Both women groaned.

"Cynthia, what words of wisdom are you holding?" Matthew asked.

"A disturbance in your life will eventually bring you great joy," she recited wryly. "I don't like the sound of that."

Lisa picked up the check and started to calculate her part of the bill. "And with those words of wisdom, I think it's time to go."

"This is my treat." He snatched the bill from her hand. "It's nice to have a meal with other humans. Once I've taken care of the bill, I'll walk you ladies to your cars."

As Cynthia drove off, Lisa pulled her keys from the bottom of her purse and turned to her car. Matthew took the keys from her hand, unlocked her car door, and handed the keys back to her, as they dangled between his fingers.

Lisa reached for her keys but stopped halfway. Her breath caught in her throat when she saw the smoldering light in Matthew's eyes. *I can't do this,* she thought. *He isn't right for me,* She took her keys from his hand, making sure her fingers didn't touch his, and got into her car.

"Thank you," Matthew said. "I know you didn't plan to spend the day with me." Without warning his hand snaked inside her car door window and touched her cheek, stroking the soft flesh until it tingled. Leaning through the open window he lightly kissed her lips. The kiss was as soft as a summer breeze.

Moving away, he smiled. "Drive carefully," he cautioned, and jogged away. At his car, he turned, and saluted her as she sped away.

* * *

A tubular-shaped package wrapped in an array of red-and-white ribbons awaited Lisa's arrival Monday morning. *What the heck is this?* She wondered, turning the package over in her hands.

Curiosity got the best of her and she pulled the bow and ribbons along the length of the cardboard tube and off the edge. The ribbons landed in a heap on her desk. With impatient hands she tugged at the sheet inside the tube and produced a poster. A note slipped from between the ends and glided to the floor.

"Soup cans." She smiled at the reprint of Andy Warhol's Campbell soup cans. Matthew must have bought this. *Oh, how sweet.*

She picked up the note from the floor and read, "It's not my thing, but I know you admired it. Enjoy and thanks for a wonderful day. Matthew."

Lisa's soul was filled with joy. He surprised her at every turn. Each time she thought she understood him, he would do something so thoughtful Lisa had to fight the feelings that threatened to overflow.

Searching through her desk drawer, Lisa found a box of multicolored pushpins. She placed the poster on the partition above her desk and anchored it with the pin to the soft gray-padded wall.

What was she going to do about Matthew? He continued to make his presence felt whether he was with her or not. The poster offered a new tool to keep him in her thoughts, her life. Oh-h-h, the man was good. He knew how to press his advantage without uttering a single word.

She could easily fall in love with him. But there was more at stake than her feelings. Matthew's needs rated well above her own.

Lisa ticked off her options. Maintain the work façade, minimize any outside connections, and get on with life. That would be a neat trick considering she'd agreed to take him house hunting. But she had to do it! At least she hoped she could do it.

The better part of her morning was spent gazing at the poster. From the moment she'd found the gift on her desk, her mind continually returned to Matthew. His scent lingered, waltzing around her, making her head spin.

And the feelings Matthew stirred within her were becoming more and more difficult to ignore.

Nine

I can do this, Lisa reasoned Saturday morning as she stepped into a pair of olive silk trousers and zipped the matching sleeveless top. A sunflower appliqué with petals of mauve, blue, and gold decorated the right breast and added a bit of spice to her somber outfit. The flower's stem ran down the right side of the blouse and along the pant leg of her trousers.

"Nothing to it," she stated loudly, struggling to gain the degree of confidence she needed to make this day with Matthew a success. Applying the final touches to her makeup, Lisa spent an additional moment admiring her image in the mirror. She fluffed the ends of her new do. The auburn color did wonders for her skin tone and she loved the way her hair spiked around her head. A new look and a new attitude might make all the difference in her future.

On her way to the balcony to check the weather, Lisa continued her pep talk. Clear, cloudless skies meant no way out of this commitment today. *Oh well, you agreed to help Matthew. And help him, you will.*

Lisa paused for a moment, enjoying the boisterous and rambunctious play of the children in the courtyard.

Secretly, Matthew's request had surprised her. She felt flattered that he valued her opinion and wanted her along.

Cynthia's maneuvers had landed Lisa in the position of tour guide, but she planned to make the best time of the situation. Her dad always told her to seize every opportunity to learn something new and different. Today, during their tour, Lisa planned to pump Matthew for information about running a business. After all, she wanted to open her own consulting business in the future and rule the world.

The gentle chime of her doorbell penetrated the silence. Taking one final glance at the reflection in the mirror, she summoned all of her courage, squared her shoulders, and marched to the door. Remember, pleasant and professional.

"I can do this," Lisa stated again with more bravery than confidence, feeling her stomach cramp uncomfortably. Eyes shut, she sucked air deep into her lungs and let it out slowly. Opening her eyes, she planted a generic "smile" on her lips and opened the door.

Discreetly, Lisa's gaze ran from the top of his shower-damp hair along the silk shirt rolled back from the wrists, revealing muscular arms sprinkled with black hair. His fresh male scent mingled with Royal Copenhagen cologne was dangerous! No doubt about it, Matthew looked good. Real good!

Straightening from his casual position against the door frame, Matthew shoved his hands inside the pockets of his navy blue Dockers. "Hey," he greeted in the husky voice that brought goose bumps to the surface of her skin.

Ohmigosh. His smile was practically wicked and as intimate as a kiss. Rooted to her spot, Lisa's heart did a jig in her chest when she imagined what rewards hid beyond Matthew's enticing smile.

Fingering the gold chain at her neck, her hard-won composure slipped, baring her deep longing before she concealed it behind a welcoming smile. Realization, swift and true, filled her. *I can't do this.*

I'm no coward. I will do this. Smiling at male perfection, Lisa stepped back from the door and waved him inside. "Welcome. Come on in," she said.

"Thank you," he answered formally.

"Can I offer you anything before we go?"

He stepped inside the hallway, shut the door behind him, and looked around. "What've you got?"

"Mmm. Juice. Soda. I have a bottle of White Zinfandel, if that's what you'd like," Lisa offered. "Come on in. I'll give you the five-second tour."

He asked, in a low, husky tone, "Five second?" His blank stare of confusion made her giggle.

"My place is pretty small." She shrugged, grinning. "But, it suits me. I like it. It's home."

"That's all that counts."

He followed her down the hallway to her living room. Standing next to him, an unexpected ripple of excitement passed between them. *Get on with this,* she thought. Recognizing the attraction that grew stronger each day, she wished she'd had the foresight to add Cynthia to this little adventure.

Matthew moved around her living room, stopping here and there in admiration. Nothing escaped his attention: the cranberry carpet, crème leather sofa, and matching chair all received a moment of his time. A blue plastic folder sat on the glass and chrome cocktail table. *Oh, I meant to put that away before he arrived,* she thought, and headed toward the table.

Matthew beat her to it, picked it up and turned it over, running a hand over the plastic. "Homework?"

"No. Just some stuff I'm working on." She replied and removed the folder from his hands. "Can I get you anything before we take off?"

"Coke would be good. If you have it." Matthew pointed at the folder and asked, "That's not work for Games, is it? I'd hate to think you have so much work that you bring the stuff home."

"No. I'm helping a friend with a project. Now, you said Coke. I think I have a can or two." Lisa headed to a desk located against the living room wall. She opened the center drawer and placed the folder inside and shut the drawer with a final snap. "Let me check."

Moving across the room, he glanced out the balcony window, then pointed at the sliding door. "Do you sit out here?"

"Mmm, hmm." Lisa stood beside him. "In the spring and summer I like to watch the kids play in the courtyard."

Matthew stared out the window for a beat, then asked, "Noisy, isn't it?"

"It can be. But I don't mind. I love kids."

"That," he began, grinning back at her, "I've gathered." Scooting around her glass and chrome dining room table, he glanced out the door, watching the goings-on in the courtyard. "I see patio furniture. Where do you put it during the winter?"

A heat wave of emotions flared between them when Matthew's large frame shifted closer. Trembling, Lisa stepped away, putting as much distance between them as possible without drawing attention to herself. "Look to the left. I have a storage lockup attached to the balcony. I shove everything in there, lock the door, and forget about it until spring."

"Convenient."

"Yes, it is. That's what sold me on this place."

Matthew trailed her through the apartment to her kitchen. "I like your kitchen," he complimented, pulling up one of the stools, sitting down, and leaning forward on the counter. "Compact and efficient."

She grinned, removing a can of Coke from the refrigerator. The cool breeze nipped at her heated flesh. "Spoken like a man who seldom cooks. Am I right?"

"Little bit." He popped the tab on his soda. "But—" he pointed a finger in her direction "—I know how to cook."

"Oh, really? And what items can you cook?" she challenged, folding her arms across her bosom. A teasing note was in her voice, at the same time that a skeptical gleam sparkled from her brown eyes.

"I can fry chicken. Grill steaks. Prepare salads and I fix a top-notch garbage-can omelet." He sipped his soda and winked at her. "Maybe one morning I'll prepare you one."

Was that an open invitation? Surprised by his naughty suggestion, Lisa kept her mouth shut. But those images sent her pulse into palpitations. Visions of them together at his breakfast table, eating omelets and planning their day filled her head and made for a load of secret urgings she fought to keep under control.

Moving back along the hallway with the soda can in his hand, he asked, "How many bedrooms do you have?"

With her back to him, her jaw dropped. That question was a heart stopper if she ever heard one. Matthew presented one surprise after another.

"Two. And the second is the guest room. Mine has its own bathroom, which I love. Growing up with three brothers and a sister made me crave the privacy of a bathroom of my own."

"I never had that problem. Mother had her bathroom and I had mine."

Matthew gave the living room one final visual sweep before saying, "Your place is great. It suits you. I can see you living very comfortably here."

"Thanks. And I do." She tilted her head toward him. "I like comfort."

"And that's what we're going to find for me today. My own personal castle." He drained the last of the soda, placed the can on the table, fished in his pocket, and produced his keys. "Ready to go?"

"Whenever you are." Lisa answered, retrieving her purse from the sofa.

"Let's hit it." He started down the hallway. "I talked to a couple of people and they gave me a few locations to check out. In case you were wondering, I've got a full day planned for us."

"Oh, do you now?" She asked mischievously.

"Oh yeah."

Several hours later, Matthew's hand rested at Lisa's elbow as they strolled down the corridor to her apartment. The evening news theme music drifted into the hallway from under the door of one of Lisa's neighbors. The heat from where he'd placed his hand seared her skin. She felt tired, but satisfied with the progress they had made. The day had been a huge success.

"Thanks for showing me around today." Matthew's smile contained a sensuous edge. "I really appreciate it. First thing Monday, I'm going to call my realtor about that house we saw on Lakeshore Drive."

"Oh, I really like that house. Let me know how things go, okay?"

"I will." He turned her to face him, rested his hands on her shoulders, and offered for the third time, "Are you sure you don't want to do dinner? It's still early and I've had you out most of the day. It's only fair. I'd like to repay your kindness."

"No. I'm fine. There's no need," Lisa reassured him, stroking his arm. "Besides, we ate those monstrous ice cream cones. I've had enough calories for one day."

"Relax. Didn't you know we ate fat-free ice cream?" Chuckling, Matthew rubbed his hand up and down her bare arm, sending a shockwave of sensations through her while her breath caught in her throat. "Anyway, it didn't seem to hold you back. You made fast work of yours."

She enjoyed the afternoon and their sparring, and added her two cents. "It's not polite to comment on a lady's eating habits."

"Sorry." Matthew's hand tightened as he pulled her toward him, leaving bare inches between them. Lisa raised surprised eyes to his. What she saw made her insides quiver with excitement.

Matthew's kiss surprised her, gentle while stirring the spark of desire. Her eyes fluttered shut as she experienced the full impact of his dynamic possession. His lips covered hers and lingered before exploring the texture hidden between her lips, learning her taste and scent. Parting her lips, she pressed herself against him to meet his kiss.

Her own eagerness shocked her even more. It wouldn't take much to get used to this.

Matthew crushed her to him, dipped his head a second

time, and reclaimed her lips. His talented fingers danced around her neck, stroking the sensitive skin at the base of her throat. It felt so good. She wanted it to continue.

A door opened and shut, disrupting their sensual cocoon. *What am I doing?* she wondered, pushing against the solid wall of his chest. *Ohmigosh.* She dropped her arms and stepped away.

Frowning, Matthew asked, "What's wrong?"

"Nothing," Lisa explained, checking the hallway. "It's just . . . um . . . this is a high traffic area."

"True." Matthew glanced pointedly at her door and carefully phrased his next question. "Maybe we should go inside?"

"No." She shook her head, fighting the edge of hysteria and desire.

Placing a finger under her chin, he stared into her eyes and asked gently, "Why not?"

Uneasiness settled inside her belly as she forced the words past her stiff lips. "I'm not ready. I need to think. This is happening way too fast. Take your pick."

"I know what you mean." His understanding smile calmed her. He drew her into his embrace, rubbing his chin across her hair. "But, it's a good thing, right?"

"Maybe. I don't know."

"It can be." He ran a caressing finger along her cheek, sending a ripple of desire surging through her. "But I won't push. Thanks for playing tour guide for me today. It really helped."

"No thanks needed. It was fun." She unlocked her door and stepped inside. "Good night. See you Monday."

Lisa switched on the lamp, thinking, what had she done? Had she lost her mind? Matthew was her boss. With all the knowledge and experience she'd gained from her engagement to Stephen why wasn't she smart enough to stop repeating the same mistakes.

Confused, Lisa wandered aimlessly around her living room. It would be so easy to let herself get caught in Matthew's web, she admitted silently. If she didn't get a handle on her emotions, this thing would soar out of her hands and then she would really be in trouble.

Her mind relived the velvet warmth of his kiss. That kiss had been a serious no-no. She couldn't deny it was an earth-shattering experience that made her feel alive for the first time in months. But there were too many strikes against her to start a new relationship. Stephen had taught her the perils of on-the-job romance. Once the news came out about her broken engagement, she'd hated the false sympathetic murmuring and snickering behind her back she'd gotten from the office staff.

No. Matthew wasn't for her. And she'd best remember it before she found herself neck deep in trouble.

"What should I do?" She paced the floor. No way would she let this hang over her head, but bringing up the topic at their next meeting didn't feel right, nor appropriate for the office. No, she shook her head. Too tacky. Besides, what if she misread his intentions? There was still the possibility that he'd gotten carried away by the moment and it would never happen again.

She would need to ask Matthew to be sure. There must be a better way, she considered, fidgeting with the chain at her neck. If Matthew suggested dinner or another outing, she'd clear the air, and explain her position about dating coworkers. Once she accomplished that, she'd focus on keeping everything strictly business. Easy, neat. She could do that.

Ten

"Hey man. How's it going?" Jacob asked as he entered Matthew's office.

"It's going." Matthew rose from his desk with a mug of coffee in his hand. "It's going."

Yeah, things are going on, but not the way we'd planned, Matthew thought. "Want something to drink?"

Jacob grinned, shrugged off his leather backpack. "Yeah. Martell. Straight." Jacob removed his laptop from his leather backpack, plugged it into the electrical socket, hit the switch on the computer, and waited for the Microsoft window to appear.

"I hear you." A kernel of suspicion struck Matthew as he made his way to the bar. He stopped, turned, and studied his friend for a beat. Jacob's blond hair stood on its ends as if he'd run his fingers through it a hundred times. His clothes were wrinkled and looked as if they'd been slept in. Plus he oozed a high-energy giddiness that always signaled that Jacob was working an angle. Something was definitely up.

That was the thing about Jacob. Once he got going, he acted like a husband on the trail of an adulterous wife; nothing stopped him. That brilliant mind of his always worked at top speed. Jacob didn't let go until he'd found the problem or solved the riddle.

"Kinda early in the day for hard liquor, isn't it?" Matthew asked, a note of reproach in his voice.

Jacob glanced at his watch, then replied with an edge to his voice. "Not really. It's after three. I haven't been to bed for twenty-seven hours, so I need a boost. Don't give me any grief about it."

Matthew crossed the room and stopped behind the bar. "Sorry, man. Didn't mean to criticize."

"It's cool. I'm a little jumpy." His hands raced across the keyboard as he spoke, "I can't sleep when my brain is going like this. It's like unstoppable. I don't mean to snap at you." Glassy, red-rimmed eyes focused on Matthew. "Bear with me, okay?"

"Okay," he removed a tumbler from the bar and filled it with cognac, then returned to the conference table, placed the glass beside the laptop, and took the opposite chair. "Jay, that means you're on to something. Right? What've you got for me?"

"A couple of interesting pieces to this puzzle have come my way. I figured with the firewall and all, it's damn near impossible to hack through from the outside. There would be a trail I could follow," Jacob explained, sipping on his drink. "Believe me, I tried so I could confirm my suspicions. It didn't happen. We've always assumed the thief copied the files and walked out of here with them. That idea got my brain fired up. So, I decided to dig through the company's systems. I surfed around and found bits of an e-mail. It left a crumb of a trail."

Matthew leaned closer, rubbing a hand back and forth across his chin. "Trail?"

"Yeah. The e-mail had been deleted, but not written over, so I was able to re-create a small portion, a few words from the text, and part of the URL address. This changed my idea about how things are being smuggled from here. Now I believe whoever stole the software is using the company e-mail to transfer the test software out of here."

Anger gripped Matthew and his hand clenched with the need to do violence. A thin chill hung on the edge of his words. "You're saying they're using my own system to steal from me?"

Jacob nodded. "That's pretty much the sum of the situation."

Matthew squeezed his eyes shut, beating down the urge to throw something. "That miserable jerk."

"Matt, get a handle on it, man. We've got too many things to fix. I need you at one hundred percent."

"God, I hate this." He drew air deep into his lungs, released it in slow, even increments. "Whose e-mail? Which employee?"

"That's the rub," Jacob's brows crinkled above his red-rimmed gray eyes.

"What do you mean?"

"It's an employee that left the company long before the information disappeared."

Matthew sagged against the back of his chair. His felt as tired as Jacob looked. "Old employee access codes are being used?"

"That's it." Jacob took a long swallow of his drink and gave Matthew a hard stare. "Which brings us back to Ms. Daniels."

"How?" Matthew asked.

Jacob sat silently for a moment, then asked, "What did you learn?"

"If she's the thief, I can't find anything to link her to this. I've been to her house. It's nothing extravagant. Nice apartment in a nice area of Chicago." Matthew leaned forward and tented his fingers together. "She drives a two-year-old Mercury Sable. Nothing special. Her clothes are nice. Again, nothing special or particularly outrageous. I'm stumped. If she's selling my software she must be doing it for her retirement."

"She's got parents? Right? What about them? Could she be doing this for them?" Jacob drained his glass. "Helping them out? Paying for their home? Maybe supplementing their senior years."

"I don't know? Never met 'em."

"That's where we need to go next."

"Jacob, Lisa and I have gotten to know each other and I

don't believe she's behind this. She doesn't seem the type. Have you looked at other folks? Somebody in the Human Resources department perhaps. They know as much about the employees as Lisa does; as a matter of fact, she gets her info from them. What about that Stephen Brock? He strikes me as someone on this side of shady."

"I'm looking into that angle. To be honest, I don't see it coming from that direction. Why would your top man in personnel want to do something like this? I mean, I've checked his background, finances, and home life. Everything is in good shape."

"The same thing can be said for Lee. I don't see her doing this." *Damn, that was a bad slip.* No way would Jacob miss it. He squeezed his eyes shut. Shamefaced, he swiveled the chair away from Jacob's probing eyes.

"Lee?"

"You know who I'm talking about. Lisa Daniels." The name came out defensively. "I can't see her as the mastermind behind this. It just doesn't click. There must be another explanation. How about the software design area? Maybe someone from that department is behind this. Any employee with a computer at their disposal."

"And that can be anyone at Games," Jacob reminded.

Matthew tapped his pen against the conference room table. "You know, I've heard rumors about this Dale Smith. He worked for Mitchell in a top-level position. Something happened and Mitchell demoted him. The man is always making derogatory remarks about the company and Mitchell. Now, that's a grudge we can't ignore."

"I've heard the rumors. That's my next step, I'll dig into it and see what I turn up." A skeptical expression entered his eyes. "Don't you think he's just a little bit too obvious. I mean, he's setting himself up for a fall. My advice, don't expect too much from this source. He's too convenient."

"I know. I know. Just check it out, okay?"

"Sure. Now, let's get back to Ms. Daniels. Weren't Stephen Brock and Ms. Daniels engaged at one time?"

Matthew nodded. "That's what I've heard."

"Could they be in this together?"

Swallowing hard, Matthew shook his head, keeping his face as impassive as possible while at the same time his insides curled and twisted into knots. He didn't like that idea at all, remembering how he'd found Brock in Lisa's office and the tension that gagged him when he'd entered her cubicle.

"I'd bet on someone else. Not her. And not with him," he stated. "She won't say much about him or their relationship. It's like she's wiped him out of her life."

Jacob's eyebrows rose. "Are you sure those aren't personal feelings instead of professional ones talking?"

"No." Matthew glared at his friend. A warning spark beamed from his eyes. "Those are my observations after spending time with the woman."

"I've got one more comment about Ms. Daniels." Jacob scratched his ear, shut down his laptop, and offered, "Don't let yourself fall, buddy. You're pretty close. It's there in your face and in the tone of your voice. All you need is a little push or one step forward."

Matthew refused to comment on Jacob's remark. He knew exactly what he felt, and he didn't need Jacob to tell him.

"Mmmm," Matthew muttered, stroking his chin. "What about Lisa's friend, Cynthia. She's in and out of Lisa's cube all the time. Plus, she's a computer geek and one of the best software programmers in the area. It's not a stretch to see her selling software. All we need to do is fit the pieces together."

"I saw her." Jacob tilted his head to one side and his expression softened. "She's hot."

"What does that have to do with anything?"

"Nothing. Just an observation."

Jacob, man, sometimes you can be a royal pain, Matthew thought as he drew in a deep breath and let it out in small increments. "Anyway, have you checked her out? What's her background?"

"One step ahead of you. I thought of that angle and did my homework." Jacob's brows did a significant lift and he said, "Who knows, that hottie and Ms. Daniels could be in cohoots."

Matthew's head jerked up and he snarled at his friend. Was Jacob trying to get to him? If he were, it was working.

"Well, we can't rule out the possibility." Jacob rose from the chair with the tumbler in his hand and strolled across the room to the bar. "I did a little checking. Parents abandoned her before she turned three. Never saw them again."

"That's rough," Matthew muttered.

"Yeah, it is. But Cynthia is a survivor. Foster parents raised her. And she never lost that rough edge. Her defiance. Lots of problems in school and probably on her way to more serious stuff when she met your Lee. Ms. Daniels took her home and changed her life. Made her part of the family. She finished high school and college and we see the results now."

"Is there a rough enough edge to take a second look?" Matthew asked.

"Yeah." Jacob nodded. "Cynthia is definitely worth a second look. She's got the skill and connection to do just about anything. I'll tell you what. Why don't you concentrate on finding out everything you can about our prime suspect? And I'll do the same with her buddy. I think you're wrong here. Cynthia turned her life around. She's made something of herself and I don't believe she'd go that route."

"I feel the same about Lisa."

"I'd like to get to know her better and this presents the perfect opportunity." The smile in Jacob's eyes sparkled with sensuous promise. "It should be interesting."

Matthew watched his friend, getting the buzz of something much more. "What gives? Are you telling me you like what you see in Cynthia?"

"Yeah." Jacob's eyes widened. His answered appeared to have surprised him. "I guess I am."

"What about Zoe?"

"What about her? She left me, remember?"

Matthew nodded, then asked, "What if Cynthia is the mastermind behind the thefts? How will you handle that?"

"Like the professional I am." He shrugged. "If she's the one, she's got to go down, man. And I mean down. Prison. For a good while. Until her hair is gray and all."

"That seems cold, man. Real cold." Matthew tented his fingers together and admired his friend. *I'm glad you can separate your feelings because I truly having trouble with the concept.*

"Got to do what you've got to do. And you've got to find out what's happening with your company before it goes up in smoke. See if there's a connection between Ms. Daniels and her family. Is there a way you can learn more about her family?"

"Yeah," Matthew answered hesitantly, running the back of his hand across his forehead. "Her family's having a barbecue soon. Maybe I can squeeze out an invitation. Then I can check them out."

He didn't like this at all. He felt sneaky and dishonest. Plus, his behavior was coasting on the edge of unforgivable. Everything might backfire and ruin his chances with Lisa. He said, "I'm telling you now. If I don't see anything at her parents that links her to Games, we're going to cut her loose as a suspect before I get caught."

Refilling his glass with Martell, Jacob studied his friend. "I hope you know what you're doing."

I hope so too, Matthew admitted silently. "We're not going to call off the investigation and I still plan to prosecute everyone involved. We're going to refocus the investigation on other suspects. Deal?"

Jacob drained his glass and said, "Deal."

Matthew stretched, shut and locked his briefcase, and lifted it from the desk by the handle. The light from the half moon shined through the window, coating the room in a soft evening glow. *Man, I'm tired,* he thought, rubbing his hand over his face. He locked the door, crossed Georgia's office, shut the door, and turned the deadbolt with the key.

Strolling among the maze of cubicles, Matthew noticed how different the office looked at night. It felt lonely. *I need to drop these software programs on Lisa's desk,* he thought, running down the stairs to the twenty-eighth floor. Silent and empty, a gentle light bathed the floor.

Matthew entered Lisa's cube and her fragrance filled his nostrils. He hit the light switch and smiled when he noted the Campbell's soup can poster on her wall. It made him feel good to know that she placed the poster where she could see it.

Moving across the cubicle, he placed the packages in the center of her desk and reached for a yellow sticky to write a note. As he drew away, his hand touched something cold and metal. Picking up a silver picture frame, he gazed at a picture of Lisa and her family. All the smiling faces were so similar, so familiar. She and her siblings all looked like Lisa's parents. He traced the image of the woman in question with a slow, caressing finger and Jacob's warning came to mind. "Don't fall," he warned.

Yeah, right. He was halfway there already. Before he got in any deeper, it was time for him to view this situation in a rational manner. He needed to separate his feelings before he lost the ground he'd gained with her. If Lisa found out he was having her investigated she'd be furious. What if she got so mad that he might not be able to make her understand later? That thought scared the hell out of him. He couldn't allow that to happen, no matter what.

Jacob was on to something. And from the sound of things, it was the right thing. After weeks of waiting, Jacob had found the way the software was being transported from the building. Whoever the thief was, he had nerve. It took a bold person to use your own Internet system against you. Damn creep had put every employee's job at Games in jeopardy. The employees were his friends and coworkers. How could he not care about what might happen to them?

But what if it was Lisa? he wondered. Ice slid down his

spine as he remembered how Stephen and Lisa had reacted to his unexpected visit. Neither had been pleased to see him. And what about that blue folder? What was in it?

He liked Lisa. Really liked her and didn't want to see her go to prison. Unfortunately, the possibility was out there unless he found the real crook.

Eleven

I need a cup of happy to get going this morning, Lisa thought, pouring water into the coffeemaker. Within seconds the aroma of the brew filled the room. Mug in hand, she inhaled the scent and waited for the coffeemaker to finish doing its thing. The doorbell rang and her lips parted in surprise.

Who in the heck is that at my door on a Sunday morning? Lisa wondered, setting the mug on the countertop, knotting the belt on her red cotton robe, and starting down the hallway to the door. Lisa stood on her tiptoes and stared at her best friend through the peephole. Cynthia was dressed in a teal-green silk jogging suit. Groaning, Lisa ran a hand over her tussled hair and smoothed it into place. *I'm not ready for this.*

She opened the door and asked, "Cynthia, what are you doing here?"

"And good morning to you, too."

"Do you know what time it is?"

"It's nine-forty." Cynthia touched the edge of Lisa's hair and complimented. "Oh, nice do. I like it."

"Thanks."

"Did you do that for Matthew?"

"No," Lisa said, gripping the ends of the belt. "Why are you here?"

"For the first time in almost a year you went out with a man. I'm here for all the details. Look, I brought breakfast." Cynthia lifted her hand and revealed a brown grocery bag.

"Bagels and cream cheese. I've got your favorite: cranberry and walnut. Plus a little something-something." She winked slyly and brushed past Lisa. "To get your juices goin'."

"Happy does that for me." Lisa followed Cynthia down the hallway to the kitchen.

"You can have that anytime."

Lisa nodded at the bag, "What you got there?"

"Champagne and orange juice."

Surprised, Lisa's eyebrows lifted.

"We're going to have mimosas while you spill your guts."

"That sounds dangerous." *But I'm not telling you my business,* Lisa decided.

Cynthia stepped around Lisa, kicked off her shoes, and removed her jacket, revealing a black tank top. She then continued to the kitchen with her bag of goodies.

Sighing deeply, Lisa followed her friend back through the apartment. As Lisa neared the kitchen she heard drawers opening and closing. No point in fighting the situation. Cynthia planned to stay until she got what she wanted.

"Your happy is ready, Lisa. Come and get it."

She stopped on the opposite side of the island, pulled up a tall stool, and waited as Cynthia placed a mug and napkin in front of her. "Drink up. We've got lots to talk about and I want you to have your happy before we start."

"Did you see David?"

Cynthia halted in the center of the small kitchen, her face an impassive mask, then with deliberate steps she resumed her course across the room. "Mmm, hmm. We got together yesterday." A burning, faraway expression filled her eyes. She puttered around the kitchen, removing plates and glasses from the cupboard, and set them on the table. If Cynthia's tight, uncompromising expression offered a clue, things hadn't gone well. "Do you have any fruit?"

"There's a pineapple and basket of strawberries in the refrigerator."

"Good."

She sipped her coffee and watched Cynthia wash and prepare the pineapple and slice the strawberries. "What did you and David decide?"

Cynthia's hand faltered for a split second before she took the bowl of fruit and placed it in the center of the dining room table near the balcony. Seconds later, Lisa heard the pop of the champagne cork. "Come have breakfast."

Hopping off the stool, Lisa turned to the table. "Wow!" The table was beautiful. A white linen tablecloth covered the surface. Yellow roses sat in a vase in the center of the table. Lisa sniffed one of the roses and caressed the velvety petals. Gold-rimmed china, champagne glasses, toasted bagels on a platter with garden vegetable cream cheese and a bowl of cubed pineapples and sliced strawberries made a perfect presentation. "You went all out. I never use this stuff."

Surveying her handiwork, Cynthia answered with pride, "It looks good. Come on, let's eat."

Lisa sat opposite her friend and spread a napkin across her lap. "You didn't answer my question. What have you and David decided?"

Cynthia reached for a bagel and concentrated on spreading cream cheese on it. Her dark eyebrows slanted into a frown. Using her fork, she nabbed a chunk of pineapple and munched on it. "We haven't decided anything. He wants what he wants and I refuse to compromise."

"You'll never get together if neither one of you gives a little."

"Well, thank you," she muttered in a quick, nasty comeback. "The thought never crossed my mind."

"Cynthia, I'm sorry." Lisa spoke with friendly concern. "I don't mean to repeat the obvious. You're my friend and I want you to be happy." She reached out and laced her fingers with Cynthia's. "All I'm saying is stop and think about what you're doing. You've loved David for as long as I can remember. Do you really want to be alone now? This is a time for the two of you to be together, preparing for the future."

"I didn't come here to talk about David." Cynthia shook off

Lisa's hand and picked up her glass. "I'm here for the four-eleven on you and Matthew."

They sat quietly for a moment. "I'm going to let it go for now." Lisa promised, leaning back in her chair. "Don't get comfortable. We are going to have this conversation. Understand?"

"Oh yeah. I understand." She toyed with the stem of her glass. "But I'm not going to talk about David and me. Right now we're at an impasse until he begins to consider my position. There's nothing to discuss. End of subject."

"Talking could help."

"No, it won't. And that's that." The shrillness of her voice made Lisa back down. No. Cynthia wasn't ready to talk and pushing her would only make things worse. "Now, how did the house hunting go? Did Matthew find a place? What about you? Did you have a good time?"

Lisa bit into her bagel and chewed slowly, debating how much to reveal. Swallowing her food, she decided to give her the basics. "House hunting was fun. We went down Lakeshore Drive, then on to Winnetka. Boy, the homes." A dreamy expression entered her eyes. "I loved them. I tell you, the rich are different. Those houses are like palaces."

Cynthia rested her chin on her hand. "Did you enjoy yourself?"

Had I had a good time? "Yes," Lisa admitted. Surprised by her answer, she took a minute to think about how easy and comfortable her time with Matthew had been. Yes. She really had enjoyed the day and him.

"And?"

"He was really nice." Lisa's full lips smiled in delight.

Grinning, Cynthia drained her glass, reached for the pitcher, filled her glass, and topped off Lisa's. "You should see your face. Your eyes are twinkling and your face is bright and happy. You like him, my friend. Guess what? He likes you, too. When you two are together it's like sparks are flying all around the two of you. And anyone who gets in the way will get burned."

"You're exaggerating. You know that, don't you?"

"Come on Lisa, admit it," Cynthia's soft voice urged. "He's a nice guy and you like him. Who wouldn't? He's sexy as hell. Rich and single. Did I mention single and rich? Admit it. You like him."

Coyly, Lisa said, "Maybe."

"That man likes you, big time. Those gorgeous eyes sparkle when you're around and they follow your every move. Like that day at the meeting, I thought he was going to eat you whole. Whether you want to admit it or not the chemistry going on between you two shoots off the periodic table."

Lisa shrugged.

"You can fool some of the people all of the time and some people some of the time. But remember this, you can't fool me anytime. So come on, admit it." Cynthia smacked her friend playfully from across the table.

"Okay!" she blurted out. "Yes, I like him."

"Then ask him to the Memorial Day barbecue."

Shutting her eyes, Lisa could see Matthew at her parents', mingling with her friends and family, assessing and watchful. Ice spread through her. "No."

"You have to. This is your chance. Are you going to spend your life on what-might-have-beens, maybes? Ask him to the barbeque."

"I don't have anything to offer a man like Matthew," Lisa said in a tortured whisper. Her hands clenched tightly around the stem of her champagne glass.

"Let me get you straight because Stephen left your brain in a hot mess." Her generously curved mouth thinned with displeasure. "My dear, you have plenty to offer any man. Not just Matthew James. How long are you going to allow Stephen to control your life? Hurt you with his callousness? That relationship is dead and buried. He wasn't the right man for you." She held up her hand to silence Lisa. A burning fire reflected from her brown eyes. "Where was he when you needed him?"

"Stephen found it difficult to handle things."

"No. He refused to try. And that's what I hate about him. I understand the disappointment. You guys had your life mapped out a certain way and when things changed he took off. But what about you?" Cynthia asked. "What about what you needed? He didn't give a damn. It was all about Stephen."

Lisa covered her face with her hands, feeling desperate and confused. "I can't go through this a second time. I'm sorry. I don't have it in me. Stephen hurt and humiliated me."

"That jerk ignored what you needed." Cynthia removed Lisa's hands and squeezed them reassuringly. "So to hell with him."

"Truthfully, I understand his feelings, but I thought we had more going for us. Our lives were going so well and then it all fell apart. Could I have been that wrong in my choice of men? Stephen was everything I thought I wanted in a man. Then one day, I realized I was making plans to marry a man who'd become a stranger. How could he say he loves me one minute and walk away the next?"

"It's simple. Stephen doesn't know how to love."

"You're wrong. He did love me. I know he did."

Shaking her head, pity touched Cynthia's face and hurt her as much as Stephen's betrayal. She didn't want anyone's pity. "Sorry, my friend. Steve loved Steve."

"What about Matthew? Couldn't the same thing happen with him?"

"Don't be afraid," Cynthia soothed. "You're smart. Use your head. You can make him see things your way. Besides, if he truly wants to be with you, he'll understand and accept you with all the problems that come with a relationship. Let go of the past and start living again."

Lisa took a quick sharp breath and grimaced at her thoughts before confessing, "Matthew and I are like night and day."

"You guys are more alike than you think," Cynthia contradicted. "For one, you want to run your own business. Matthew runs a business. Two, you're looking for love and I think he is, too. Three, you both have an appreciation for art. And four, I'm not going to let you back away from Matthew. I think you need someone like Matthew James in your life."

"Where did you get that idea?" she snapped, jumping to her feet and placing her hands on her hips. "I don't need *any* man."

"Oh Lisa," Cynthia checked Lisa softly. "I'm sorry you took my comment the wrong way. I'm not saying you need a man like you need food or air. We all crave companionship—a friend, maybe even a lover. Wouldn't it be sweet to have someone to care for you, share your dreams and disappointments, someone to laugh with? Someone to hold you while you cry?"

"Maybe," Lisa answered quietly. "But when you least expect it, reality pushes its ugly, unwelcome head through the door and it shatters your dreams."

"I don't believe that will happen with Matthew."

"Good to know you have that much faith in him. I'm still reserving judgment." Lisa took a long swallow of her champagne. "Let me play devil's advocate for a minute. Say I get something going with Matthew and things really start to sizzle. Sooner or later he's going to ask about Stephen."

"Yeah, Matthew will. I'd be very surprised if he didn't. Everyone has something in their past that has the potential to blow up in their face. You're no different. What I suggest you do is give it to him. Tell him all the facts and let him make a decision about whether he's willing to go into a relationship with you. If you do this up front, then you've set the tone. After that, it'll all be good."

"Okay. That's one of the problems." Lisa waved a hand back and forth between them. "What about the fact that he's our boss? That he owns the company? Been there, done that. Don't want to go there again. Not ready for a repeat."

"I hate to break it to you, but you're in the middle of a repeat." Cynthia grinned broadly, then winked at her friend. "Obviously, you're attracted to powerful men. And vice versa."

"What was Stephen? Who was he in my life."

"Your first love. That's okay. We all have them. Sometimes those relationships are long term. Most times not."

"Oh girlfriend, what would I do without you?" Lisa got up from the table to wrap her arms around Cynthia and hug her close.

"I don't ever want you to have to try."

"You're a good friend, Cynthia. I really appreciate your listening to my moaning and groaning."

"I'm your bud. If anyone should listen to you, it's me. And I'll always be in your corner, no matter what." She reached for the pitcher of mimosas and filled Lisa's glass. "Now, enough heavy stuff. Let's soothe the woes of our world with champagne."

"Sounds good to me." Lisa sat down and picked up her glass.

"Ask Matthew to the barbecue. You'll be safe. Your family will be there to protect you."

"No."

"Yes. He can come as a friend. He's new to town and would probably be all alone on the holiday. It's a nice gesture. Then, you get a chance to see how things come together. Ask him."

"Yes Mama." Lisa said.

"You're welcome." Studying the plate of bagels, she offered one to Lisa. "Hey, I didn't go all the way to the Bagel Nook for you to ignore the cranberry and walnut bagels. Eat."

Long after Cynthia left, Lisa sat at her dining room table and sipped the last of her drink. The sun rose to its highest peak and filled her room with its warmth. She rose from the table and took the remaining bagels into the kitchen.

Lisa placed the tray on the island and returned to the dining room for the glasses and dishes. The last thing she'd expected when she got out of bed this morning was a visit from her buddy. She planned to drink her mug of happy and vegetate all day. Instead, she'd spent the morning debating the merits of a relationship with Matthew James.

Clearing the table, Lisa shook the crumbs into the trash from the tablecloth, then tossed it into the laundry basket. Sometimes Cynthia's lectures hit their mark. Today was one of those times. Lisa wasn't a quitter, but the thought of starting a new relationship scared her silly. Besides, what if she was misinterpreting the signs and Matthew was only being friendly?

Lisa flushed under the skin when she remembered how she responded to the kiss she'd shared with Matthew. Not a friendship kiss. And it was good. Too good.

With Matthew she felt vulnerable, naked. That frightened her more than anything else. Deep within her soul, she knew he had the power to sweep into her world, hurt her deeply, and leave her with nothing. Lisa suspected, if the truth were told, being hurt by Matthew would be a hundred times more painful than anything Stephen had done to her.

Loading the dishwasher, she glanced out the balcony window, watching the children playing in the courtyard. Was she a coward?

No. There was chemistry between them and she wanted to explore it. Find out how they fit together.

Lisa snapped the lock on the dishwasher. She was going to do it, ask Matthew to the barbecue.

Twelve

Lisa checked the clock for the fifth time. *Matthew will be here any minute.* Her heart drummed against her chest as she raced around the living room, shaking lilac potpourri into a dish on her end table. She removed her mug from the coffee table, headed to the kitchen and rinsed it and a few dishes in her sink, placing them in the dishwasher.

Returning to her bedroom, she posed in front of the mirrored closet door and studied her reflection. The black capri pants that ended midleg offered a nice glance at her calves. Black high heel mules left her painted toes bare and a T-strapped black satin camisole completed her outfit.

I hope this isn't too much. Indecisive, Lisa tapped her foot against the carpeted floor and bit her lip, evaluating her outfit once more. "I don't know," she admitted softly. "I haven't had a date in six months."

I should call Cynthia, floated through Lisa's head. Cynthia would know what to do. She rushed to the nightstand next to her bed and picked up the receiver. As quickly as she lifted the telephone from its cradle she returned it.

"This is ridiculous," Lisa muttered matter-of-factly. "This isn't even a date. I'm inviting a lonely friend to a family barbecue." Matthew was no different from any other friend she'd brought home.

Right, the tiny voice in her head responded. *Tell yourself another lie. This friend is your boss and more.* Much, much more. *Don't go there,* she warned silently. *There's nothing more. Not for you and not with him.*

A mental image of her brothers, swarming Matthew and interrogating him as if he'd just shot the president, sent chills racing through her. She didn't want her brothers pouncing on Matthew like he was a prospective date. To their way of thinking, Matthew was a man Lisa brought home to meet the family. There must be something serious to the relationship.

My brothers will know something is up if I show up dressed like this. Lisa ran around her bedroom, drew the camisole over her head, kicked off her shoes, and wiggled out of her pants. Frantic, she searched her closet for something less revealing to wear. She spied the perfect outfit.

The doorbell sounded throughout the apartment as she zipped her knee-length, clay-colored shorts. "Ohmigosh, he's here," she exclaimed, taking a final look at herself. Much better. She felt less conspicuous with the shorts and cranberry, scooped-neck top.

Strolling down the hallway, she stopped at the door, put her hand on her chest, and drew in a deep breath. *This is going to be a good day,* she promised silently, planting a welcoming smile on her lips, then opening the door.

"Hi." Matthew's spicy cologne waltzed under her nose. She inhaled deeply.

"Hi yourself." Smiling, Lisa's eyes slid over his tall frame. *My, my. Don't you look wonderful,* she thought, admiring how his striped polo shirt laid smoothly over his broad shoulders and tight abs. "Come on in and have a seat."

"Thanks."

Although he'd been to her place before, he examined her apartment with interest. He dropped onto the sofa and watched her step around the coffee table and sit on the edge of the matching leather chair.

"Umm, Matthew," Lisa began, playing with the watch at her wrist. "We've got a few minutes before we need to take off. I thought I'd give you the four-eleven on my family."

"Oh." His forehead wrinkled into a frown. "Do I need it?"

"Possibly." Her head bopped from side-to-side while she considered his question. "Umm, umm," she muttered, debating how to say this. "I'm not trying to scare you off, but I want you to be aware of what you're walking into."

"Are they vampires, demons, or ghouls?"

She giggled, imagining her brother David with fangs. Now that would be something. "No, but they can be overwhelming, especially when they're all together. I'd be remiss in my duties as your hostess if I let you walk into that group uninformed. So, I'm giving you a heads up on what to expect from them."

"This sounds interesting." He placed his left ankle on his right knee, leaned back into the sofa, and said, "Go for it."

Lisa linked her fingers and focused on the carpet. "You already know I have three brothers. David, Eddie, and JD." She swallowed hard, drew her tongue across her dry lips and reseated herself on the edge of her chair. "This is a little embarrassing for me. But, you need to be prepared for the cross-examination. My brothers are very protective of Vanessa and me. Showing up at the family gathering could signal warning bells. Since my broken engagement, they're determined to keep me safe."

"Which means?" he asked in a level tone. A spark of amusement glittered from his multicolored eyes.

She remembered how her dad had showed up at her office to have a talk with Stephen and how the pair had treated her coworkers to a verbal battle until Dad left. It had been an embarrassing time, one she hoped to never repeat.

It means you're in for a rough hour or two, my friend, she answered in her head. But Lisa sugarcoated her verbal response. "They believe they need to check out any man that I bring to family parties. They'll probably interrogate you. Want to know your intentions." A note of apology crept into her voice. "Warn you against hurting me. Basically, give you a hard time."

He nodded. The humor that lit his eyes a moment before

had disappeared, replaced by a somber spark of understanding.

Gnawing on her bottom lip, she asked, "Aren't you going to say anything?"

"What do you want me to say?" Matthew hunched his shoulders and rubbed a finger across his chin.

"I don't know." She lifted her hands, palms up. "This makes sense to you? You understand?"

"Believe it or not, it does and I do." He leaned forward and captured her hands between his. "They love you and they don't want to see you hurt. If I had sisters, I'd feel the same way. I'd want to protect them."

"That's pretty much it." Relieved, Lisa sighed, sinking in the cool, soft folds of her leather chair. "Please be on your guard because they're going to hit you hard or all together. The minute they see you, expect to be grilled." Lisa took his hand between both of hers.

"I can handle it. Their feelings are justifiable."

She smiled.

"What?" Matthew asked.

"I'm surprised how much you understand about siblings."

Eyebrows arched above his dual-colored eyes, he asked, "Why?"

"You don't have any brothers and sisters, right?"

"Correct," he answered. "It was just my mother and me."

Shaking her head, she lifted her hands in an act of surrender. "Yet, you seem more understanding than I would expect from an only child."

"It doesn't take a brain surgeon to understand family."

"True." She leaned forward, her voice turning sympathetic. "Sometimes only kids are spoiled rotten and they always want their way."

"Oh, I want my way. I just don't always get it." Matthew let go of her hand and drew away. Lisa felt as if a door had been shut in her face. Sadness filled her as she watched that expressionless mask settle into place.

"Sometimes," Matthew answered in a neutral tone,

"Mother traveled a lot. So I spent much of my time with baby-sitters and nannies."

Lisa shook her head. "Nanny. That's so hard for me to comprehend."

He watched her steadily. "That's the way I was raised."

Suddenly, she realized that Matthew wouldn't welcome or want her sympathy. He was a proud man and from everything she'd learned about him, he didn't want or desire her pity.

"The idea of a nanny is so different from the way I was raised," Lisa said. "Things might have been easier if you had a brother or sister. You guys could rely on one another."

"So, I became very self-sufficient."

"I don't mean to put down how you were raised, Matthew. The differences are what make us unique, right?"

"Right. Mother had to be away, promoting, advertising, making deals when and wherever the opportunity presented itself and a lot of times those situations took her away from me."

A shadow of vulnerability flashed across his face and was gone. Lisa questioned whether she had truly seen it.

"I can't deny that there were times when I felt lonely," Matthew admitted in a straight-to-the-point tone. "Very lonely. That was the life we lived."

"I'm sorry."

"No need for that. I survived and I'm fine." He rose from the sofa, seemed to shake off his mood, and said, "Forget about all that. Let's get gone and see what your brothers have in store for me. Do they know that I'm coming?"

"N-o-o-o-o-o. Only Ma and Dad."

He chuckled. "This should be interesting. I'm a surprise on top of everything else."

"Trust me. It'll be okay." *Hopefully,* Lisa prayed. She strolled to her bedroom. "Let me get my purse, then I'll be ready to go."

Remembering his mother's call to his office, Lisa thought of that cold, stiff conversation she'd overheard. Matthew refused to let Mrs. James come for a visit. There were some serious issues between Matthew and his mother.

While her own parents were loving, they also worried about the men in her life. And they had no qualms about telling her what they thought of anyone she brought home. Matthew wouldn't be an exception. His position as her boss would cause a stir and questions would crop up about whether she really knew what she was doing.

Locking her apartment door, Lisa and Matthew strolled from her building and into the afternoon sun. It felt warm against her bare legs as Lisa walked quietly through the parking lot at Matthew's side. Opening the passenger door to his Lexus, he helped her inside before running around the back of the car to the driver's door. Lisa stepped from the car, her lips pursed and her fingers drummed against the top of his car. Her glance shifted from Matthew's to her own car and back again, a thoughtful expression on her face.

"What's up?" He asked, fidgeting with the keys in his hand.

"Let's take my car," she announced with gentle authority.

Surprised, he stared at her with a puzzled expression on his face. "Why?"

Lisa gnawed on her bottom lip for a moment before explaining, "This is a big to-do. A lot of people come to this barbecue. Parking will be a nightmare. Last year my brother's Corvette got sideswiped. I'd hate for anything to happen to your car."

He waved her comment away with his hand. "It's just a car."

"True. But it's your car. And I would feel really bad if something happened to it, especially since I invited you to the party. Plus, I wouldn't enjoy myself. The whole time I'd worry that something might happen to your car while it's parked at my folks."

"It's not a problem. I'm not worried about leaving it on the street."

"Please, humor me." She offered him her most engaging

smile. "I'd feel a lot better if we left your car here and took mine. It's safer here. Trust me."

"Whatever." He shrugged, reached inside the car, and came out with a brown paper bag.

"What's that?" she asked.

"A gift for your parents."

Matthew shut the door and hit the car remote.

Lisa strolled toward her car with Matthew on her heels, calling over her shoulder as she fumbled in her purse for her keys. "Good. I'm glad that's settled. Don't be afraid, I'm a good driver. Remember, I had three brothers to teach me."

"Yeah, I've seen you drive," he answered with a dubious expression on his face. "You've got a little lead foot going on."

Indignant, she drew back. "I do not."

He grinned. "Oh yeah, you do."

"I'm going to pretend I didn't hear that." She unlocked the car and opened the door. "Hop in."

"As long as you don't kill me."

"Trust me." Lisa rolled her eyes at him and moved around the car to the driver's door. "I'm not going to hurt myself."

"Famous last words," he teased.

Lisa shifted into reverse and backed out of her parking space. She watched as Matthew worked himself into a comfortable position. He reached for the seat belt and buckled himself in while she suppressed the urge to giggle. *I'm not that much of a bad driver,* she thought.

Her brothers always called her a speed demon on wheels. Lisa found it interesting that Matthew had noted the same thing. *I'll fix you,* she thought, glancing at the speedometer. She eased her foot off the accelerator pedal. *I'm going to drive a bit under the speed limit.*

Matthew turned to Lisa, brows lifted, and smiled. *He knows what I'm doing,* she thought, feeling heat rush into her cheeks.

Lisa glanced at him and her heart leaped into a gallop. She really liked Matthew. Less than an hour ago, she had been worried and nervous for him. Now, she was driving him to the barbecue. If things had been the least bit different, she might have let herself get closer to him, but as things stood between them, she was on the edge of his life.

Her brothers would no doubt suspect she and Matthew were involved and give him hell for it. Her instincts told her Matthew would be just fine. Wimps don't become owners of million-dollar companies.

He had no idea how intense her brothers became when they felt their little sister might get hurt. That was one of the reasons she had changed her clothes and gave him the four-one-one on her family. She didn't want to cause a problem for him. The best thing she could do for him was stay at his side and protect him from her family.

Stopped at a red light, Lisa glanced at the SUV on the right side of her car and smiled at the kids playing in the backseat. Two little boys waved at her and she returned their greeting. *Cute kids,* she thought, unable to miss Matthew's profile. For a moment, his handsome face took her breath away. She drew in a deep, unsteady breath. *Get a grip, Lisa. Get a grip.*

Matthew watched the kids for a beat. He smiled at her and she squeezed his hand, then returned it to the wheel. She felt Matthew's loneliness with everything in her.

In some ways Matthew reminded Lisa of Cynthia. An unhappy or lonely childhood ruled their view of the world. Part of her wanted to help him, let him see the world in a different way.

Today he would get a taste of how a real family works, or at least how her family worked. Ma and Dad collected strays from the neighborhood and schools all the time. Matthew's turn had arrived. After the initial grilling, he'd be welcomed into her family. He was in for a new experience. A pleasant one, she hoped.

She accelerated down the ramp to the freeway and merged. As they cruised along, Lisa took her eyes off the road and noticed the evidence of a three-car accident. Holidays brought out the worst in some drivers. That was what she had tried to explain to Matthew about his car.

There were tons of cars up and down her parents' street during the Memorial Day barbecue. She didn't want to see his beautiful Lexus sideswiped or totaled by a careless or drunken driver. This is better, she decided.

Approaching her exit, Lisa switched on her turn signal and merged right with traffic. Relieved, she sighed. Boy was she glad that they'd switched cars. If Matthew's car had been damaged at her parents, the guilt would eat her alive. Matthew's car was safe and they could relax and enjoy the party. Now the only thing she needed to worry about was her brothers and Dad. But she'd handle that by keeping Matthew at her side.

Lisa slowed as she approached her turnoff. A few minutes later, she parked her car three blocks from her parents' home. "This is it," she announced, grabbing her purse from the back-seat.

Thirteen

Matthew and Lisa rounded the corner of the two-story brick colonial to the scent of charcoal and freshly cut grass. Marvin Gaye's smooth tones cooed from the stereo system set up on the patio as he sang "Let's Get It On."

A white metal awning covered the patio, extending from the back of the house over a quarter of the yard, while smoke billowed from the huge black drum that served as a barbecue pit. Spare ribs, chicken, hot dogs, and hamburgers filled the grill.

Guilt hit Matthew in the chest when he remembered his true reason for being here and Jacob's suggestion: "Check it out, see if you can find any motive for Lisa to steal from Games. Maybe she's helping out her parents."

Matthew felt like a cheat and a fraud, using Lisa's invitation to spy on her family. Worried, he rubbed a finger back and forth across his chin as he considered the possible consequences of his deception. If the truth ever got out, there would be hell to pay.

There were other reasons for his visit today. He really liked Lisa and wanted to get to know her better. If her invitation meant anything, finally she was showing a tentative interest in him. And for that he was grateful.

People filled the backyard. Young, old, light, and dark gathered into groups around the yard, gently swaying to the music as they discussed world events and life in the big city.

Lisa turned to him with a sheepish expression. "Oh. I forgot to tell you, my parents are big fans of sixties and seventies music. That's all you're going to hear around here."

He chuckled. "It sounds like a good thing to me."

"Only if you don't have to listen to it twenty-four-seven. Believe me, I knew all the lyrics to the Isley Brothers, Marvin Gaye, and the Jacksons tunes. Are you okay with it?"

"It's fine."

"Great." A smile of relief brightened her eyes and she reached out and caught his hand in hers, then started through the crowd. "Come on. I want to introduce you to Ma and Dad."

As they headed for the patio, Matthew lagged back a bit, focusing on the pair nursing the meat on the grill, while bopping to the music. They had to be Lisa's parents. Mrs. Daniels was a knockout. Here was the origin of Lisa's beauty. She was 5'8"; her auburn hair mixed with gray streaks was cut into a short style. Confidence oozed from her, making him believe she could handle any crisis without hesitation.

On the other hand, Mr. Daniels had the build of a football player and the face of a bulldog. A vision of Mr. Daniels barking out orders to preschoolers entered his head. Deep lines were etched into his dark, chocolate skin and he'd lost a good portion of his hair. The strikingly attractive woman and this man made quite a contrast.

"Lisa," a woman's voice rose above the hum of the crowd. Matthew got a good look at her as she zigzagged her way across the yard. She stood a little over five feet with hair pulled into a dark brown ponytail. She stopped in front of the pair and gathered Lisa into a huge bear hug. "I didn't think you'd show."

"Hey, Jen." Lisa hugged her back. "Family do. You know I have to be here or Ma and Dad will hunt me down like a fugitive." She drew back and gave the other woman the once-over. "How are you feeling? Are things okay?"

"Just pregnant," she answered and patted the barely visible bump. "And picking up weight each day."

"That's the truth," confirmed a tall brown-skinned man.

This must be Lisa's brother. Matthew remembered him from the photos on her desk; he watched as the man wrapped his arm around Jen, drew her against his body, and kissed her hair.

Although they were not touching, Matthew sensed tension building in Lisa. He looked closer. That sadness was back in her eyes, so clear and painful that he fought the urge to draw her into his arms, right then and there in front of everyone. His gaze shifted back to Jen. What was the deal? Maybe Lisa didn't like her sister-in-law. No. There appeared to be genuine affection between them. Then what?

It all started when Jen mentioned her pregnancy. The baby. Could that be it? No. He'd seen Lisa with the infants at the hospital. She was great with them and had nothing but cute anecdotes about the kids in her apartment complex. It had to be something else. But what?

"How are you, Little Bit?"

"Good, Eddie. I'm good."

Eddie shifted toward him. His eyes were dark and assessing.

"Ohmigosh, I'm sorry." Turning to Matthew, Lisa extended a hand toward the pair. "Jennifer is my sister-in-law, and the man holding on to her as if she might disappear is her husband and my brother, Eddie. Jen, Eddie, this is Matthew James. Eddie's a math teacher and Jen's a counselor at the same high school."

Amused, Matthew watched as Jennifer's eyes opened wide and she gave him a thorough once-over. When her gaze returned to his face, she hid her expression behind a pleasant smile. "You have the most beautiful eyes."

Matthew's eyebrows lifted. "Thanks."

Unlike his wife, Eddie's skeptical gaze slid over Matthew.

He nodded at Matthew, but kept his distance, waiting quietly by his wife's side.

I've been summed up and found wanting, Matthew thought.

"Who's here?" Lisa scanned the crowd.

"Everybody," Jennifer responded.

"David and Cynthia?"

"No shows, so far. They called and said they'd be here at four," Jen answered, smirking. "You know what they're probably doing."

"I can imagine," Lisa answered, shifting from one foot to the other. "But, it's not my business."

"I just . . . their relationship fascinates me."

"Where are JD and Vanessa?" Lisa asked. "I don't see them."

"You know JD. He's in the house playing Spades and Vanessa's doing dishes."

Lisa's head snapped back a bit. "No Bid Whist?"

Jen giggled. "He couldn't round up four people. So, he settled for two hand."

Lisa laughed out loud. "That's my brother. Maybe I'll go in and help him out after I talk to Ma and Dad." Lisa touched Matthew's arm and his muscles leaped under his skin. "Do you play?"

"Not since college." He found it hard to concentrate with her hand on his arm.

"That's okay. We'll teach you. Let me give you a word of advice about the Daniels clan." Jen whispered behind her hand in a conspiratory manner. "Bid Whist is serious business. If you can't take it, don't sit down at the card table with them. Prisoners are shot dead the minute they play the wrong card."

Matthew chuckled.

"Look, I promised your mother that I'd make the deviled eggs. I've got the eggs boiling." Jen pointed at the house. "So, I better get gone." She turned away with Eddie on her heels and called over her shoulder, "Nice meeting you, Matthew."

"Back at you," he replied.

Matthew followed Lisa through the maze of people toward the patio. Friends, neighbors, and family stopped them. Curious, he stepped back and watched Lisa. Her bright, relaxed smile made Matthew crave more of this pleasant, easygoing person. Truly, her family brought out the best in her.

Finally reaching the patio, Lisa said, "Hi Ma," as she hugged her mother, then her father. The appetizing aroma of spare ribs and chicken filled Matthew's nostrils as he stood to the side and observed the interplay.

"We missed you, Little Bit." Mrs. Daniels said, rubbing a hand up and down Lisa's bare arm and asked with a trace of concern in her tone. "You okay?"

"I'm good." Lisa grabbed Matthew's hand and drew him closer. "This is my friend Matthew James."

"Thanks for taking pity on me and allowing me to visit for the holiday," Matthew said.

"You're more than welcome. Lisa said you're from out of town?" Mr. Daniels wiped his hands on the edge of his apron that read, "Don't ask me, I'm with the cook," and grabbed Matthew's hand in a firm handshake.

"Actually, he's only been in Chicago a few months," Lisa explained. "Matthew moved here from California."

"Mmm. Chicago must be a big change for you. Where did you two meet?" Mrs. Daniels lifted the top from the grill, removed the meat, and placed it in a blue roaster.

Lisa cleared her throat and played with the chain at her throat. "Work."

"Work?" Mrs. Daniels stopped what she was doing and glared at him, openmouthed.

"Ma, close your mouth."

Mr. Daniels stepped closer, eyeing Matthew. "I take it you've met Stephen Brock?"

"That's enough, Dad."

Matthew nodded.

"Ma, do you need me to help with anything?"

"Mmm, hmm. I certainly do." Mrs. Daniels picked up the roaster. "Come into the house and help me sauce the meat. I want to talk with you."

"Okay. Matthew, will you be all right? Or do you want to come in with me?"

"Matthew will be fine with your father," Mrs. Daniels vetoed.

Matthew studied Mr. Daniels's expression and knew it was time for "the talk." Better to get it over with now. "I'll hang with your father."

Once Lisa and Mrs. Daniels got out of earshot, Mr. Daniels took his eyes off the grill to bore holes into Matthew. He shoved his hands inside the pockets of his jeans and moved around the patio. "So, you work with my daughter?" He asked in a quiet, but somewhat menacing tone.

Matthew nodded.

"I'm a plain-speaking man," Mr. Daniels stated, pacing around the younger man. "So, I'm going to say what I've got to say. Don't hurt my daughter. She's had a few rough months and she doesn't need anyone to push his way into her life and hurt her again." His voice rang with command. "Understand?"

What could he say? *There's no need to worry. I'm really here to spy on your family.* Boy, would Mr. Daniels be mad. "Understood."

"Good." There was satisfaction in that one word. "I can show you a whole lot better than I can tell you. Because I'll have a lot to say if you hurt my girl. If you've met Brock, then you know the whole sorry mess. Lisa's fragile, vulnerable. Don't take advantage of it and don't cause her any grief."

"I won't." What was that saying, 'parents were number one with the guilt trip.' *Oh, hell,* Matthew fumed silently, *can't argue with that.*

Now that he'd made his point, Mr. Daniels's demeanor changed. He slapped Matthew on the back. "Enough said about that topic. What do you drink?"

Drink? A shot of Martell would do the trick to pull him back together. Maybe two shots. But he didn't want Lisa's family to think he was a drunk. His gaze settled on the bottle sitting on the table next to the grill. "Beer?"

"Beer it is."

Thanking Mr. Daniels, Matthew stood on the patio waiting for Lisa as he sipped his beer. The bite of guilt took a huge chunk out of his hide when he remembered why he was here. He hated this charade, disliked pretending and snooping around Lisa and her family.

A slight nudge brought his attention back to the present and he found Cynthia at his side. She winked, giving him a knowing smile. "So, how's it going for you?"

He did a double lift of his brow. "It's going."

"Looks like Dad gave you 'the talk.'" Cynthia used her fingers to indicate quotation marks in the air.

Matthew nodded, taking a swig of his beer. "You've hit the nail on the head."

Cynthia patted his arm reassuringly. "Don't worry. Dad and Ma are really good people. They love their kids. And nobody will get away with hurting them. Lisa's had a rough time recently, so you have to forgive her family. They want to protect her whether she wants it or not."

"I got that." He kept his tone dry so that other feelings wouldn't show through.

"Trust me. It's all good from this point forward. I promise."

He looked down at Cynthia, remembering how close she and Lisa were, and then asked, "What about you? What do you want for Lisa?"

"I want her to be happy," Cynthia answered without hesitation. "She deserves that."

Once those words were out of her mouth, Matthew realized that he wanted the same thing for Lisa. He wanted her to be happy.

"Hey, Cynthia," Lisa greeted, tossing an arm around her friend's shoulders. "When did you get here?"

"Few minutes ago." Cynthia hugged Lisa back. "I thought

I'd keep the boss company until you got done helping your mom."

"Thanks." She turned to Matthew and asked, "Everything okay?"

He saluted her with his beer. "Great."

There was silence for a minute; the music from the sixties had been replaced by a slower, more contemporary sound. The crowd began to couple off and moved toward the edge of the patio.

The sensual tones of Gary Taylor filled the backyard. A broad-shouldered, dark-skinned man touched Cynthia's arm. She faced him and Matthew noted how her face morphed into a radiant smile of welcome.

"What happened to the sixties music?" Matthew asked.

Lisa grinned and pointed at her brother. "My brother loves Gary Taylor."

"Mmm, I see," Matthew muttered.

Lisa, Matthew, Cynthia, and David exchanged pleasantries, then David nudged Cynthia. "Dance?"

"Yeah." Cynthia floated away on David's arm.

Matthew watched the couple cling to each other as they swayed to the music. His gaze cut to Lisa. He'd love to have her in his arms for a bit. "Want to dance?"

Smiling, she nodded and stepped forward. Matthew wrapped his arms around her, drew Lisa close, inhaled her delicate scent, and felt as if he'd just received the prize of the year. Gary Taylor's voice filled his head as thoughts of Lisa filled his heart. The lyrics of the song encapsulated his emotions as they moved to the music.

"So special. I just want to let you know," Gary Taylor sang. "You caused my love to grow. You are . . . so special."

Yes, she is, Matthew acknowledged silently as he drew Lisa closer. *Very special.*

This has been a great day, Matthew thought as he watched Lisa's siblings play Bid Whist. He glanced around the small family room and Jacob's request took center stage in his head. There was no evidence that Lisa was stealing to help her parents. From everything he'd seen so far, her parents lived a comfortable life, not extravagant. The Daniels home was pleasant, nothing more.

From the moment he'd stepped into the backyard, he'd seen a totally different person from the woman he saw at work. And that person had totally captivated him. Lisa was open and friendly.

Although Lisa had warned him about her family, he hadn't been prepared for the depth of their collective and separate interrogation. Everything hadn't gone as smoothly as he would have liked. The interrogations had been intense, but he'd gotten through them without any blood being shed. Her brothers, Eddie and David, had been cordial but reserved. He understood. If he had a sister, he would feel the same way toward any potential boyfriend.

Their instincts were to protect their sister and Matthew presented a threat that they wanted to neutralize at the earliest opportunity. And her father had made it clear that he wouldn't tolerate anyone hurting Lisa. Her family accepted Matthew as long as he obeyed the rules and didn't hurt her. Lord help anyone that did the unthinkable. Their attitudes made him wonder how much damage Stephen Brock had done to Lisa.

If being interrogated made it easier for him to come back for a second visit, he'd work his way through it. Because he wanted to be welcomed back into Lisa's family, not just for her but because he liked this family and their friendly, warm interaction.

Eddie threw down his cards and rose from the table. His partner, Jen, did the same. Matthew rose from the recliner and moved across the room. He wanted to be part of this family, if only for a little while.

"Lisa?" Matthew pointed at the table. "Want to try a couple of hands?"

Her eyes widened, then she grinned. "Why not?"

"Cool."

"Remember what I told you," Jen reminded as she offered Matthew her place at the table. "JD's serious about his cards."

"I remember." He chuckled. "No guts. No glory."

Laughing, Jen said, "It's on your head. You've been warned."

Fourteen

So special, swirled in Matthew's head as he flipped down the car's visor against the late afternoon sun. *Yes,* he thought, *Lisa is more than special.* As she maneuvered the car around a bus, his eyes eagerly roamed over her soft features while desire took a sharp bite out of him.

This Memorial Day had been very special, unbelievably so. Not only was Lisa special, that label easily applied to the members of her family. After the initial interrogation, the Daniels clan had warmed up and welcomed him. He felt a sense of peace and belonging he hadn't felt since he was a child. Someday his family would be as close and loving as what he had found today with Lisa's family.

His mouth quirked with humor as he spoke, "Remind me to never play partners with JD. My life passed before my eyes when I gave up that ace."

Lisa's laughter was infectious. She turned to him with an I-told-you-so twinkle in her eyes. The soft, enchanting sound floated through the enclosed space and wrapped its warm tentacles around him. He drew in a deep breath and took in the enticing floral scent of Lisa's perfume.

"I tried to warn you. JD takes his cards very seriously," she reminded in a low silvery voice.

"So I learned at my own expense." Matthew shifted toward her, intent on watching her animated profile. "We did pretty well as partners."

"Yes, we did." She turned to him with a big grin on her

face. "It was fun. We got things together over the last couple of hands. It felt fantastic to beat my brothers. I loved that we won the last hand."

"That was high drama."

"Ohmigosh, yes." Lisa sighed, placed a hand on her chest. "I thought my heart would jump through my chest when you played that last trump card. I was so sure JD had it." She turned into her apartment complex entrance and drove through a maze of cars toward her designated parking area.

"I had a great time. Thanks for inviting me." Matthew squeezed her hand and lingered a moment longer than necessary on her skin. He loved the way it felt, soft and warm. "Your family is something. I'd like to be invited back again."

Hope rose within him. He hadn't realized how much her answer meant to him. Being a friend was only the beginning of what he wanted from her.

"Invitations aren't necessary," Lisa assured. "You're welcome anytime. My parents' place is home to lots of our friends."

"Am I?"

"Are you what?" She glanced at him for a second with a frown of puzzlement on her lovely face.

"A friend?"

"Yes," Lisa confirmed in a quiet tone. Awareness sizzled through the air and made his insides churn with excitement. An odd light entered her eyes while she studied him, then returned her attention to the road. "Very much so."

Watching her profile, her beauty struck Matthew again. He exhaled a long sigh of satisfaction. Good! They were making progress.

Without warning, the serene expression morphed into confusion, then Lisa's mouth dropped open.

"Hey!" She pointed at the front windshield. "Isn't that your car?"

Matthew's glance followed her finger, then nodded. The

Lexus was parked at an odd angle. His heart did a tango in his chest. Had he parked that way? No way. "I don't remember it sitting like that."

Lisa parked in an empty space near his car, then sagged against the bucket seat. "Oh Matthew," she moaned, scrunching up her face and touching his hand. "Somebody hit your car!"

"Damn," Matthew growled as he forgot everything but the rage tearing through him. The car was less than six months old. Now it was junk. Shaking his head, he got out of Lisa's Sable. Taking in the crumbled silver metal, bashed-in driver's door, and broken glass, he answered, "You're not wrong."

Matthew looked around the parking lot for a hint of who might have done this, saw nothing, and returned his attention to his car. He thought she lived in a pretty decent place. Maybe he made the wrong assumption. After all that talk about leaving his car parked because she wanted to keep it safe, he should have vetoed her idea and taken his own car.

"Well, I thought you lived in a nice neighborhood. And that my car was safe."

"I do live in a decent neighborhood." Lisa defended hotly, eyes flashing a warning message at him. "But, it's a holiday weekend and people drink and drive. I have no control over that or who drives through this lot."

Matthew took in a deep, calming breath and studied Lisa for a beat. He sensed how badly she felt and he wasn't helping the situation. Chalk it up to male pride about his car. "You're right. I'm sorry."

Now that his rage had subsided, he began to think rationally again. She feels guilty enough without you adding to that.

"I'm so sorry."

Matthew squatted down next to the Lexus and checked the car's frame. Green and red liquids dripped from the underbody. He rose, wiped his hands on his handkerchief, stuffed it back into his pocket, and ran a hand over his face. "I won't be driving this baby home today."

"This is my fault." Lisa covered her eyes with her hand. "I feel so bad. If I hadn't insisted that we take my car, everything would be fine."

The look of guilt on her face touched his heart. He saw that she was very upset and he wanted to make her feel better.

"Don't think like that. It might have been your car. My insurance will cover everything. That's what I pay for." Matthew placed an arm around Lisa's shoulders and drew her against his side. Her warmth seeped through his clothing and spread like sweet wine through him at the same time Lisa's unique scent filled his nostrils and head. "I figure it will take about a month for the car to get fixed and it'll look better than new. They'll repair all the little dings and scratches I'm always ignoring."

She smiled up at him. He felt as if the sun had moved from behind the clouds and filled the sky with sunlight. "Are you trying to make me feel better?"

"Mmm, hmm." Eyebrows arched, he asked, "Is it working?"

"Some."

"Good. That's all I can ask for. There's no point in speculating about what-ifs. We made a decision to take your car and now we have to live with it." He ran a soothing hand up and down her bare arm and steered her toward the apartment building. "Come on, let's go inside. And if you don't mind, I need to call the police, my insurance company, and a tow truck."

Lisa nodded and led the way. Minutes later they stepped through the front door of her apartment. She moved gracefully across the living room, picked up the cordless phone, and placed it on the desk. "Use my desk. You'll be more comfortable."

"Thanks."

"Can I get you anything?"

"Yeah." Matthew answered, pulling his wallet from his back pocket. "Coffee would be good."

"No problem. There's paper and pens in the middle drawer. Help yourself."

"Thanks."

He dialed 911 and was immediately transferred to another number. While he waited on the line, Matthew opened the desk drawer. The blue folder seemed to jump out at him. Should he open it? Risk the possibility that Lisa might come into the room while he was reading her personal business? A quick glance over his shoulder confirmed that she was busy in the kitchen preparing coffee.

Lifting the folder from the drawer, Matthew stroked the flap. Lisa had been very protective of this folder. He needed to know how this folder fit into the situation. And if whatever was in this folder shed some light on the events at Games, he needed to see what Lisa was hiding. This might be his only opportunity to learn the truth.

Anchoring the telephone between his chin and shoulder, Matthew laid the folder on the desk and stared hard at it. *I've got to do this.* He turned so his body blocked him from Lisa's eagle eye and removed the legal-looking document from the folder while the word "rat" screamed in his head.

Lease agreement? Baffled, he frowned, flipping through the pages until one name shot out at him. Stephen Brock. Stunned, he stared at the document. Lisa signed a building lease with Brock. Why?

She'd talked to him about starting her own business. But with Brock? Matthew shook his head. That idea didn't click. A cold shiver spread over him as he remembered the morning he had made that unexpected visit to her office. The tension he felt between Lisa and Brock had been filled with flashing eyes and clipped retorts.

Had they been arguing over this lease? That made sense, but the rest didn't. Matthew glanced over his shoulder to make certain Lisa hadn't returned to the living room. Again, Jacob's words hit him like a slap across the face. Were Lisa and Brock in cahoots? Could they be planning to open their own business using the money they'd stolen? That thought made his heart palpitate uncontrollably.

"No. Not Lisa," Matthew muttered to himself. "Come on, man. Don't condemn her until you know all the facts." He rubbed a finger back and forth across his chin. "I'm out of my league. Time for Jacob to do some legwork." Taking an additional glance at the door, he jotted the name of the leasing agent and the building on a piece of paper before stuffing it in his pocket. He returned the document to the folder and replaced it where he found it. Best to leave this situation alone until Jacob did an investigation and got all the hard facts.

Besides, this was not the time to question Lisa. The police were due any minute. Matthew needed a clear head for that. And he needed some time to form the proper questions.

The operator came back on the line and Matthew put everything related to Games out of his head and concentrated on giving the right information. Hanging up, he dialed the number for his insurance company, and then the road service.

"How do you take your coffee?" Lisa stood in the doorway with a steaming mug in each hand.

"Black's fine."

"Good." Her head tipped toward the telephone. "How's it going?"

"Done." He watched Lisa closely, searching her face for a clue that would put all the pieces together. "The police are on their way. It's Memorial Day. It'll take hours for a tow truck to come today, if at all. So, my road service will pick up the car tomorrow. I told them to have their driver look under the mat for the key whenever they show up. That way no one has to be around when they put in an appearance."

Nodding, Lisa strolled across the room, handed a mug to Matthew, then sank into the leather chair and tucked her feet under her. "I know I've said it before, but I'm really sorry. If there's anything I can do for you, let me know."

"Do me a favor." He scratched the side of his face. "Stop saying you're sorry. It's done."

"Okay. Okay. I don't know what else to say. I just feel so bad." She shrugged.

Matthew strolled away from the desk, sat on the sofa. Between sips of coffee, he said, "You don't have to say anything. I told you before, it's done. Forget it. Now, what I need from you is the number for the local cab service."

"This I can do. You don't need a cab." She tapped her chest. "I'll take you home."

"No can do. You're already home," he vetoed, stood, returned to the desk, and retrieved the telephone. "I'm not going to have you come out of your safe environment to take me across town."

"Yes, can do. So, don't argue with me." She rose, placed her mug on the coffee table, and started down the hallway. "I'm going to get my purse. Once the police arrive and take their report, I can take you home."

He smirked. "For a tiny thing you can be really bossy."

"And to think I'm trying to be nice to you."

They waited in the parking lot next to Lisa's car as the policemen took notes, inspected the car, and gave Matthew his copy of the accident report.

"Well they got here quicker than I expected." Matthew watched as the policemen returned to the squad car, backed out of their parking space, and headed for the complex exit.

"Actually, I was surprised they got here at all," Lisa admitted. "This being a holiday weekend and all."

"You're right. We were lucky. I'm glad they got here so quickly. I don't want you to be out too late by yourself." He turned to her and smiled. "Chauffeur, are you ready to take me home?"

Lisa waved a hand at her car and said, "Your limo awaits."

"You know," Matthew began in a thoughtful tone, as they approached her car. "I think I should drive."

"Why?" Lisa glared at him with her hands on her hips. "This is my car."

"I know." He held out his hand for her keys. "It'll be quicker and easier than giving you directions. Besides I don't feel right about you driving around late at night by yourself. Maybe this will get you home quicker."

Lisa stood at the rear of the car, arms folded across her chest and her lips pursed while she considered his suggestion. "You're right." She tossed the keys to him.

Matthew helped Lisa inside, then ran around the hood to the driver's side. Once he was behind the wheel, he shifted the seat away from the steering wheel and turned the key in the ignition. Preoccupied, he drove in autopilot.

So special still floated in his head. He still believed Lisa was special. Unfortunately, there were more pressing issues crowding out that wonderful time he'd spent with her and her family today.

That blue folder had turned into his personal Pandora's box. Now, he had an additional set of questions that needed answers. What did the lease agreement really mean? Were Brock and Lisa in cahoots? Partners? How was all of this connected to the company?

Was Lisa planning to resign and start her own business? With Brock? No, he refused to accept that. The thought of Lisa with Brock ate into his belly like acid. He hated it.

Matthew had a hard time believing Lisa was behind the thefts. His day with her and her family had revealed a strong moral fiber. Or maybe he just wanted there to be one because he liked her so much.

Look how upset and guilty she felt when she saw his car and that wasn't her fault. Poor baby. When she saw his car, she practically cried. Guilt was written all over her face. All he could do was try to comfort and assure her that she wasn't responsible. The car was parked and someone hit it. That could have happened anywhere.

He shook his head, which brought him back to the same question: What did everything mean? There had to be an explanation. An answer that made sense. He rubbed a hand back and forth across his chin.

Matthew opened his mouth to ask her about the folder, then shut it. He couldn't read her face in the dark. Besides, he needed to keep his eyes on the road. Maybe he'd wait until they reached his house, invite her in, and then hit her with the questions that were driving him insane. Yeah, that would work.

Or he could just let Jacob do the research and find the answer. That's what he paid him for. Jacob was already working on this case; this was an additional tidbit to add to the their growing list of suspicions.

Until then, he'd enjoy this time with his Ms. Daniels.

Fifteen

Matthew cut the car's engine in his circular drive and turned to Lisa. "This is it." She noticed the full moon through the windshield.

For the hundredth time, she said, "I'm so sorry."

Irritation flashed across his handsome face, then it was gone. "I told you forget it," he dismissed, stretching his arm along the back of her seat. "It wasn't your fault."

She twisted the soft gold chain around her finger. Her logical mind knew that, but her heart felt something different. "I know. But I feel so bad."

The soft brush of his fingers against the back of her neck made her pulse quicken. His touch should have soothed her. Instead, it started a tingling in the pit of her stomach that had nothing to do with sympathy and everything to do with Matthew's touch and her response.

Lisa touched his arm and felt the muscles jerk under her fingertips, sending currents through them. "I-I-I," she stammered. For a moment her train of thought was lost. "If I hadn't insisted we take my car, we would have taken yours and avoided all of this mess."

Matthew's hand brushed the hair from her forehead and skirted gently along her cheek. "It's all right," he said in that husky voice that ran through her. "I have my truck to drive."

"I know you're right. I just feel bad," Lisa admitted in a breathless whisper and twisted her hands together.

Gently, Matthew grabbed her hand and held it. A faint light

twinkled in the depths of his eyes. "I've got a proposition for you."

Eyebrows lifted, she quizzed, "Oh?"

"Mmm, hmm." He nodded. A husky note lingered in his voice. "If you forget about the car, I'll let you come in and see my new house."

"House?" Preoccupied with her own miserable thoughts, Lisa hadn't noticed or cared where they were going. Finally taking stock of her surroundings, Lisa's lips parted in shock. "Ohmigosh." Turning to him, she said on a note of surprise, "You bought the house."

His mouth twitched with humor. "That I did. I wondered how long it would take you to come out of your blue flunk and notice."

"Obviously, too long," she responded, a bit of self-mockery in her tone.

Covering her hand with his own, Matthew asked, "Remember the day we found it?"

She nodded. Her lips curved into an approving smile. Of course, Matthew would purchase the house they both fell in love with that Saturday afternoon.

"We were both so enchanted with it, I instantly knew this was the one. It felt right for me. That Monday morning, I called my realtor and made an appointment. Once I saw the inside, I made an offer. Seven weeks later I closed and moved in." Matthew tilted his head toward the house. His car door swung open and he stepped from the car. "Let's go in so you can see what I've done with the place."

Excitement bubbled up within her. "This I've got to see," Lisa said. "This is too good to pass up."

Lisa followed Matthew from the car and stood in the driveway. With arms folded across her chest, she ran a keen eye over the exterior.

The house was a wonderful, red-brick colonial with white pillars on each end of the porch. Large red ceramic flowerpots decorated the porch with azaleas. She climbed the concrete steps and stood at Matthew's side and waited while he unlocked the carved front doors, then disarmed the security system.

Greeted by the warmth of the small, elegant foyer, Lisa felt as if she'd been wrapped in a wool blanket on a snowy night. Her gaze followed the high-beamed ceiling, admiring the dark gleaming wood contrasting against vanilla walls.

The foyer contained an enormous marble drum top table. A staircase filled one corner of the foyer, each step covered with a brown, crème, and blue rug. Cut roses stood elegantly in a tall, narrow-necked Waterford crystal vase placed in the center of the table. Passing the table, Lisa couldn't resist stroking a scarlet velvety petal, and inhaled the delicate fragrance into her lungs.

Silent, Matthew shut the door and leaned against the door frame. Stroking his chin, he exhaled a long sigh of contentment, enjoying Lisa's examination of the room. He grinned devilishly. She was a delight to watch.

White Diamonds perfume sizzled in the air like a delicate potpourri and made Matthew's nostrils flare. Smiling, he recalled the day that he'd stopped some strange woman on the street and asked her what perfume she wore because it reminded him of Lisa.

Matthew stood in the shadows, giving Lisa the run of the place. He made no attempt to hide the fact that he was watching her. This was a treat he hadn't expected to enjoy so soon. In the past, there had been women who caught his attention. There had even been a time or two that he believed he was in love. But nothing compared to the feelings he had for Lisa. The more he saw of her, the more he wanted to see and know. Even the mushroom cloud threat of uncertainty about Games couldn't dampen his spirits.

There were still things standing between them that needed to be addressed. Games still had to be his first priority, with whatever Lisa knew about the thefts coming second. That lease agreement and all its secrets drew a quick third, and fourth and most important, what were her feelings for him?

He'd been wrong to believe he could question her tonight.

This wasn't the time or the place. Plus, he didn't want to break the mood, or create unnecessary tension that would make her shut down.

Tonight he'd put aside all concern for the company and its problems. This was going to be his night—correction—their night. This was an opportunity for them to grow closer. And he didn't plan to miss it.

"Can I?" Lisa pointed at the great room. A hopeful gleam blazed from her eyes.

Matthew reached around the door frame and switched on the light. It bathed the room in a gentle golden glow. "Knock yourself out."

"Thanks." Lisa's smile widened as she hurried across the hallway and slid gracefully into one of the Queen Anne chairs. Like a proper debutante, she perched on the edge of the chair and glanced around her.

"This house is gorgeous," Lisa muttered, wiggling in the chair. She took note of the cathedral ceilings, a natural stone fireplace, hardwood floors, and an oriental rug splashed with brown, crème, and blue. At the opposite end of the room, a large bay window with a half-moon-shaped cushion pillow overlooked what Lisa suspected were the gardens.

Somewhere outside the great room the telephone rang. Matthew pushed away from the wall and pointed to the hallway. "I've got to get that. It might be about the car or Games. Will you be okay?"

"Yeah. I'm fine. Go take care of your business." She shooed him away with a wave of her hand. "Oh, before you go. Do you mind if I look around?" she asked, barely able to contain the eagerness in her voice.

"Enjoy," he answered indulgently. A half-smile appeared on his lips before he left the room.

"That's my ticket," she muttered, springing from the chair once he'd left the room.

After examining every nook and cranny of the great room, Lisa turned her attention to the formal dining room. A Queen Anne cherry wood table with high-backed chairs filled the room. Plus, a buffet and china cabinet completed the set. The brown, crème, and blue pattern continued with the same soft fabric base covering the seat cushions. Here, too, roses spread their fragrant cheer throughout the room from the vase in the center of the table.

Moving along the hallway, she heard the deep rumble of Matthew's voice behind a door. She peeked in and found him pacing the room with the telephone glued to his ear. Good, she could move around without worrying about bumping into him. Not wanting to disturb him, Lisa pulled the door closed and hurried down the corridor.

A chef's dream awaited her when she entered the kitchen. The black surface of the appliances sparkled against the black-and-white ceramic tile floor while the fresh aroma of pine cleaner lingered in the air. A matching ebony range and Jen-Aire grill found their home inside the walnut kitchen island.

The breakfast nook connected the two rooms. A carved wooden table and four matching chairs filled much of the space. The black-and-white ceramic tile pattern continued throughout the breakfast nook.

Hesitating at the back stairs, she rationalized her next move. Matthew told her to make herself at home. Well, checking out the place was part of making herself at home.

Lisa headed up the stairs. At the landing, she paused, taking stock of her surroundings. A ripple of excitement zipped through her when she peeked into the first of seven rooms. *Boy, this place is gorgeous.*

With a hand on the doorknob Lisa entered the fourth bedroom. Strings of music floated through the opened door. Shadow Fax's new age music filled the room and drew her inside with an invisible hand. "Very nice. Now, this is the way to live," she complimented, admiring the DVD player tucked inside an entertainment center, accompanied by a television and VCR. A brick-colored leather sofa sat in front of the fireplace; smoked glass and chrome coffee and end tables completed the set.

"Jay, I don't have it with me." Matthew appeared in the room with the telephone attached to his ear. "Let me check the suit I wore yesterday. I might have left it in the pocket."

Paralyzed, Lisa stood next to the sofa with her feet nailed to the floor. Her stomach twisted into knots. She wondered, had her exploration gone too far? Would Matthew be upset to find her on the second floor?

He looked up, saw her, and halted. The smoldering flame she saw in his eyes startled and excited her all at once.

"I'll call you back," Matthew said into the phone. "No. Tomorrow. I'll call you back." He disconnected the call and tossed the phone on the sofa. Smiling, he strolled with nonchalant grace to within inches of where she stood. "Hi," he greeted in that husky, sensuous voice.

"I'm sorry. I'm so sorry," Lisa chanted, embarrassed to the roots of her hair. "I-I-I-I'm sorry. I invaded your privacy. I got caught up in seeing the place. I'm sorry."

"No harm done." Matthew swept a hand across the room and said, "So, you've seen everything."

Lisa shook herself mentally. Get a grip, girlfriend. "I'll go back downstairs now."

"Don't go. You wanted to see the place. I understand your interest. After all, we found this house together. Let me be your guide." He touched her arm and a thousand sensations exploded within her. "The minute we saw it, I knew this was going to be my home. And it is. This is the master suite. Bet you've already figured that one out. It has a total of three rooms. A sitting room, master bedroom, attached nursery, and his and her bathrooms."

"I love this place. It's warm and beautiful. Intimate."

Glancing around the room, Matthew's lips curled into a smile. "I love this house, too. But there's one thing I'm missing."

The suggestive note in his voice struck a vibrant chord in her. Her heart hammered in her chest. Matthew required a response. Lisa summoned up all of her courage to ask, "What's that?"

"I need someone to share it with me," Matthew muttered in that husky voice, "I'd like you to be that someone."

Lisa swallowed hard. She wanted to be that person, but couldn't, studying his face, remembering the times they had been together.

An even more frightening realization washed over her. *I'm falling in love with Matthew.* That's why she couldn't get him out of her head or heart.

"Matthew." Lisa wet her lips, searching for the right words to say. Wringing her hands together, she needed to stop him before he said something he couldn't take back.

"No. Wait. Listen to me first." His hands rested on her shoulders. "I understand you're scared to get involved again." He stroked her cheek with the back of his hand, reached for her hand, and took it between both of his. "We can't let this opportunity for us to be together pass us by. If you need me to take it slow, I will. No problem. I won't let you go, Lisa."

"I can't do this," Lisa whispered back, shaking her head.

Kissing the palm of her hand, Matthew persisted, "Why? Why can't you?"

"There's a lot you don't know or understand about me," she answered in a weak, miserable voice.

"Tell me. Help me to understand," he lowered his voice to a persuasive purr. "You can tell me anything."

Just talk to me, Matthew begged silently. *Tell me what's really going on and I'll help you. But I can't do anything without you giving me the facts.* If she just admitted her part in the software crimes he'd find a way to clear her. But Lisa must admit the truth before he could act.

Silent, Lisa stood in front of him wishing things were different.

Drawing her into his arms, the warmth of his body seeped into hers. Matthew said, "Okay. We'll let things go for now. But know this. Whenever you're ready to talk, I'll be here to listen."

His gentleness was her undoing. It was unexpected and genuine. The intoxicating scent of Matthew overwhelmed her, making all of her fantasies bubble to the surface. Until now she'd always been able to resist his smart remarks and flip answers, but his tenderness tore down the barriers and left her heart open to him. Lisa turned away, fighting back her tears. It would be easy to just let her fears go and pretend everything was perfect, to love him completely.

One hot tear slid down her cheek while her heart sank in her chest. He stroked her cheek with the back of his hand, wrapped his arms around her, and ran soothing hands along her spine.

His hands moved upward and cupped her face between his warm palms. The touch created delicious sensations. Matthew bent his head and nibbled at the corners of her closed lips, first the left side, then the right.

Lisa gasped, unable to control her reaction. His nearness made her senses spin out of control. Need took over and her lips parted. He took advantage and covered her lips with his. A wave of giddiness wormed its way through her as he settled her against the warm, hard planes of his body, deepening the kiss.

This was a far cry from what she expected when she offered to drive Matthew home. She couldn't fight him or her feelings anymore. Truthfully, she didn't want to. The need to love him consumed her. And she refused to deny herself a moment longer.

Surrendering, she wrapped her arms around his neck, drew him closer, and returned his kiss with all the love in her heart.

Sixteen

"Trust me, sweetheart," Matthew whispered against her ear while his busy hands made quick work of the buttons on her shorts. The garment slid off her hips and landed in a heap on his sitting room floor.

Desire, hot and all consuming, raced through her like lightning flashing across the sky. Matthew's fingers trailed across Lisa's lips. The gentle stroke felt as soft as a whisper and ignited an untapped flame within her. He took her lips in a powerful, persuasive kiss.

"Just trust me," he repeated huskily. "It'll be good. I promise."

Lisa tore her lips away from his. "Matthew, maybe, maybe we should think about this." She panted into his ear, struggling to focus on the logical thing to do, seconds away from being swept away by the tide of sensations his persuasive touch evoked.

"Later," he whispered in a deep velvety purr as his arms slid around her waist and drew her against the hard planes of his body. His lips skimmed the side of her neck and sent her blood bubbling like hot lava through her veins. "We'll think about it later."

Lisa gave in. A gleam of sensual fire smoldered from Matthew's eyes while his hands rested low on her hips and stroked the soft flesh above the waistband of her black lace briefs. Her eyes shut as he captured her earlobe between his lips. Hungry for her, his hot, moist tongue suckled on her flesh, sending shivers that raced down her spine.

Exerting a light pressure, he drew her closer, his lips fastened onto hers. He tasted of beer and the hearty essence of Matthew. Her fingers slid over his hair and settled at the base of his neck. She drew him closer.

Within seconds, the T-shirt followed the same path as her shorts. Lisa stood in the center of the room dressed in her black bra and matching panties. Cool air circulated around her and made her nipples harden beneath the lace—or was it Matthew? He scooped her into his arms, lifting her from the tangle of clothing at her feet.

Surprised, Lisa gasped and her arms crept around his neck. He marched across the floor into his bedroom with his prize.

Lying among the sheets, the sensation of silk against her back felt cool. Lisa swallowed hard as the rising tide of passion consumed her. Sensual heat spread through her like a wild fire out of control.

Matthew dropped down next to her and pulled her close. "I want to make love to you," he whispered against her hair. His lips rained hot kisses along her throat and made every spot sizzle with excitement. *Yes,* she thought, *oh yes.* Lisa closed her eyes and savored the vision of his magnificent body entwined with hers, lips caressing, souls touching.

No words were needed; she planned to use her hands, mouth, and body to let him know how much she cared for him. Her long fingers trailed through the mat of dark hair that narrowed into his jeans as his nipples tightened.

"Lee, you're playing with fire," he warned.

"I like fire," she answered in a liquid gold tone that promised everything as her fingers caressed his flesh through the fabric. "Fire draws me. I like to watch it spread and burn."

"Wait." He hooked his thumbs inside the waistband of his jeans, yanked them and his shorts below his knees in one fluid motion, then bicycled the garments off his legs and dropped them next to the bed. His aroused shaft sprung forth and drew her attention to this treat.

"Let's get you out of this thing." He slipped the straps off her shoulders, stripped the panties away from her body, and tossed them both to the floor next to his jeans. Leaning on his side, Matthew did a slow study of her nude form. The expression in his eyes melted her bones and shattered all resistance she had about making love with him.

"My turn, sweetheart. I want to see you burn." He cupped a breast in each hand and smiled at the expression in her eyes. Lovingly, he flicked his thumbs across each sensitive node then watched the tip turn turgid. Arching herself against his hands, she cried out, wanting more.

Matthew suckled a brown tip between his lips and concentrated all of his energies on drawing nectar from this special passion fruit. She turned her head into the pillow and tried to stem the cry of pleasure that threatened to escape her lips. Her efforts were unsuccessful.

"Oh-h-h . . . yes," she moaned.

He smiled down at her, sending her pulse into hyperdrive. "I don't want the other one to feel neglected." His tongue created a moist path to the twin globe and administered the same treatment to its double. "Beautiful."

Gentle, but arousing hands swept over her breasts, down her belly, and explored the cluster of dark curls that guarded her womanhood. His finger separated the folds and rotated the bud with his thumb. Her pulse skittered into orbit.

"Don't stop." Panting, she moved her hips in harmony with his fingers.

"I don't plan to." His deep voice promised, combining with the touch of his hand, inflaming her passion. "Touch me."

Her fingers slid through the pelt of hair that covered his chest. Smooth, unblemished skin felt firm to her touch. Her fingertips glided over the hard plane of his chest, stomach, and along the smooth broad shaft. She stroked him, gliding up and down the broad shaft.

Matthew gasped, his face a mixture of emotions. He removed her hand, rolled her onto her back, and whispered huskily against her neck, "I want to be inside you."

"Oh Matthew, I do want you . . . in me . . . with me." Lisa guided him to her wet passage. Needing no further encouragement, Matthew buried himself deep within her core with one powerful stroke.

He gasped, trying to control the tremors that threatened to take him as he settled himself within her wet warmth. Almost withdrawing, Matthew plunged deeper into her and began their dance of love.

I love you, Lisa's body shouted with each stroke. *I'll always love you, Matthew,* she promised silently as her tongue slipped between his lips.

"Matthew . . ." Lisa pleaded. He stretched and filled every part of her. She responded to his every touch, caught up in the scent, taste, sound, and feel of their mating. With each thrust the tempo increased as he caressed her wet passage. His hands slipped beneath her, drawing her closer.

"Come with me," he whispered against her ear. "Come with me."

She met every thrust of his hips with her own. They danced the exquisite dance of lovers, climbing from peak to peak, seeking completeness. Higher and higher they climbed. The flame ignited by their lovemaking burned unchecked. Lisa's nails dug into Matthew's back while his tongue met and waltzed with hers. His body slid into hers uncontrollably. A gasp slipped from her lips as the first contractions rippled, building to a volcanic eruption. One final stroke took them both over the edge into a world of brilliant lights and vibrant colors.

The warm, hot rush of his release filled her. Lisa held tight, refusing to let him slip away. Contented, he remained inside her, sharing the afterglow of lovemaking.

Sated, Lisa drifted somewhere between wakefulness and sleep, wrapped within Matthew's embrace. Without breaking contact, he rolled onto his back and took her with him. She landed on his chest and gazed into the heavy-lidded eyes of this very satisfied man.

"I didn't want to crush you. But I want to keep you with me." He pressed the back of her head into the crook of his arm and ran his hands along her spine. She complied eagerly.

Kissing her forehead, he held her tightly against him. "We need to talk. But you can barely keep your eyes open. And neither can I. Let's go to sleep, sweetheart. We'll work everything out in the morning."

Lisa felt far too content to comment. Matthew's hand continued to caress her spine in a slow sensual slide and finally rested possessively on her nude bottom.

Sleep eluded Lisa, although her body felt satiated and limp. Her mind was crowded with one hundred and one questions and no answers. She lay close to Matthew and listened to the unfamiliar sounds that were part of his house. She recognized the occasional car that crept down the road, the sprinkler system soaking the lawn in its nightly ritual, and the deep, even breathing of the man sleeping in the bed beside her. His body sprawled completely relaxed and nude on top of the sheet.

What she'd feared had finally happened. Not only had she fallen in love with Matthew, she had allowed him to make love to her. Love was a much fiercer opponent than she had anticipated.

Rising quietly from the bed so she wouldn't disturb Matthew, she picked up his terry-cloth robe from the back of a chair. The brown fabric was old and faded from many years of wear. Both elbows were threadbare and the hem frayed, but it offered the measure of protection and comfort she needed.

Lisa flopped down on the sofa and stared into the empty fireplace. The moonlight cast a shadowy covering over the darkened room.

He'd kept his promise, Lisa thought. She'd never experienced anything like it. Loving Stephen hadn't made her feel the way she felt with Matthew.

Now, what was she going to do? She twirled a lock of hair around her finger. Her eyes strayed to the man on the bed. Images of them together played out in her mind like a videotape. She could almost see them together, loving each other with all the desperation of new lovers.

She still wasn't sure he was the right person to have a relationship with. He was a good man who deserved much more than she could offer.

It was time to leave Games. But this wasn't the best time to start a new business, or quit her job. Putting her feelings aside, she enjoyed her work and the challenges it offered.

In one evening, she'd destroyed all the promises she'd made to herself when she'd split from Stephen. Now she had to live with the consequences of her actions. As soon as the weekend ended, she'd start preparation for her business. Hopefully, within a few months she would be able to leave Games and Matthew. But for tonight, she wanted to be completely and truly his.

Matthew escaped the tangled covers and padded nude across the carpeted floor to where Lisa sat. Silently, he stood in the shadows and watched the woman on the sofa. Lost in thought, she had no idea how beautiful he found her. His gaze dropped from Lisa's face to her silken shoulder, to her soft enticing breasts that winked at him from between the vee of his robe.

Lisa stiffened and turned to find him leaning against the wall. "Hey." He smiled and dropped to one knee on the oriental rug in front of her. He wanted to draw her into his arms, hold her close, and tell her what she meant to him.

Instead, he asked, "What's going on in that head of yours?"

She shrugged. "Nothing."

"Why don't you come back to bed?" He stood and offered his hand to her. "Tonight is not the time to contemplate life as it exists. We both need some rest before morning." His heart pounded happily when she put her hand in his and allowed him to pull her to her feet.

"Is that what you really want to do?" Lisa wrapped her arms around his neck and brought his head down to hers. She gave him the sweetest of kisses, then slipped her tongue between his lips.

Ending the kiss, his eyes shimmered. "What have you got in mind?"

"Oh, a little exercise that will make us both rest better," she answered, taking his face between her hands and kissing the left corner of Matthew's mouth, and then the right.

On her toes, she swayed toward him and buried her face in his neck.

"Mmm. Why don't you show me?" he whispered, carrying her back to the bed.

"I can do that," Lisa promised.

Seventeen

Matthew awoke first. He watched Lisa sleep for a few quiet moments. Enticed by the smooth peanut-butter color of her skin, his fingers traced her shoulder blade and his lips followed his fingers. Her intoxicating perfume lingered on his skin. Matthew inhaled deeply, enjoying her fragrance as memories of the previous night returned to him.

The doorbell vibrated loudly in Matthew's head and throughout the room. "What the hell!" he mumbled, reluctantly untangling his limbs from Lisa's warm flesh. Careful not to disturb her, he rolled onto his side and glanced at the clock. Eight o'clock! The bell reverberated a second time and he eased from the bed, scrabbling around on the floor for his jeans.

"Who is that at my door?" Shoving his legs into his jeans, Matthew zipped up, rushed out of the bedroom, and hurried down the stairs in his bare feet to stop that racket before it woke Lisa.

He muttered a fine string of obscenities under his breath at this intrusion. "What is the deal?" he complained as the bell rang for the third time. It was Sunday! A day of rest and relaxation!

When Lisa woke up, there were a few choice questions he needed to ask Ms. Daniels, including a question regarding the riddle he called their relationship.

Let me see who this is, Matthew glanced through the great room window and spotted a black limousine in the circular drive. His face scrunched up. Limo? Who would show up at his house in a limo? Returning to the foyer, he snatched the door open and immediately felt the urge to slam it shut.

"What took you so long?" His mother demanded, glancing pointedly at his shirtless state and bare feet. One finely arched eyebrow rose suggestively. "Were you busy?" She asked in a smug, know-it-all tone.

Surprised, his mouth dropped open. They stared at each other across a sudden ringing silence.

Amusement flickered in the eyes that met his. His reaction seemed to tickle her. But it didn't slow her down a bit.

Coherent thoughts fled his brain as he watched his mother. She turned to the driver and ordered the poor soul to carry in her luggage.

Carolyn James stood five feet seven inches tall at sixty-two years of age. Her high cheekbones, skin the color of warm mocha, and toffee eyes gave her an exotic, fragile air. Matthew knew better. His mother had a will of iron, one that matched his own.

Determination flashed from his mother's eyes. He took a step away from her. She was on a mission. He'd bet Games on that. That certainty gnawed at him like an aching tooth.

"I'm welcome, correct?" She asked with quiet firmness. Her eyes clouded with uncertainty before her more familiar mask dropped into place. Although her voice sounded and appeared strong and firm, an insecure note crept into her tone.

Matthew's lips puckered in annoyance; he crossed his arms and maintained his vigil at the door. Every line of his stiff body shouted disapproval. With unwelcome frankness, he said, "I thought we'd agreed that you'd wait until I got the house organized."

Mother gave an impatient shrug and stepped close to kiss the air near Matthew's cheek. Then she moved past him to inspect the foyer. "I planned to wait, but things slowed down at the company. So I decided to take the plunge. After all, you're my baby, my only child, and I wanted to see how things were going for you." Her mouth spread into a thin-lipped smile. "Besides, you know as well as I do that you'd never invite me. So, here I am. Easy, pezy, Japanezy."

"You're here all right," he gritted his teeth and muttered under his breath like a disobedient child.

Mother waved a graceful hand toward the limo driver struggling up the walkway with her luggage. "Pay the man."

He choked back words of anger at the sight of the driver hauling the last of Mother's luggage. Just how long did she plan to stay?

Matthew dug in the back pocket of his jeans, pulled some bills from his wallet, and handed them to the driver. After thanking him, he took a moment to reflect on how much he wished he could stuff his mother back in the limo, lock the door, and tell the driver not to stop until they reached the airport.

In a fit of frustration, he slammed the door shut and went in search of his parent. Chanel perfume created an olfactory trail through the entrance and the connecting hallway. His search led to the great room where he found her black silk jacket tossed across the sofa, much of it in a heap on the floor.

He shoved his hand inside his back pocket and paced the floor while contemplating this new development. For months Mother had been threatening to visit. To keep her out of his life, he'd used every trick he knew.

Matthew wanted her in Chicago as much as he wanted to reconcile with her. His stark, lonely childhood played as a vivid reminder of her lack of interest in his life and he didn't want her to the fill the void at this point.

Holidays and special occasions, she'd flown away on business, leaving him with baby-sitters and nannies. No, he refused to be part of any happy family reunion or reconciliation, whatever she wanted to call it. He'd open his home for a while, a short while, because he had no choice. But, he'd make damn sure he stayed out of earshot of her tearful regrets. Too little, too late.

Running his hand through his hair, Matthew moved

through the house. Where did she go? After a search of the first floor, he returned to the great room. The only place left to search was the upstairs. Lord, this woman was going to be the death of him.

Muffled voices drifted down the stairs. In the quiet of the morning, he heard, "Ohmigosh!"

Fist clenched, he shouted in his head. *No! Lisa!*

"Oh!"

Followed by his mother's, "Sorry, darling."

"Hell!" Matthew shook his head at the heavens as fear and anger knotted inside him. Taking the stairs two at a time, he crested the second floor at record speed, turned down the hallway to his bedroom, and pushed the ajar door the rest of the way open. The pungent scent of sex filled the air and made it obvious what had transpired.

Mother's sharp whiplash tongue was notorious. Lisa needed his protection from her.

"I guess you were busy." Mrs. James grinned at her son.

Lisa stood like stone, bare toes curled into the carpet. Her eyes were downcast and her knuckles white as she clutched the two ends of the sash that held his brown bathrobe together. She looked as if she wanted to evaporate into the air. Poor baby. He needed to explain everything to Lisa, so Mother needed to leave.

"Hello," Mother strolled closer to Lisa and drew herself to her full height, towering over Lisa with an outstretched hand. "I'm Caroline James, Matthew's mother. And you are?"

He stepped between them, pushed her hand away, and demanded, "Go away, Mother. This is none of your business." He glanced around the room. "There's no place here for you."

"She's cute, Mattie." Her head tilted as she ran an appraising eye over Lisa. "Although very different from what I'd expect from you."

Lisa's gaze lifted from the carpet and held Matthew's for a

moment, blistering with harsh emotions, then turned to his mother. "Don't talk about me as if I'm not in the room."

"My, oh my. She can speak. I had my doubts. And there seems to be a brain in there, too." Mother turned to him. "That's a new feature for you. Isn't it?"

"Stop . . . this . . . now, Mother," Matthew grounded out between clenched teeth and jerked his thumb toward the door. "Get out."

"Excuse me." Mother again drew to her full height and placed her arms on her hips. "Who do you think you're talking to? I'm your mother."

Fear and worry gnawed away at his confidence. Watching Lisa's closed expression, he realized that if Mother refused to leave, every baby step forward with Lisa would be lost.

"Yes, you are. And there's nothing I can do about that. That's why I'm giving you an opportunity to go under your own steam." He turned from Lisa and trapped his mother with a piercing stare that he hoped got his point across, and spoke in a rough and ruthless tone. "So leave."

"I didn't do anything. You didn't tell me you had company," Mother protested, as she moved to his side, reached out, and clutched at his arm. "Honestly Mattie, I just peeked inside this room, searching for a place to put my things. I didn't expect to find anyone up here."

"You're working my last nerve, Mother." He warned, grabbing her arm and steering her toward the door. "I won't ask you again."

"All right." Mother shook off his hand and looked past him again. "It was interesting meeting one of my son's friends. Enjoy," she tossed over her shoulder and disappeared through the door.

Now, he must make things right for Lisa. "Sweetheart, I'm sorry." Arms outstretched and an explanation on his lips, Matthew walked to her. "Mother's visit was unexpected," he explained as he wrapped his fingers around her upper arms and drew her stiff frame into his embrace. "She showed up without an invitation."

"This whole situation is beyond me," Lisa pushed the words from tight, grim lips. Her words seemed worn, thin, and hollow and it worried him. "I'm not sophisticated enough to know the expected protocol. So, I think the best thing for me to do is get gone."

"Look, Lee, I understand. But we need to talk and because my mother is here, it'll have to wait. You get dressed and I'll get Mother settled, then we'll find someplace for me and you. How about breakfast?" He suggested in a persuasive tone, holding Lisa's gaze with his own. Again, a chill ran along his spine at the withdrawn, unresponsive expression in her eyes. "A restaurant would be a good thing. What do you say?"

"I've got a better idea. I'll get dressed and go home. You've got problems of your own in the shape of your mother. That's where you need to concentrate your energy. This isn't the time or the place for any deep discussion. Give me a minute to get dressed and then I'm out of here." She took a deep breath and brushed passed him to stand in the bathroom doorway. "I'll chalk this one up to experience."

Matthew gathered fresh clothes from his closet and headed across the hallway to the empty bedroom for a shower. At this point he believed it was damn near impossible to get Lisa to listen to him. Once she cooled down and reconsidered things, then he could talk to her.

He slammed the bedroom door, gaining a bit of satisfaction from the childish gesture, stalked across the room, and dropped his clean clothes on the bed.

Last night on the verge of sleep, he had such high hopes for today. His last waking thought had been of spending uninterrupted time with Lisa, talking everything out and making plans for their future. Instead, here he stood in the opposite bedroom, alone.

Mother, he thought. Her presence caused so much trouble. From the minute she arrived on his doorstep, she had stirred up problems. Why hadn't she stayed in Dallas? Life would have been so much sweeter.

He had thought his heart would pop through his chest when he heard Lisa's surprised cry. And when he stepped into his bedroom and saw her embarrassed expression, all he wanted to do was take her in his arms and reassure her that everything would be fine.

Damn! His mind screamed as he stripped off his jeans. He made his way to the bathroom and twisted the hot water knob for the shower. Steam rose from the enclosed space, and he added cold water, before stepping inside the stall, closing the door, and reaching for the soap.

How had a morning with so much promise, gone so wrong? Finally, he'd broken down a few of Lisa's reservations and found the real woman, only to have her withdraw into her shell once his mother intruded into the warm cocoon they'd created.

Lisa and I have too many things to discuss to be pestered by Mother, Matthew thought, lathering his body with soap. That stuff about the lease agreement still bugged him. Stephen Brock's involvement in Lisa's life and Matthew's relationship with her were at the top of his list that needed to be addressed. Matthew turned in the shower, rinsed off, then reached for his hair shampoo and squeezed a few drops into his hands.

As Matthew worked the shampoo into his hair, he wondered if he would have a second chance to share the closeness he'd found with Lisa the previous evening. That time with her had been spectacular. Making love represented only a portion of it. The giving and sharing of their bodies and feelings had rocked him. *Got to have that again,* he promised.

Leaving the shower, he grabbed his towel and began to dry off. A second towel covered his damp hair when he returned to the bedroom. To get Lisa back in his arms and bed, he needed to resolve whatever issues his mother had on her agenda. He stepped into a clean pair of briefs and a fresh pair of jeans, adding a black Tommy Hilfilger T-shirt and running shoes.

He drew the brush over his short hair, then ran a hand over his head. Mother needed to be dealt with. What did she want? True, she had been calling him every week for the past month or two. Each time he had blown her off. Hell, he had a life that didn't include her, and he liked it that way. While she was here, it was up to him to deal with her if he wanted to move her through her vacation and back to California.

But not before he spoke with Lisa. She must understand that Mother had swept into his home and his life with all the force of a summer storm and without his permission.

Matthew picked his wallet off the bed, deposited it inside his back pocket, and headed for the door. Now that he was dressed, Lisa became his priority. He planned to catch her before she slipped out the front door and make her understand that his mother presented a temporary distraction that would disappear just as quickly as she had appeared. Lisa needed his reassurance that his mother would not come between them again.

Eighteen

Lisa stood in Matthew's empty hallway, gnawing on her bottom lip, debating what her next move should be. Maybe she should slip out the front door without a word or leave a note on the drum top table in the foyer. *No. Do the right thing, Lisa.* She needed to find Matthew and let him know that she planned to leave.

A door at the opposite end of the corridor opened. Tense, her breath caught in her throat. Poised to flee, she waited. *Please, don't let it be Carolyn James.* One encounter with that woman provided more than enough unpleasantness for this lifetime. Her shoulders sagged with relief and she let out a ragged breath. Good, she was safe. Matthew stepped from the room and into the hallway.

His presence filled the small space and she shrank a bit. All of the embarrassing images came back to her in a rush, filling her head.

Fear crept through her soul. Lisa took a tentative step away from the imposing male silhouette as he stepped from the shadows. On closer examination, she modified the idea that she might be safe. He looked fierce, ready to pounce. Mrs. James may not be here, but Matthew had that furious we're-going-to-straighten-this-out expression.

Lisa's heart galloped as Matthew approached her. He sauntered down the hall as if he had all the time in the world. The wheels were turning inside his head.

He stopped several feet away from her. Silent as night, they stood, enduring the silence.

Matthew must have showered in one of the other bedrooms, Lisa surmised, because the fresh scent of soap and aftershave invaded her senses and filled her nostrils. The polo shirt accentuated his broad chest and the finely pressed blue jeans emphasized his long runner legs.

In contrast, Lisa felt grubby, standing before him in her clothes from the previous day. It increased her need to get away from this house and Matthew.

Matthew's eyes moved over her then returned to her face. He gave her a curt nod of greeting and Lisa knew that he'd come to some sort of decision. The determination glittering from his eyes turned her fear up a notch. Unexpectedly, his hands shot out and wrapped around her upper arm. Her eyes grew wide with confusion. He drew her into the warmth of his embrace at the same time his head dipped, seeking her lips.

"No," Lisa spat, turning her head from side-to-side, avoiding his lips. Unnamable sensations ran through her as Matthew's lips grazed her cheek, sending her pulse out-of-control. *Oh but I want to,* she admitted silently.

"No?" His eyes narrowed and his hand cupped her chin, holding her firmly as he forced her to look at him. "Why not?" Matthew challenged in a husky growl. "We did a helluva lot more last night."

Her gaze shifted away from the anger and frustration she read in his eyes. "Because." Unsure if she knew the answer, she responded defiantly.

His brows crinkled into a scowl and he chuckled unpleasantly. "That explains it."

"Because enough has happened here today and I'd like to go home before I become a fatal casualty in whatever is going on between you and your mother." She stood tight and tense in front of him.

"Forget Mother. We live very separate and different lives,"

he dismissed. "I'm more interested in us, and where we're headed."

Lisa took a step close to Matthew and her quiet response was definite and final. "Let me make it clear for you. You and me are not going to happen."

Shock flashed across his face and Lisa spotted a hint of hurt before he hid it. His lips curled into a nasty snarl. Matthew held her gaze with his own. "Oh? You think not? Making love with me meant nothing?"

Lisa tried to mentally shield herself from her obvious lie and his anger.

Suddenly, his eyes twinkled with humor. "Obviously, I didn't do my job. I remember mountains moving and the heavens opening up for . . . both of us. Where were you?"

"Look—"

"Where were you?" He asked a bit louder and with more force.

"This is not the time or place."

"Oh no," he shook his head in dissent. "You're not getting out of that comment that easy. You brought it up. Where were you?"

"I-I-I," she stammered. Embarrassed, she felt the hot rush of heat fill her cheeks.

Matthew demanded, evenly spacing each word, "Where—were—you?"

"With you." Lisa opened her mouth to say more, then shut it without another word. Enough had been said already.

Matthew nodded. "That's what I thought."

"But it was all a mistake. I made a mistake." She stated before pushing her way passed him to the staircase.

Matthew shot down the stairs and blocked her path with an outstretched arm across the railing. She halted several steps from the bottom.

"I don't think so. You didn't make a mistake." He corrected in a deadly calm voice that dared her to contradict him.

Her lips pressed together and she stared at the carpet.

"Contrary to what your mother believes about me, I am not a whore."

"In my eyes you've always been a complete lady. And one I truly respect." Matthew whispered in sweet reverence while his hand caressed her cheek. "What my mother says or does means nothing in this house."

Lisa shut her eyes, absorbing the feel of his cool hand against her flesh. "Maybe so. Maybe no."

"There's no maybe. It's a fact." Matthew growled, dropping his hand to his side. His eyes flashed with angry fire. "What Mother thinks doesn't mean a thing. "All you need to know is our being together was more, much more than a one-night stand. It was." He drew in a deep breath, shut his eyes, lips curved into a smile as he relived those moments in his head, "special."

Yes, it was, she admitted silently, replaying every second they'd spent together in her head.

"Second, we are having a love, L-O-V-E affair," he spelled out, cutting off his words with a finger to her lips. "What we shared last night was wonderful, unique, and so special. It doesn't happen like that for everyone."

Lisa knew that. What she shared with Stephen never reached the heights she felt with Matthew. But she refused to admit to anything he said. It would only make things harder in the end.

"Right now you refuse to admit your feelings, but last night your body told a wonderful story. We have more than sex here. You know it and so do I. All you need to do is say the words."

She stood silently before him.

"Look at me, Lisa," he demanded.

She lifted her head and wished she had the strength to look away. Matthew looked ferocious. A muscle jerked unchecked at Matthew's temple, but his words were soft and tender.

"I want to give you anything you want, anything you need. All you have to do is tell me. Talk to me. Let me inside your head and heart. And I'll give you everything within my power."

Pretty words, she thought. *I want to believe. But can I?* Better to leave now than risk her heart a second time, she decided, stepping away from him and heading for the front door.

"Where are you going?"

"Home," Lisa answered.

"I'll come with you. Then we can talk."

She turned, stared, then hurried from the house. "No. You won't."

Matthew grabbed his keys off the drum top table and hurried out of the house after her. "Wait!"

Lisa fished her keys from her purse and unlocked the car door. "I'm going home alone."

"You can't stop me." Matthew blocked her car door with his body so that she couldn't open the door.

"I think you have bigger problems right here." Lisa pointed at a second floor window. "And they need your attention, now."

He followed the direction of her hand and saw his mother in the bedroom window seconds before she stepped away. The silence that followed her comment sizzled with tension. After a moment, Matthew stepped away from the car.

Before she climbed into the driver's seat, Matthew touched her shoulder, detaining her. "I don't want you to leave believing everything we shared can be reduced to some bodily itch. You are important to me. I care about you. And if you let me, I'll be there for you."

She blinked back tears. One tear spilled from the corner of her eye and slipped down her cheek. Brushing it away with the back of her hand, she returned Matthew's declaration with silence.

"I'll give you a little bit of time to come to terms with what's going on. We will talk again. Believe my words, we've just begun."

Matthew leaned close, took her face between his hands and

gently kissed her. Her lips parted of their own will, allowing Matthew access. His tongue danced with hers, lingering for several moments before he released her lips and stepped away from the car. "Remember, this is just the beginning. I promise."

Checking the rearview mirror, Lisa noticed Matthew standing in the driveway watching her.

Matthew's clever mind immediately started to develop a plan as he watched Lisa's car disappear down the drive. Questions regarding where he and Lisa were headed filled his head. After dancing around each other for weeks, he believed he'd finally put their relationship on track and, voilà, Mother showed up like a zit on his nose the morning of the big date. Mother barged into his home uninvited, disturbing the quiet time he and Lisa needed to cement their very new relationship and answer the questions on his mind about Games.

Lord, when he entered his bedroom and looked into Lisa's strained face, all he wanted to do was take her into his arms and warm her so that the color would return to her face, put the smile back into her eyes. Poor baby. Lisa didn't understand how formidable his mother was. Mother belonged in a class all her own. Hell, there were times when he couldn't win an argument with her.

There wasn't a snowball's chance in hell that Lisa would return to his house as long as his mother was there. Honestly, she'd probably never come back even if his mother left tonight. He had to find a way to persuade Lisa.

Mother represented the biggest problem and the logical place to start. Find out how long she planned to visit, get her whatever she wanted, then get her out of his house posthaste.

This isn't going to be easy, he thought. The old girl hadn't traveled all this way to be rushed home. She had an agenda.

First things first. Resolve hardened Matthew's features. He

needed to learn exactly why his mother came to visit and what he could do to expedite her exit.

Reentering the house, he stumbled over his mother's luggage. Six bags suggested a lengthy visit. God help him if that were the situation. Matthew made a mental note to address this issue first. How long did she plan to visit? What did she want?

For the second time today he went in search of his wayward mother, following the lingering fragrance she wore and locating her in the great room. Draped across his couch, her feet tucked under her, a glass of red wine in one hand, Mother looked like the perfect "Fabulous You" commercial.

"Hello dear," she uncoiled from her relaxed pose and moved to the edge of the sofa. "Did you get your little friend sent off safely? She seemed a little shell shocked."

His arms dropped to his side with an exasperated sigh before retorting, "What did you expect?"

"I told you. I was searching for an empty room to put my stuff." Her brows drew together as she studied him. A sense of disquiet filled the room. "Now that you've mentioned her, I have a question for you. She's someone special, isn't she?"

"Not going there today, Mother."

"Why not?" she asked between sips of wine. "What's so different about her? Everything else has been fair game."

"Because she's not." Angrily, Matthew pointed a finger at his mother. "I don't want you to embarrass her again with one of your crass remarks."

"Oh, our little girl has been talking. This relationship must be serious. You've never cared what I say about your friends." She watched him intently, leaning comfortably against the sofa. "Hmm. Interesting."

Marching to the sofa, he leaned over her intimidatingly, his voice hardened ruthlessly. "Listen to me, and listen good. Don't hurt her again. Understand?"

"Now, why would I do that?"

"Who knows?" he muttered. His hand trembled as it ran

over his hair while the edge of anger receded. After all these years he still felt the bite of betrayal. "You didn't need a reason in the past. Unless there's been some great change in your life, you are the same person I grew up with. But I'm getting into another area that should be saved for another day. I've counted six bags in the hallway. How long are you planning to stay?"

"Actually, I don't have any definite timetable. This trip happened without a schedule," she explained between sips of wine. "I'll be here until I've accomplished what I set out to do. Is that a problem?"

"Could be." He shoved his hands into the pockets of his jeans. "But a more important question is, what do you want?"

"I told you months ago. I want us to get reacquainted. To have a relationship with my son. You're my only child and I don't know you. I plan to change that."

Matthew's sharp hiss cut through the room like ice, chilling everything. "Look Mother, we can't go back and there's no way we can change things. That time is gone. We have separate lives." He made a dismissing gesture with his hand. "Go home and get on with your life and I'll do the same here."

"I don't think so. It's past time for us to clear the air. I'm not leaving until we do. And I mean talk, really talk. Pull all the skeletons out of closet and examine them." She swallowed the final drops of wine, placed the empty glass on the cocktail table, and stood up.

Facing him, they stared at one another across the length of the table. Tension crackled between them like a burning log in the fireplace as their strong personalities played a mental game of tug of war. Only this wasn't a game. They were fighting for the superior role in their relationship.

"I'm here and I plan to stay," Mother promised with a cynical twist of her lips. She turned on her heels and sashayed toward the kitchen.

Well, she could take her little family reunion and leave right now. He'd gotten his invitation but didn't plan to attend this particular party. He had his life and he enjoyed it just the way it was. He'd be even happier with Lisa. His mother needed to get back to her own life and leave his alone.

Nineteen

Matthew smelled food. Bacon, coffee—his nose led him to the kitchen like a bloodhound on the trail of a convict. His stomach rumbled, answering the wonderful breakfast aromas that filled the air.

Coffee, he needed coffee badly. It would help him screw his head on straight, clear the cobwebs from his brain and get the day started.

His housekeeper, Viola, never cooked, so who could it be?

Instantly awake, Matthew stopped dead in the doorway. All thoughts of food and coffee vanished when he saw his mother, standing over a skillet of frying bacon, using a back-handled fork to turn the meat, wearing a two-piece jogging suit, running shoes, and a red apron.

This was indeed a Kodak moment. His mother had stopped preparing breakfast for him around his seventh birthday.

Mother walked into his house three days ago, but this was the first time she'd cooked for him. Indeed, this was the first he'd seen her since she steamrolled her way into his house.

"Good morning," Mother waved him into the kitchen. The warmth of her smile echoed in her voice. Her toffee eyes ran over his clothing, took in his casual attire. She pointed the fork at the counter where the coffee brewed. The black percolator expelled the final drops of liquid with a strangled sound. "Coffee's ready. And your breakfast will be ready in about five minutes. Sit. We can visit while you wait."

Sunlight, bright and clear, poured through the kitchen windows, warming the room and teasing his half-awake state with its brightness. Repressing his anger at her obvious manipulation, he took a mug from the cupboard and poured himself a cup of coffee. He cradled the mug between his hands and felt the warmth of the brew penetrate his fingers when he blew on the liquid to cool it. Ignoring the chairs at the table, he leaned against the Formica-covered counter and watched his mother flutter around his kitchen like it was an everyday occurrence.

Her dark brows drew together over the bridge of her nose as she eyed his black running shorts, loose T-shirt, and battered running shoes. "Are you going to work today? You're looking rather comfortable for the office."

"Not for a while. I've got to do my run, then I'll come back for a shower and change."

He strolled across the kitchen and dropped into one of the chairs, then stretched his long legs casually before him.

"How many miles do you run each day?"

"Seven or eight. It depends on my time and the weather. But that's not the only reason I'm dressed this way. Everyone's dressing casually because we're having a picnic. I'm closing the office at noon today."

"Sounds like fun. Do you mind if I tag along?"

"No can do, Mother. I don't want my employees to feel uncomfortable."

"By employees I suppose you're talking about your little friend."

"Yes."

Mother gave a curt nod of her head, took a deep, unsteady breath, and turned back to the stove and tended to his breakfast. Silence followed.

"How come you're up so early? Aren't you on vacation?" He sipped his coffee. The bitter brew slipped down his throat, spread through his veins, and nudged his brain into a functioning state.

"Yes. I wanted to do something special. It's been years since I've cooked for you."

"Mother, I take care of myself."

"I know," she answered. An uncomfortable stillness settled between them, filling every crevice of the room, while each shuffled through their limited selection of topics for a neutral subject. "This kitchen is gorgeous. I love it. It has everything a woman could want." She opened the refrigerator door and removed the butter and jam. Cool air flirted around the legs of his chair and brushed against his bare ankles. Mother slid a plate of bacon and eggs in front of him before moving to the counter to fill her cup with coffee.

"Thanks." Matthew watched her sip black coffee. "Aren't you going to have anything?"

"No. I'm not a breakfast person. I'll just have coffee."

"That's not very healthy."

"True, but breakfast always slows me down, makes me sluggish and it takes a good part of the morning for my edge to return."

"I didn't know that."

"There's a great deal you don't know about me. I'm willing to share," she offered, sitting down in the seat across from him, a hopeful catch in her voice. Her white teeth flashed a grin and her eyes crinkled at the corners. "Remember when you were little and you came down for breakfast every morning and asked for panacakes? Didn't matter what I prepared; waffles, eggs, whatever, all you wanted were panacakes."

A muscle twitched in Matthew's jaw and he pleaded, "Mother, don't start."

"Don't what?" Her hands dropped to her hips. "I'm trying to have a conversation with my son. What's wrong with that? It's been a long time. I would like to think you'd enjoy some time together."

"If I remember correctly, you were never home to have any meals with me. Is that why you orchestrated this Soul Food moment?" Matthew responded in a voice filled with blame. "Are you trying to soften me up with food and warm memories before hitting me with your plans for our big family reunion?"

"No," she protested, twisting her hands together. Her deep toffee eyes were troubled. "I just wanted to spend some time with you. Maybe get to know you better and let you learn more about me. There must be some common ground that we can build on." She was hurting. He read her hurt; it blazed from her eyes, unchecked. But she'd hurt him for many painful years.

"You can't recapture my childhood," he pointed out. "That's gone. You missed it. Maybe I should say, you chose to miss it."

"I know, I know," she lowered her dark lashes to conceal the expression in her eyes. "We can't change that. But I can be your friend now. If you'll give me a chance, we don't have to spend the rest of our lives at odds. We can have a friendship that's full and enjoyable."

Shoving back his chair, Matthew stood, massaged the tight cords at the back of his neck. Shaping the words in his mind for the greatest impact, he absently watched the birds in the yard. "Mother, you and I can't be friends. Do you understand me?"

His words didn't slow her down. She plodded on. "Why not? Many parents and grown children develop meaningful, strong relationships, even when they've had difficult years growing up. Why can't we? You're just being stubborn. Open your mind to the possibility. Open your heart."

"Okay Mother, let's have open dialogue." Matthew snapped, took a deep breath, and folded is arms across his chest. "Do you remember Debbie?" He almost laughed out loud when Mother's jaw dropped, eyes widened and for once she didn't have one of her snappy retorts ready. "Does the name tickle your brain cells?"

"Why are you bringing her up after all these years?"

"Why indeed?" He asked sarcastically. "Because that was the one time you chose to give me your full attention by driving away the one person I cared about."

A look of tired reservation passed over his mother's features before her mask once again settled into place. He'd always marveled at the way his mother rallied and pulled herself together like a queen no matter the situation or circumstances.

"Don't bother lying. I know you paid her off. Debbie and I ran into each other a few years back. She nearly broke her neck, getting to me so that she could provide me with the details of your arrangement. Debbie left nothing out."

"Mattie." She met his accusing eyes while her hands drew invisible patterns on the tablecloth. "I was trying to protect you. Keep you safe from her. She only wanted to use you. Debbie knew about Fabulous You and wanted in on the gravy train. Think back; you were hurt at first but you weren't really in love with her. Infatuation, that's what it was. Puppy love. She didn't want you, she wanted my money. You don't know how lucky you were to get away from her."

"I didn't need you to save my ass. I had a right to make my own decisions and live with the consequences."

"Is that why you were so protective of your little friend?

"Leave Lisa out of this. What we're talking about has nothing to do with her. Lisa and I are none of your business."

"You thought I might interfere. That's not why I'm here. You're an adult and I believe you know how to sum up a situation and make the right decision."

"That's big of you. How did you come to that decision?"

"Mattie, let's not argue anymore. That's ancient history. It's time to put that in the past and start fresh."

"No. There'll always be a wedge between us. Debbie's only one of those reasons we can't be friends. "

"Mattie, please. We can—"

"No Mother. We can't." Matthew stood, implacable.

"Baby, please."

"Do you need more reasons?"

Head bowed, she answered quietly, "Yes."

Matthew admired the sheer tenacity of the woman. She allowed nothing he said to penetrate her armor. Her single-mindedness and determination kept her strong. But so was he! The game had just begun.

"Maybe this is the time to get some of those issues out in the open. Discuss them and try to work past them." She held his gaze with her own. "Tell me what else stands between us getting to know one another."

"You're asking for it and I'm more than willing to give it to you. How many times have you put Fabulous You before anything else? Where were you when I graduated from high school? College? Did you even know I graduated at the top of my class? Or that I almost joined the military after graduation?" Matthew stared at his hands surprised to learn that he was trembling. The look of surprise and shock on his mother's face would have been comical if it weren't so sad.

The silence that followed fueled his anger and belief that he was right to keep his mother out of his life. "I didn't think so," he muttered disdainfully.

"Oh, Matthew." She reached out to stroke his cheek. He flinched away. "I convinced myself that you were old enough to understand. I didn't consider your feelings. I'm truly sorry. I love you." Her toffee eyes beckoned him to believe her. "I'd never deliberately hurt you. Please understand that I've made some bad choices and you suffered for them. Forgive me. Don't let it continue."

Unable to conceal his overwhelming pain, he asked, "Why did I always come second with you? You tell me you love me so much but you missed every major event in my life. Not content with that, you bought off the one person that meant anything to me. That's not love. What you love is Fabulous You Cosmetics." He spun away, fighting the need to shout, growl, and hit something. "No, Mother. We can't be friends."

Tears slid down his mother's cheeks. For a moment Matthew's heart opened and he felt her pain as keenly as his own. He turned away, refusing to allow her tears to weaken him, furiously wishing she'd stayed away and spared them both this torment.

He wanted to believe her desperately and needed the love she offered. His heart said "maybe." But his head said "careful, buddy." How could he trust her? She'd let him down so many times. Could he risk getting hurt again, destroying the barriers he'd worked so hard to erect—the walls that kept his heart safe from more emotional injury?

"Enough," he barked out, starting for the door. "I'm tired of walking down memory lane with you. I'm out of here. Feel free to find something to do or maybe go home. There's nothing for you here."

Storming through the house, Matthew headed for the foyer. He grabbed his car keys off the drum top table on his way out the door. *Breathe, James, breathe,* he instructed. *Don't let her get to you. That's what she wants to do.*

At his truck, he stopped and worked hard to get a handle on his feelings. He was so upset, the key refused to go into the lock. *Calm down,* he thought. *Get a grip.* The key went into the lock, turned, and the door opened.

Why didn't Mother stay out of his kitchen? Let him have his coffee in peace and quiet. Instead, she played the role of parent and cooked breakfast, something she hadn't done since he was a child and something he didn't want her to do now.

"Damn! Damn! Damn!" he yelled, pounding the steering wheel with his fist. Why didn't Mother stay where she lived, spare them both this unexpected and ugly family reunion? There were way too many bad memories and too much distrust between them. He didn't want to cause her pain and vice versa.

And if Mother didn't believe it was too late for them, he'd just remind her of what happened when she interfered in his relationship with Debbie. God, he could hardly remember how she looked. But, Mother and Debbie's betrayal were like a fresh burn, stinging and blistering. He wished Mother would go home. Go back to California and get on with her life, while leaving him to his.

Mother had already put a ding in one of his relationships. Lisa was special. And he didn't plan to lose her.

Twenty

The Sears Tower felt cool this morning. The central air-conditioned breeze waltzed around her bare legs as she crossed the lobby to the bank of elevators. Lisa shivered, rubbing her hands up and down her arms. Feeling a bit underdressed, she glanced around the lobby, then at her knee-length shorts, T-shirt, and sandals.

Today, Games People Play planned to close at noon and the staff and their families were invited to participate in a picnic sponsored by the company at Grant Park. From the excited buzz generated among the employees, the picnic was being toasted as a major event.

Lisa shook her head in reluctant admiration. Matthew was a born leader. He had created another avenue to make his employees aware of how important they were to him and the company.

Suddenly, the hair at the back of her neck rose at the same time her body stiffened. Gray Flannel cologne shot up her nostrils seconds before Stephen Brock appeared at her side dressed in a pair of jeans with razor sharp creases, a yellow polo shirt, and canvas rubber-soled shoes.

"Lisa." He nodded at her and his eyes dropped from her face to her shoulders and lingered on her breasts.

She flushed red hot, then chilled all over. Sometimes he was a major pig. "Can I help you?" She responded in a tone that was coolly disapproving before turning her back on him.

"No," he answered, making a close study of the elevator door.

Silence separated them like a dense mist. They stood shoulder-to-shoulder. Lisa cut her eyes in his direction, trying to assess his unreadable features. *I need to talk to this idiot, but I must be diplomatic if I want to get things settled. And I can't let it go on any longer.* Ready to do battle, she faced him and asked, "How's that deal going? Have you done anything about it?"

Stephen's eyes darkened dangerously as he glanced down at her and shifted his briefcase from one hand to the other, "No."

Lisa felt her blood pressure soar and set her teeth on edge. *What did I ever find attractive in a loser like you?* After weeks of arguments, debates, and negotiations, she believed they had finally reached an understanding. An agreement.

Hands balled into fist, Lisa reminded, "You promised."

"So, I did." He agreed with a smug lift of his eyebrows.

Lisa, be calm. Flying into a rage won't accomplish anything. Reason with the man. "When do you think you'll get to it?" Containing her anger, she asked in a cautious tone.

"Don't know."

"You promised you'd handle things," she reminded.

"Guess what?" He shot her a twisted smile. "I'm not going to keep that promise."

Her stomach clenched into knots. If Stephen didn't resolve this situation soon, everything would fall back on her and she didn't have that kind of cash.

Remember, this is a delicate matter. Deal with him gently, carefully.

Jabbing a finger at her, Stephen growled, "You're on your own. I'm not taking any responsibility for it."

Oh buddy, yes you will, Lisa promised silently. *You're going to own up to your part in this.* Shaking her head, she drew closer to him and lowered her voice to a fierce whisper. "Wait a minute. You were right there with me and agreed to clear up everything. As a matter of fact, you found the place."

"True." He stepped closer and got in her face. The bitter aroma of his morning coffee lingered on his breath. "And now I'm not touching it. It's all on you."

If she hadn't been so angry, she would have used more caution. "You can't leave me holding this bag of garbage alone." Her voice trembled with indignation. "We went into this together."

"So we did." He agreed with a quick tilt of his head. "Now, you're alone."

She refused to be intimidated. If she gave an inch she'd end up with a new set of lies. "Liar!"

With an icy expression in his dark brown eyes, Stephen looked down his broad nose at her and chuckled. "Call it what you want." He grabbed her arm, pulled her close, and answered with a silken thread of warning in his voice. "But you're still going to handle this one all by your lonesome."

You're such slime. I should never have trusted you. She snatched her arm away. Her heart thumped erratically, her tongue curled, ready to throw a string of insults at him. She stopped, recognizing her limited choices. That wouldn't help the situation.

A forewarning tingling started at the base of Lisa's spine and spread upward. *Matthew,* she thought, seconds before his large frame eclipsed the sunlight. *Straighten your face,* she warned, pulling herself together. She locked her feelings behind an emotional door and smiled brightly at Matthew. *You don't want him to know how stupid you've been.*

Matthew nudged his way between the pair like a referee separating boxing opponents at the prizefight. He glanced from one to the other, his brows creased. "Trouble here?" he asked in that deep husky voice that could melt a stone.

Clearing her throat, Lisa shrugged and answered, "No. No. A bit of a lively debate between colleagues. No big."

Stephen stepped close to Lisa, wrapped an arm around her shoulders, and explained in his smooth, urban drawl, "One of our lively conversations. Nothing more."

Matthew's eyes narrowed to slits, following Stephen's gesture.

Surprise, then satisfaction beamed from Stephen's smug gaze. Dropping his arm away from Lisa, he stepped around Matthew, patted his flat belly, and said, "I'm headed over to the deli. I need a bagel or something." With a finger at his temple, he saluted them. "See you later."

Fuming, Lisa watched Stephen walk across the lobby and entered Louie's Deli. One part of her felt relief at his departure, but a larger part wished Matthew hadn't heard them. There were things she and Stephen needed to resolve. She took a quick peek at Matthew and noted the frown crinkling his handsome brow. *What's going through that clever mind?* she wondered. *How much did he hear?*

"How are you?" he whispered in the velvet voice he reserved only for her. It ran through her veins, firing every nerve.

Lisa suffered the dull ache of desire at the thought of Matthew. All the things they did together that one night came back to her with vivid clarity. He'd done things that made her heart and body sing. Those memories of shared joy reflected back at her each time their gazes locked. Not one word about that fateful night had passed his lips since that day. But his eyes revealed so much more. She groaned as her heart swelled with the love beyond her control.

Their encounters at Games were businesslike and professional. But she sensed a watchfulness in Matthew. For what, she had no idea. Sometimes she wanted to scream at him to tell her what he wanted. Instead she kept her mouth shut. As long as he never touched her or mentioned what happened that night, she felt strong enough to maintain the thin façade that passed for professionalism.

To complicate everything, each day her love for Matthew grew stronger. The prospect of being in his arms, close to him, caused a spark of excitement to flare within her each time they met. She loved him and found him in her thoughts constantly. His remark about a love affair had been closer to the truth then he realized.

Lisa took a giant leap of faith when she made love with him. By morning light she had almost convinced herself they could make a relationship between them until Mrs. James put in an appearance, adding her two cents to the cauldron, making Lisa feel like a cheap whore he had found on the streets.

His multicolored eyes glittered and moved along the compact length of her; moving closer, his unique scent rose between them. "You're coming to the picnic, right?"

She retreated a step, nodding. "Yes. I feel odd coming to work like this."

"Don't worry. You look great." Matthew's grin was irresistibly devastating, and his compliment didn't hurt either.

Lisa's heart hammered in her chest. She found it impossible to not return his disarming smile. The bell chimed and she started through the elevator doors. Matthew followed her, much too close for Lisa's peace of mind. She punched the button for both their floors then leaned against the wood paneling, fighting the wild fantasies that crowded out intelligent thoughts. He looked fantastic in a pair of jeans and a Tommy Hilfiger long-sleeved T-shirt.

"You okay?" he asked with sensual possessiveness. This disturbed her nerves even more.

"Fine," Lisa answered, ignoring the intimate message in his question. *You're not pulling me into your web,* she thought. "And you?"

"Good." A light twinkled in the depths of Matthew's eyes as he moved closer and the heat from his body warmed hers. "But that's not what I'm asking. And you know it."

Lisa put a hand to her forehead, massaging her temple as if it hurt, and said, "I'm sorry. You've lost me."

"You've always impressed me as a very forthright and honest woman. Why are you pretending now?"

"I don't pretend."

"Right," he drawled. "That's why you're acting as if you don't understand a word I'm saying. Because I know you do.

But I will give you a little reminder." He brushed a gentle hand across her cheek and the electricity of his touch surged through her. "Things aren't over between us. I also promised I'd give you a little time to come to terms with everything that happened between us."

Her eyes opened wide. Matthew's nearness overwhelmed her.

"But not too much time." He closed the distance between them, invading Lisa's personal space with his presence and scent. Shifting away, he tapped the red "stop" button on the panel, causing the elevator to jerk and grind to a halt. He crowded her into a corner with his large, powerful body.

"What are you doing?" She dodged left, reaching for the control panel while a myriad of emotions welled up inside her. Matthew intercepted her fingers in a firm grip, all the while running his thumb back and forth across the back of her hand in a slow, caressing motion. Lisa felt her pulse leap with excitement.

Pleasure surged through her, causing her attention to switch from the button to his sensual touch. "Stop," Lisa demanded, trying to pull her hand away.

A glint of amusement flickered in the gaze that met hers. "Stop what?" He asked in the husky tone that tripped every sensual alarm within her.

"You know." Annoyed by his act and her response to him, she added, "Touching me."

An answering smile flashed across Matthew's lips and one dark eyebrow rose. "Oh, do you mean this?" He asked, turning her palm up, bringing it to his lips and touching the moist tip of his tongue to her palm, sending her pulse into a gallop. He ran his free hand over her soft spiked hair and made her scalp tingle each place his fingers touched.

Under her T-shirt, Lisa felt her nipples harden. She hunched her shoulders, hoping he hadn't noticed. The hard nubs were clearly outlined. "Matthew."

"Shh." He stroked a finger across her bottom lip. Heat rippled under her skin everywhere his talented fingers touched her. Lisa watched the flare of dark hunger form in his eyes as his large hands framed her face. Her breath caught in her lungs when she read the simmering need.

The intoxicating scent of his body sent shock waves rippling through her as her heart lunged madly when his lips touched hers and shattered the hard shell Lisa had built around herself. Slow and thorough described his kiss, as desire built in deliberate increments. Matthew's tongue traced the soft fullness of her lips then moved inside to explore, tasting mint toothpaste. Lisa felt the heat of his body. His male hardness seared her skin through the thin layer of clothing.

Finally, his lips left hers and she felt that loss as keenly as if she'd lost a part of herself. But Matthew wasn't finished with her. His lips searched for a new location. He nibbled on her earlobe. Every sensitive spot received his attention as he wove magic with his tongue, then returned to her lips, taking them like a tornado, uprooting a house, leaving nothing behind.

Finally, Matthew released her lips and he slowly raised his head, looking deep into her eyes. A pure male grin of satisfaction spread across his face.

"Okay, I'm attracted to you." Looking at her hardened nipples, she continued, "That's pretty obvious. So, what are you trying to prove?"

"Nothing. Everything. I wanted you to have a little reminder that we hadn't settled anything yet." Lowering his head, he ran his tongue across her lips. "But, we will."

Forget about him! Lisa almost laughed. She could barely remember her own name after that kiss. His image, touch, scent, and taste were imprinted on her very soul.

"I told you I made a mistake," Lisa retorted. "Why can't you leave it at that?"

Unwrapping himself from their embrace, Matthew snapped the button into the start position and retrieved his briefcase from the floor. "Because it's not true. Remember, this is just the beginning for us," he promised between tiny kisses. "I know you have doubts, we'll clear them all up. Give the situation a little time and finesse and it'll all be good. I promise."

The elevator doors opened and Lisa stepped onto her floor on shaking legs. She pulled her scattered wits together while she pushed her T-shirt into her shorts, smoothing the wrinkles from it with her hands. Royal Copenhagen cologne mixed with Matthew's scent clung to her clothes. Why had she allowed Matthew to do those things to her? Kissing her, making love to her with his words, and holding her so close that she responded to every muscle.

Every movement she made brought his image floating under her nose, making it impossible to forget what had happened in the elevator. That dog! He did this deliberately. Everywhere she went or each time she moved, he'd be there with her.

This morning, men had ruled over her. First, Stephen had reneged on their agreement after making a promise to her. And then Matthew had kissed her, making her feel everything she had been trying to forget.

Twenty-one

Matthew eased between his black silk sheets and rested his head on his hand and sighed contentedly. The warm breeze ruffled the sheer curtains, signaling the end of spring and the first days of summer. Crickets protested at their unauthorized shower courtesy of the sprinkler system. He turned, looked out the window at the half moon glittering from the bedroom window, and wished Lisa was laying there beside him.

Every bone in his body started to relax after the grueling day he'd put in. Boy, was he glad his mother had found something to do with herself away from the house. A battle with her was the last thing he needed or wanted. He'd achieved his greatest ambition for tonight: hot shower and bed.

Glancing at the clock, Matthew wondered idly. It was past midnight and she hadn't returned home. *Where was Mother?* Oh well, he didn't keep tabs on her and vice versa.

On a whiff of Chanel perfume, Mother entered the room, following the briefest of taps on the door. Closing the door behind her, she leaned against it for a moment as her eyes adjusted to the moonlit room.

Speak of the devil, Matthew thought, sniffing Chanel perfume. "What is it, Mother?" He drawled with obvious vexation, raising himself on his elbows. "I'm tired."

"I know and I'm sorry for bothering you so late. This can't wait any longer. You've foiled every attempt I've made to talk to you. So I've created my own window of opportunity."

So much for his plans for the evening, he thought, sighing heavily. "To what purpose? Can't this wait until another time? Whatever you've got to say can wait until I get home from work tomorrow."

"No. It can't. Nor will I. I've been patient long enough. You've dodged me for the past two weeks." She spoke with quiet, but determined firmness. "We're going to have things out now."

"No can do, Mother."

"Yes. You will," she snapped.

"I don't think so," he answered. His voice was equally firm, definitely final. "I'm not going to deal with you at this time of night. Not ever. Good night, Mother."

Mother rushed to his side of the bed and placed a warm hand on his bare shoulder. "You don't have to fight me. Just listen. To work toward any type of relationship we need to clear the air and put all the misunderstandings and mess on the table."

"I've told you already that any possibility of us being close is gone." Matthew answered in a dead voice. He knew his mother planned to make every effort to reunite them. This was another attempt on her part. But he wanted no part in it.

"I refuse to allow us to continue at cross purposes for the rest of my life. I want to be a welcome guest here. When you have a family of your own I plan to be here and enjoy my grandchildren like any other grandmother. The only way I know how to do that is to talk to you and make things right between us." Mother took a deep breath and plunged ahead.

It seemed obvious that she was here for the duration. It was up to him to sit out the ride and then she'd go away.

"All I ask is that you listen and try to understand. So here goes. When I started my business, hell, before that I was fighting to keep a roof over our heads and food in your mouth. I used the house for collateral to start Fabulous You. It was the only thing we had left."

What was she talking about? Did she really think he'd believe this sad story? Maybe she believed he had been too young to understand how things were. Dad had plenty of investments to keep them comfortable. Had she forgotten that he had been there with her?

Feeling those painful memories all over again, Matthew said, "Mother, I'm not interested. Let it go."

"You should be interested. It's past time for you to hear the truth. Everything." Her tone sharpened as if she were readying her battle skills. "This is not going to be easy." She paced back and forth and mumbled more to herself than to him. "When I started the company women didn't own their own businesses. Especially not black women. But the bank had no choice, they had to give me the money because the house was ours, free and clear. That wasn't the end of it though. They were on my back the whole first year, waiting for me to fail so they could foreclose." She wrapped her arms around her. "Everyday I fought like an animal to make the company solvent and keep our home."

"Yeah right. Whatever." Disbelief oozed from his voice as he took his pillow, fluffed it up, then placed it behind his back. "You've forgotten something. I'm a businessman myself. I know better. There's no way Dad didn't provide for us before he died. There must have been life insurance, bank accounts, something. Dad wouldn't have been that irresponsible where his family was concerned."

Mother dropped her hands to her sides. In the moonlight, he saw deep sadness. "There was a time when all that was true. People and situations change. And so did your father. I didn't want to tell you this." Her tone had become wintry. "I've never let anyone tarnish his memory because I believed it was important for you to remember your father as a hero. And I'm sorry after all these years I have to be the one to shatter that image."

"No!" He growled, throwing his legs over the side of the bed. He was ready to get up until he remembered his nude state under the light sheet. "I won't let you dirty my father's name when he isn't here to defend himself. Keep your lies to yourself."

"Mattie," she cut in, stood next to the bed, and rested her small hand on his shoulder. "Your dad was a good man, but he had a problem. That addiction cost him his job, all of our savings, and eventually his life. Your dad gambled. And when he died the only thing we still owned was the house. All the savings, investments, were gone."

"I don't believe you," he roared, angry and confused. "You're trying to make him look bad so that I'll see you in a better light."

"No, that's not necessary. I don't have to lie. You already think the worst about me. What do I have to lose? Think back, don't you remember how often your father went to Las Vegas? Remember when you were eight your father stopped going to the office? We told you he was working from home. In reality he'd lost his job. Do you remember when we pulled you from St. Cecilia and put you into the local school? That happened because your dad gambled away your tuition money. But you went back the next term because he hit it big at the tables and I stashed away part of the cash."

Memories stirred in Matthew's brain. He saw through all of the lies, half-truths, and tears his mother tried to hide from him. The silent, uncomfortable meals as they waited for dad to come home. A wall cracked in his heart and all the incidents he hadn't recognized or understood cleared in his mind.

An impotent rage spread through him as the incidents his mother described crystallized in his mind. The memories overlapped one another, until all the parts came together like the pieces of a jigsaw puzzle. It hadn't meant anything at that time. After all he had been a child. He remembered the time his father stopped going to the office and told everyone that he planned to start his own business and his father's angry voice on the phone explaining why the car payment hadn't been paid.

Unable to take anymore, he pleaded, covering his face with his hands. "Go away, Mother. Please. I need to think."

"Where's the light switch?" Mother turned away and headed for the door. Her nails scraped the wall as she searched for the switch.

"No. Don't touch it," he answered in a voice rough with pain. "I can't face you right now. I need the darkness."

"I'm so sorry," she muttered back. "I never wanted you to know. But, I couldn't allow our relationship to suffer any longer. I sacrificed too much to keep that dream alive."

How could he have been such a fool? So blind to the truth?

"I was a black woman with a child and major debt, snapping at my butt. The bank loved me. They believed in a year that million dollar house would be theirs."

"Once I started the company things were happening quicker than I could handle them and I didn't have the time or the strength to explain anything to you. I assumed, hoped, wrongly, that you were too young to understand and everything would be fine."

He heard her voice in the darkness but her face was hidden from him.

"After years of being a wife and mother, I was in charge, making decisions that involved millions of dollars and I liked it, believed it was the right thing for me." Pride oozed from her words as she moved around the room. "I'd never allow myself to feel lost, alone to wonder where the next meal would come from. Your father taught me a valuable lesson—be self-sufficient and rely only on yourself."

Her voice changed, softened, turned persuasive. "I never stopped loving you. Everything I did was for you." Mother swallowed hard, ran her slender fingers through her dark hair, and continued. "I wanted your future to be secure with a company that was profitable. First and foremost, I had to put food in your mouth."

Matthew traced the pattern of his comforter with a shaky finger and gave himself additional time to think.

"You're my son. My child. Please try to understand. Think

about what I've told you tonight, then try to forgive me." She moved around the bed to sit next to him and searched for his hand in the dark.

She smelled of Chanel and the lightest mist of hair spray. But he could also remember his mother's gentle tone reprimanding him whenever his antics put him in danger. She warned him against harm in that patient parental tone he'd ignored with the logic of a child. And he remembered the hugs and kisses he had received when he came in from school each day.

"I'm not sure if forgiving is the right thing," he began slowly. "I have to consider everything you've said tonight. What you've told me turns everything I believed inside out. Putting all that aside, you weren't there for me when I was a child and needed you. Where do we go now? What's left for us? I can't do anything about Dad. I love my dad." His voice broke, he stopped, cleared his throat, and began again. "Now everything I thought about him is gone. And right now I need time to absorb everything you've told me."

"Oh Mattie," his mother cried. "I never wanted you to know. Don't judge your father too harshly. Gambling is an illness, like heart disease or diabetes. He couldn't help himself. His only crime lay in not seeking help. I couldn't help him, that decision had to be made by him." Mother ran a shaky hand through her hair. "In your father's case, he refused to recognize his problem or do anything about it. Back then, people didn't realize how insidious gambling could be or its effect on their loved ones. We lived through a rough time together and survived. We should be able to live as a family now. I don't want us to become victims of your father's illness. Please, can't we try to be friends, enjoy each other?"

Mother leaned over, wrapped her arms around his broad chest, and hugged him close. "I've always loved you and no matter what decision you come to I'll always be there for you. That's a promise." She kissed him on the forehead and Matthew almost suffocated under an avalanche of memories.

For the first time in many years, they were communicating and for now it would have to be enough. They could hash out everything else later.

Releasing him, Mother rose from the bed, fumbled in her pocket, and removed a tissue. She'd wiped away tears before pocketing the tissue and facing him once more.

"Good night, son. I love you," she whispered, taking one final look at him before closing the door quietly behind her.

Matthew shook his head, trying to accept all he had heard tonight. After all these years, Mother had decided it was time to clear the air and start fresh. Why now, instead of last year, or the year before? What really brought her here?

He laid against the pillows and shut his eyes as the hot sting of tears rolled down his cheeks. Everything he'd believed had just been blown out of the water.

Wiping away his tears with the back of his hand, Matthew tried to form a mental image of his father. Tall, always smiling, playful—that was his dad, those were the things Matthew remembered. His father had always been his idol. And his opinion meant more to Matthew than any other man's. His father was the man he strived to be like because he believed his father was a stand-up guy.

But, in the recesses of his mind, he also remembered the fights between his parents. Mother's tears. The coldness that crept into his father's eyes when things didn't go the way he wanted them to go.

Talk about the dysfunctional families, he thought, laughing out loud. *I don't need this self-examination at this point in my life.* A soft voice whispered, *Yes, you do. It's time to learn everything.*

"Dad." Matthew shook his head. *How could he have done those things to us?* His gambling almost destroyed them, forced Mother to get a job after years of being a homemaker. And left his mother an emotional cripple, unable or unwilling to commit to another relationship.

How could Dad have gambled away their life savings? Matthew had forgotten the embarrassing telephone calls from creditors.

Mother's love didn't excuse the way she treated Debbie. God, how he'd loved her. Granted, Debbie turned out to be less than the prize he'd envisioned. Red-hot anger flew through him with a vengeance when he thought about what his mother had done and how it had affected his life. All the blame couldn't be placed on Mother; Debbie accepted the money and that made her just as responsible as his mother. Obviously, she hadn't loved him as much as she had professed.

And to think he always blamed everything on his mother. Matthew always believed Mother was a rock-hard business-woman. He was wrong, there was more to this particular woman than he ever believed, like strength of character, courage, and love.

I can't lay here, he thought, throwing back the sheet and padding across the room to the bathroom. He flicked on the light and stood in front of the sink. Splashing cold water on his face, he looked into the mirror and wondered, *Who in the hell am I? Everything I believed was a lie.*

There were still unanswered questions. What really brought her here? And how much was she still hiding? *I'm going to get to the bottom of this,* he promised. Returning to his bed, he pulled the sheet over his shoulders. *Tomorrow!*

Twenty-two

Emotionally paralyzed from last night's revelations, Matthew waited at his kitchen table for his mother to appear for her morning coffee. He felt jittery and impatient for answers to the questions Mother's nighttime visit had sparked.

Scraping his fingers against his unshaved stubble, Matthew shifted in the chair, searching for a comfortable position. He gazed out the kitchen window and watched as the birds fed from the bird feeder.

This wasn't going to be easy. Carolyn James was a master at hiding things she didn't want known. He hated pressuring her this way. But they needed to let all the hurts and grief out, then try to rebuild their pitiful relationship.

"Oh." Her eyebrows shot up and she fidgeted with the zipper at the neck of her jogging suit. "Good morning," she whispered from inside the doorway, masking her surprise behind a pleasant expression, then Mother continued into the kitchen on a mist of Chanel.

"Morning," Matthew matched her casual tone and patted the empty chair next to his. "Have a seat." He rose and headed for the black-and-white Formica counter while he kept his tone neutral and even. "I'll have your coffee on the table in a minute," he assured, determined to lull her into a relaxed, talkative mood.

"Is it decaf?"

"Yes." Matthew plucked a mug from the mug tree. "The

last thing I need is caffeine to get me more jittery than I am now."

"Thanks." She took the overstuffed chair opposite his. Her eyes ran over his tattered jeans and blue T-shirt. "Are you running late? I thought you liked to get an early jump on the workday."

Pouring her coffee, Matthew returned to the table and placed a mug in front of her. Mother seemed calm and in control, but Matthew sensed something much more. Maybe it was the way her eyes darted away each time he made eye contact, or the nervous way she plucked at the zipper. "After you dumped all that stuff on me last night, did you really believe I'd be able to get on with my day? I've thought about you and Dad most of the night and now it's my turn. I have some questions of my own."

"I expected that." Mrs. James pleated the napkin on the table again and again, then dropped the linen in her lap, picked up her mug with an unsteady hand, and sipped. "What do you want to know?"

Matthew slid into his chair and faced her. "Why now, Mother? We haven't communicated in years. Why have you shown up on my doorstep *now?*"

Her eyes narrowed. Matthew got the impression she was deciding how much to reveal. She set the mug on the table and answered hesitantly, as if she were running through a mental checklist. "Several things brought me here."

"Such as?" Matthew leaned closer. Studying her, working hard to read and interpret the emotions flying across her face.

"You're my only child. I don't want us to be strangers any longer." She swallowed, took a deep breath, reached out, and touched Matthew's hand. The subtle gesture brought an unexplainable level of comfort to him. It took him back to the time he got sick with the measles; she had rocked him to sleep and caressed his forehead. "As I said last night, I don't want my life to end with us at odds."

"End?" He latched onto that one word. His calm voice hid

the icy fear twisting around his heart. "What's wrong? Are you ill?"

Mother moistened her lips with the tip of her tongue, her fingers fluttered around the mug's handle. "No-o-o-o," she answered with uncharacteristic hesitation. "Not anymore."

Noting the catch in her voice, he pounced, "Not anymore? Then when?"

"Last fall I had a heart attack."

"Heart attack!" He shut his eyes against all the horrible images, seeing hospital staff and equipment surrounding his mother. "You were critically ill and never called me?" Matthew rose. "I can't believe you kept something this important from me. Why?"

His eyes bored into hers. Was the rift between them that wide? How had they grown this far apart? Somehow he couldn't shake the feeling that he was responsible.

"I refused to come to you when I was in need, clinging like food wrap. I wanted to meet you on equal ground. We should have been two adults coming to terms with our past, not with emotional blackmail or guilt blocking the way. That's not you. Nor is it my way of doing things."

He planted his palms on the table and leaned closer. "What about the hospital, or your secretary. What's her name? Denise. No. No. Ember. Why didn't they call me? Someone should have had the sense, the common courtesy to let me know what was going on. Or did you prefer I read about your death in the local obituary or hear about it on the news?" He knew he was being cruel, but he was hurt. Deeply so.

"Sit down." Mother waved her hand at the table, waited until he flopped into his chair, then held his gaze with her own. "It was my decision and I threatened to fire anyone who violated my confidence." She answered in a tone that tolerated no back talk. "My orders were explicit. Unless I was on my deathbed, no one should contact you. I'm sorry if you're hurt. But we weren't close enough for me to expect anything from you."

"You're right," he confirmed. "Basically, I went about my business and so did you."

"At least you understand that. I called it the way I saw it. Maybe I was wrong."

"Is that why you started calling my office?"

"Yes," she answered, fingering the zipper at her neck. "Laying on your back, depending on the kindness of others will make you reevaluate your life choices. I made a decision to resolve our differences. But you stubbornly refused to return my calls. So I pushed the envelope and forced your hand by showing up on your doorstep."

"I can't believe things were this far gone."

"Well they were. While I recuperated I had a great deal of time to think. It came to me that I needed you and I didn't have the right to call you. Couldn't ask for your help. Oh, I know, you probably would have responded to my call for help. That wasn't the way I wanted it. You had your life and I had no place in it. I decided then and there that as soon as I got back on my feet I planned to do everything in my power to reconcile with you."

"Are you all right now?" The slight throbbing at his temples became a fierce ache and he massaged his forehead with his fingertips. "What does your doctor say? What about medicine? I haven't seen you take anything."

Brushing aside his questions, Mrs. James answered firmly. "I'm fine. Rich food, no exercise, stress, and lack of sleep caused my heart attack. It was the best wake-up call I could have gotten, although I would have preferred something a great deal more subtle."

"It's a hell of a wake-up call," he muttered.

"Yes, it was. One I don't plan to repeat."

"So what are you doing about it now?"

"I eat right. I walk three miles a day and I delegate so the burden of the company doesn't fall on my shoulders alone."

"Good!"

"But there's more," Mother continued. "Something more important followed that event."

"Oh? What could be more important than a heart attack?" Matthew was almost afraid to hear the rest. He'd had enough surprises for one day. But, the gods had one more in store for him.

"During my hospital stay, I met a man. He's the chief of cardiology and we've been together for about nine months. He, I mean, Vincent, wants me to marry him."

"Marriage!" Stunned, Matthew fell back into his chair.

"Yes. Vincent expects an answer when I get home."

Shocked, he demanded, "Where did you find this *man?* Are you sure he's not after your money?"

"Of course not."

"How do you know?" He asked.

"He's chief of cardiology."

"Fine." Matthew waved a hand in her direction, pacing the kitchen. "Last night you told me that you like being in charge of your life. Are you willing to give that up?"

"I don't know. I don't plan to. That's one of the things I need to consider." She stepped in his path and took his hands between both of hers. "Matthew, our relationship is the most important thing in my life. I don't want to lose you forever. I love Vincent, but before I make a commitment to him, it's important to me that our relationship be on firm ground."

"Well, Mother, I can say this for you, when you draw your weapon, you don't hesitate about firing it." Matthew rubbed his temples to relieve the tightness. "I've learned the truth about my dad, regained a mother, and now it looks as if I'm going to inherit a stepfather. My brain hurts."

Her gentle laughter rippled through the air. "Oh Mattie. I've missed you. I'm not sure this is the time to add a husband to my life. You and I are just getting to know one another."

"That won't change. I promise." He folded his arms across his chest and asked, "When do I meet this paramour?"

"Soon."

"What about getting married? How soon do you think that'll happen?"

"I haven't said yes yet. Give me a little more time," she explained. "It's a big step."

"Are you having second thoughts?"

"No. I just never planned to remarry. Your father cured me of that notion. At least I thought he had. Vincent's very different. I'm not sure how to take him," she explained, a thoughtful expression on her face. "To be honest, I'm afraid to commit myself to another relationship. I can't help it. I have been master of my own universe for far too long and it's difficult to think in terms of someone else's needs. I'll have to get accustomed to the idea. In the meantime, I'm considering sharing a household for a while before saying 'I do.' "

"Live together? Mother, don't you think you're a little old for shacking up?"

"I'm still your mother." Mother's eyes flashed and her nostrils flared. "And I don't appreciate your comment," she stated as she dropped her hands to her hips and glared angrily at him. "This is not your business."

Uh-oh! he thought. *This little old lady looks as if she might kill me.* He raised his hands in an act of surrender and offered his most engaging smile. "I'm sorry. That was tacky. It's none of my business. I do care about you and I want you to be happy. Whatever you do, I'm with you." He held out his hand. "Okay?"

"Thank you." Toffee eyes glistened and she stretched out her hand to stroke Matthew's cheek. "There's one other thing we need to discuss."

Mother's serious tone made him brace for another assault. "Sure," he answered cautiously. "What is it?"

"I owe you an apology."

"For what?"

"I should have been a better mother." She looked everywhere but at him.

"No. An apology isn't necessary."

"Yes, it is." Her fingers crawled across the table and held his. "Mattie, I'm sorry. You deserved so much more than what you got. And I'm sorry our family couldn't hold things together. Please forgive me. Forgive your dad. He loved you. Remember, he had an illness that was greater than him. You shouldn't have suffered because of your parents."

How could he not respond? Her tone was heartfelt, her eyes glittering with unshed tears.

"I forgive you."

They sat, fingers laced, across the length of the table, enjoying the comfortable silence.

For the moment, he'd leave the cardiologist boyfriend alone until he'd had him investigated, learn his motives, then if necessary persuade his mother to slow down this marriage stuff.

"Say, how about some breakfast?" Matthew stood and started for the refrigerator. "Then we can catch up a little more."

Carolyn's smile dazzled him. "I'd like that. I have a question. Can you cook?"

Matthew grinned. "Remember, you raised a self-sufficient kid. Of course. Breakfast is my specialty. Did I tell you that I make a mean garbage-can omelet?"

Matthew opened the refrigerator door and removed the carton of eggs. He placed a bowl and whisk on the island countertop next to the range and opened the carton. A sense of relief settled over him. As he cracked eggs and dropped them in the bowl, his gaze shifted to his mother as she set the table for breakfast.

Mother's perseverance sure paid off. It bugged him to think where they would be if she'd given up. Granted, he'd been pissed off when she showed up on his doorstep. Now, he appreciated the fact that she'd forced the issue and stood firm.

Given his stubborn nature, they might never have resolved

their differences. His hands shook when he considered how close he had come to losing her.

Heart attack. Those words conjured all types of evil images.

It bothered him to think that his mother had been ill and suffered alone, that she felt she had no right to call him and ask for his assistance. *She's my mother and I should have been notified.* What if Mother had died? He wouldn't have been any wiser. Her illness provided an eye-opening experience that he didn't plan to encounter a second time.

Adding salt, pepper, and milk to the eggs, he picked up the whisk and blended the mixture. Mother taking a trip down the aisle a second time didn't thrill him. This Vincent guy needed to be checked out. Once he made it to work, he'd put Jacob on the case. His bud would dig up all the dirt on this character and report back to him, then he'd decide how to proceed.

Moving to the stove, he placed the omelet pan on the heating element and searched the cabinet for the cooking spray to coat the pan. He glanced at his mother. Should she be eating eggs?

"Mother, is it okay for you to eat an omelet? Maybe we should rethink breakfast."

"Of course. I'm allowed three each week and I generally eat egg whites. I haven't had any this week. It's fine."

Matthew asked, "How about some toast?"

"I'll make it." Mother strolled to the refrigerator, opened the door and removed a loaf of wheat bread. "Wheat all right with you?"

Matthew nodded.

As the pan warmed Matthew chopped scallions, fresh spinach, green peppers, mushrooms, and tomatoes, and grated some cheese. Today, he'd skip the bacon and ham. Mother didn't need the additional fat. This omelet would be more of a vegetarian fare, Matthew decided, pouring the mixture into the skillet. He had to do everything in his power to keep her healthy. That's the only way he knew to help her and have the relationship that they deserved.

It was time, past time, to let her into his life. Maybe he'd invite her to the office and show her the company. An image of Lisa's shocked face after one of his mother's biting remarks pierced his thoughts and choked his heart. A second dose of Mother might ruin any chance they have of getting together. When Mother made her visit to the office, they'd steer clear of Lisa.

The way he'd work it, he'd invite Mother to lunch, give her the grand tour of Games while skipping Lisa's area. No point in stirring up that hornet's nest.

Picking up the spatula, he tested the edge of the omelet, then added the vegetables. After breakfast, he'd suggest she get her calendar and choose a date.

Twenty-three

"Ms. Daniels," called the voice from hell.

Queasy and exhausted, Lisa halted in the center of the corridor, glanced over her shoulder, and her eyes widened in shock. Ohmigosh, Matthew's mother. Computer keyboards, ringing telephones, and chatting employees all faded as Lisa made a sharp turn, barreled down the hallway toward her cube, and concentrated all of her energies on escaping Mrs. James.

"Wait. Ms. Daniels, I'd like to talk with you." Matthew's mother waved her hand in the air. The employees lounging about the corridor parted like the Red Sea, creating a pathway.

This is silly. *I'm a professional. One senior citizen doesn't scare me. Right?* Lisa stopped in her tracks and gave Mrs. James an opportunity to catch up. She didn't run from situations. She met them head on and worked out a resolution. She balled her hand into a fist and cheered. Right!

Fighting to catch her breath, Mrs. James stopped in front of Lisa. "Good. I caught you. Are you busy? I need a minute of your time." She took Lisa by the arm and guided her away from the watchful crowd. "This won't take long."

"I'm really busy today, can we do this some other time, Mrs. James?"

"So, which way?"

Mrs. James got that one right. Lisa didn't want to be a source of entertainment and gossip for her coworkers. As things stood, her father and Stephen had been story enough for the whole company to gossip about.

Carolyn James's eyes gleamed with determination. Sometimes Lisa felt as if she had no control over the events in her life. *This woman isn't going to leave peacefully.* Lisa extended her arm in the direction of her cubicle. "My cube is this way."

Gathering her dignity, Lisa strolled down the corridor with Mrs. James on her heels, nodding at her coworkers as she moved to her cubicle. She stepped through the entrance and patted a chair for Mrs. James.

"Have a seat," Lisa offered once they entered her cube.

For several days, the symptoms of a summer cold or flu had plagued her. A nagging pain pulsated behind her eyes and shifted to her frontal lobe. Matthew's mother might just put her over the edge. Lisa shut one eye and glared at Mrs. James.

Chanel perfume floated under Lisa's nose and made her stomach lunge dangerously. If she didn't put some distance between them, Mrs. James's white suit might be decorated with her lunch.

Even her beloved cup of "happy" had left a bitter, rank taste in her mouth this morning. Her stomach churned when she glanced at the film covering the surface of the cold coffee in her mug.

"Don't worry. I won't take much of your time." A tight little smile skirted across Mrs. James's face. "I'm sure you don't want to talk about your personal affairs in a place where everyone can listen."

Her father's rant against Stephen had been embarrassment enough. Not only had it been at Games, but in the corridor where everyone in the office could hear it.

Lisa hoped Mrs. James's visit would be quick and painless. Then, she could turn her attention to the real business of being sick without an audience. Propping her hand under her chin, she waited for Matthew's mother to complete her scrutiny of her cubicle. The other woman's eyes rested for a moment on the Andy Warhol reprint on the wall.

While Mrs. James inspected her cubicle, Lisa examined her. Her made-up face was gorgeous, except all of her lipstick had been chewed away and her hands clutched the white Coach bag as if it were a life preserver. Girlfriend was nervous, very nervous. Why?

Mrs. James scooted to the edge of her chair, picked up the photographs of Lisa's family, and studied the photo.

"Handsome family," Mrs. James complemented.

"Thank you."

Her brows drew together over the bridge of her nose and her expression grew concerned. "You're looking a little ill today, dear. Are you all right?"

Time to get this over with, Lisa decided. Well, that sure made her feel better. Having someone who looked as good as Mrs. James tell her that she looked like crap made her already awful day worse. She continued, "I'm fine. Just a touch of the flu or something like that. Nothing to worry about. Now, what can I do for you?"

"Well, this is awkward for me." Mrs. James clasped her hands together and settled them over the purse in her lap. "There's something I need to say."

Here it comes. Lisa braced for a second verbal fight with the reigning champion. *What more did Mrs. James have to say? She'd made herself more than clear at Matthew's.*

"Actually, dear, I want to apologize for my behavior the day I arrived. After all, it's Matthew's house and I had no right to make any comments. It was wrong of me to interfere and make you feel like an intruder. I was the outsider, the intruder, not you. Please don't blame Matthew for what happened. My only excuse is that I wanted my son's full attention and you had it, not me. It's been years since we've visited together and I hoped to have him all to myself. I felt jealous and my motherly instincts kicked in. I'm sorry. I'm sure it wasn't pleasant for you and I promise it'll never happen again."

That punch to the gut hit its mark, but for totally different reasons. Stalling, Lisa ran her fingers across her arched brow and tried to soothe her headache, while dissecting Mrs. James's apology. Had she heard correctly? Was Mrs. James apologizing to her? Matthew must have demanded that she do so.

"Lisa?" She queried softly.

"I'm sorry, my mind wandered for a moment. There's no need for an apology. The incident is forgotten." *There. Now go away.*

"Oh, but there is. My instincts tell me that you and my son have something special."

Ohmigosh, any minute now she'll start talking about my sex life.

"Matthew really cares for you and I don't want to come between you. I want us to get along and, in time, become friends." Mrs. James stretched her hand across the desk and squeezed Lisa's fingers. "The way I barged in caused trouble. And I want you to know if anything I said or did hindered your relationship with Matthew, please don't take it out on him. It's my fault."

"Mrs. James," Lisa began. The churning in her stomach rushed upward. She slapped a hand over her mouth and leaned away from her desk in search of her wastepaper basket. She retched into the black plastic cylinder until every morsel of food she'd consumed this wretched day was gone. Weak, Lisa fell back against her chair and drew long breaths into her lungs, fighting to regain control over her flushed limbs.

Cool, soothing fingers brushed hair away from Lisa's face. Mrs. James laid her palm across Lisa's forehead and handed Lisa a tissue. "Wipe your mouth, dear. I'll go and get you a glass of water to rise your mouth."

"Don't." Lisa raised a hand to warn her off. "I'll be fine."

Ignoring her comment, Mrs. James posed a question of her own. "How long have you been ill?"

Lisa straightened in her chair and tried to pull herself together. "Just for a little bit," she answered, physically and emotionally exhausted. "But it's better now."

"Hmm. We'll see. I'm going to the fountain and get you some water. I'll be right back." She hurried from the room and within minutes was back with a paper cup in each hand.

"Here, drink this," she ordered, sounding very much like her son.

"Thank you," Lisa answered meekly.

"What have you kept down today?" The older woman asked.

"Liquids. A sip or two of coffee. I think it's one of those bugs going around the office. I'm always picking up something. Thanks for everything. But I don't want you to worry yourself. I'll be fine in a bit. Besides, I don't want you to catch whatever I have."

"Nonsense. I seldom get sick. I don't think you need to be at work. Or alone. Relax. I'll be right back."

Now what? Lisa wondered, too ill to do more than wipe the corners of her mouth with the tissue and sip a little water. She shut her eyes and leaned her head against the back of the chair. If she could just sit here for a short while, she might be able to pull herself together and no one would be the wiser. Besides, there was plenty of work that needed her attention.

That all too familiar tingling sensation lodged at the base of her spine then surged upward. Lisa turned to the doorway and found Matthew. Summing up the situation with those piercing multicolored eyes, he strolled into the cubicle. Mrs. James's worried face observed everything from under her son's arm.

He dominated the small space, stood over Lisa, studying her pained expression. Today, the combination of Royal Copenhagen and his pure male scent did nothing for her. In fact, the fragrance almost made her gag.

"She looks terrible," he whispered to his mother. Turning to Lisa, he shot a volley of questions at her. "What have you done to yourself? How long have you been ill? Have you called your doctor? Are you taking any medicine?"

Eyes closed, Lisa answered, "Leave me alone."

"Mother, ask the secretary for a glass of water and some aspirins," he ordered.

Lisa watched him for a beat and came to her own decision. She refused to fall in with his plans like a rag doll.

"Why didn't you stay at home today? You're allowed sick days," he scolded.

In contrast to his harsh words, Matthew supported her head gently and brought the cool water to her parched lips. Lisa groaned in true horror, embarrassed and humiliated beyond anything she'd ever experienced.

"Matthew, don't fuss with the girl. She's too ill for that right now," Mrs. James chastised on the other side of Lisa. "What she needs is to go home and get in bed for a few days while someone pampers her."

"You're right. She needs to be at home. I'll take her."

"Good." Mrs. James patted her son on the shoulder. "Make sure she has plenty of orange juice and stock up on aspirin."

Lisa tried to regain some dignity, sitting upright in her chair, but a wave of dizziness assaulted her and she slid back. "Wait, I don't want you to upset your schedule. I can get myself home. I'll call one of my brothers. They'll come and get me."

"No," Matthew vetoed, shutting down Lisa's computer. "We're not going to wait for them to get here. That could take hours. I'm right here and I can take care of you."

"I'm sure you can, dear," Mrs. James added her two cents to the issue with a hand of Lisa's shoulder. "But for now, we'll take care of you."

Was she invisible? Had she lost her voice? It didn't seem to matter what she said. Everyone was going about her business, doing what they believed was best for her.

Matthew opened and shut several desk drawers before he found what he wanted. He drew her purse from the drawer and handed it to her. "Do you need anything else?"

Yes, Lisa thought. *My dignity. I've got to make one more attempt to make them understand.* "Thanks for your help. I really appreciate the help, but I got here under my own steam, I can get home." She tried to stand and failed miserably, sinking back down into her chair as the room spun around her.

"Just how are you planning to do that?" He folded his arms across his chest. "You can barely hold your head up."

She raised her head and glared at him. "My parents will send somebody for me."

"There's no need. I told you I'll take care of it. So, up you go." He secured his arm around her waist and helped Lisa to her feet. "Let's get you home before you get sick again. Mother, don't forget her briefcase."

"No, wait." Lisa pulled herself from Matthew's arms. "There's plenty that I need to finish. Who's going to do it? And what about my car? I can't leave it here. How will I get back to work?"

"Anything you're working on can wait until you get back. You need someone to look after you and I'm the logical choice. I'm your man for a little while. You'll have to depend on me."

Shaking her head, Lisa replied, "I don't think so. I can take care of myself."

"Yeah, right. You've really done a great job so far," he added. "Sorry, you don't have a choice this time. I'm in charge. Now, can you walk or should I carry you to the car?"

Horrible images of the whole office watching Matthew parade through the corridor with her in his arms made her shudder. "I can walk."

A few steps later she found she'd been wrong. The last traces of her dignity vanished when she realized how weak she felt. Appreciation and thanks for his physical presence filled her when Matthew's arm lent support to her wobbly legs. Although Lisa planned to keep that bit of information to herself.

Oh, why hadn't she just stayed home today? If she had followed her first thought, she would have been safe in her own bed right now. No one would be the wiser. Instead, the entire office staff would see her at her absolute worst.

Mrs. James trailed along behind them, carrying Lisa's briefcase and handbag. She hovered quietly in the background and waited at the elevator. When the elevator arrived, Mrs. James deposited Lisa's belongings on the elevator's carpeted floor.

"I'm sorry about the tour, Mother. Maybe we can do it later this week," Matthew said.

"No problem."

"You won't have any trouble getting home, will you?" he asked, lightly touching his mother's arm. His tone held a degree of concern.

"I've got my car. I'll be fine."

"Mother, I'll see you at home."

"You just take care of her," Mrs. James answered.

"I will," he promised.

"Lisa, get better soon." Mrs. James's grave, concerned expression was the last thing she saw before the doors slid shut.

Twenty-four

Suspended between sleep and wakefulness, Lisa snuggled her face deeper into the pillow. The room had developed a chilly nip while she slept. "It's cold in here." She searched for the blanket with the tip of her toe. Fluffy, wool fabric brushed against her nylon-covered foot as she tried to hook her foot under the blanket and drag it over her.

Lisa gave up, flipped onto her back, and sprawled across the peach and teal triangular patterned quilt that covered the bed. She opened her eyes, and blinked several times to adjust to the darkened room. Green fluorescent numbers winked from the center of her white cube digital clock. Seven forty-eight! She sprang into a sitting position. Ohmigosh, she'd been out for hours.

Stretching, her eyes roamed the familiar room for Matthew. She didn't find him, but his navy silk jacket laid carelessly across the chaise longue next to her own jacket. He must have forgotten it when he brought her home.

Lisa identified the aroma of simmering vegetables and coffee as her other senses kicked in. Her stomach rumbled. *I'm hungry.*

She realized there was somebody in her house as she listened to the noises coming from beyond her bedroom door. Running water and a muffled male voice touched her ears. Had Matthew stayed? It was one thing for him to make certain she'd made it home safely. But to stay here and cook, that was too much. Mixed emotions overwhelmed her as she tallied the hours he'd spent in her home while she slept.

It's time for Matthew to go home. She swung her legs over the side of the bed and perched on the edge of the mattress, waiting for the tingling in the pit of her stomach that always accompanied the queasiness. After several minutes of calm, she rose, moved cautiously to the bathroom door, stopping to lovingly stroke Matthew's jacket. Her eyes drifted shut as her fingers caressed the smooth silk fabric.

Cradling the garment between her hands, Lisa rubbed it back and forth against her cheek, enjoying the smooth feel of silk and Matthew's scent. For a moment, she savored the memories associated with his scent.

Whatever image Lisa maintained in public or at work, she discarded at home. No need to hide the fact that Matthew's presence affected her far deeper than anything else in her life. She loved him. Carefully replacing the garment where she'd found it, Lisa locked her heart behind her protective barrier and continued on to the bathroom.

Soft murmuring drifted her way as she approached the kitchen in her stocking feet. Leaning against the doorframe, she enjoyed the agile movements of Matthew while he sauntered around her kitchen. Brown arms sprinkled with black hair sprang from the rolled back crème sleeves of his shirt as he cradled the telephone under his chin.

Matthew turned and caught sight of Lisa. He grinned in delight, pivoting on his heels, he halted in front of her as his multicolored gaze skipped along her frame.

"See you later. Bye," he said into the phone. A slow, easy smile spread across his lips before he ended the call and placed the telephone on the counter. "Hey," he whispered. The underlying sensuality of that one word captivated her.

"Hey yourself." She smiled back at him.

"I used your phone. I hope you don't mind." He poked his thumb at the phone. "I wanted to check on my mother. Make sure she made it home okay."

"No problem. You've both been very good to me."

He studied her feature by feature. "You look better. How do you feel? Are you doing better?"

"Good. But I'm hungry." She said, crossing the room and reaching for the refrigerator door handle.

"You might want to take it a little slow until you're sure your stomach can handle things."

"I know," she agreed. "I know. Maybe something light will do the trick. Soup or something. Although I wouldn't turn down a grilled chicken sandwich."

"I'm way ahead of you. There's soup simmering on the stove and a fruit salad chilling in the fridge."

"Boy, you're really handy in the kitchen. I might consider keeping you around," she teased. As soon as the words left Lisa's lips, she wanted to call them back. Relationships in general or theirs in particular were last on her agenda.

"Can I help?" she asked, opening the drawer and gathering silverware.

Matthew marched to where she stood, removed the spoons from her hands, and guided her to a chair. "Sit," he commanded, pushing her into a chair. "I'll take care of the rest."

What choice do I have? she thought, watching him set the table.

"I'll remind you of that another time. For now, let's eat."

Picking up her spoon, she dug into the bowl of vegetable beef soup. Matthew placed a glass of milk and a smoked chicken breast sandwich on a plate next to her bowl. He sank into the chair across from her and placed a napkin in his lap. They sat silently, concentrating on their meal.

"That was good," she complimented, wiping her mouth with her napkin.

He bowed. "Thank you. Opening a can is my specialty."

"I really appreciate everything you and your mother have done for me today. Don't feel you need to baby-sit me." Lisa pushed her empty bowl toward the center of the table. "As you can see, I'm fine now."

Grinning at her, Matthew guided her from the dining room table. "Actually, I'd like to talk with you before I leave." His words caused her heart to leap uncontrollably before it returned to its normal rhythmic beat.

What do you want, Matthew? she wondered. Since the night they made love, she'd tried her darnest to steer clear of him. *What did they have to discuss?*

He led her to the sofa, made sure she was comfortable, then settled next to her. "Lisa," he began, linking their fingers. "It's time for you to fess up. You've been sick on and off for several weeks. Vomiting, dizziness. Sweetheart, you might be pregnant. We were far too busy to think about using any protection that night or the next day."

Stunned, her insides quivered with the idea of having his baby. Boy, did she want his idea to be no more than a wonderful dream.

"Close your mouth, sweetheart," Matthew suggested, patting her knee. "I see the possibility never crossed your mind.

"I'm not pregnant."

"How can you be so sure?" He persisted. "Have you had your period?"

An unwelcome blush crept into her cheeks. "That's a bit personal, don't you think?" Lisa shot back at him.

His mouth turned tight and grim and the expression in his eyes said don't-give-me-that. "No. As I've said in the past, we're beyond the hand-holding stage. In case you've forgotten, we've shared our bodies and at the time I thought our hearts with one another. I'm not going to pretend to soothe your sensitivities."

Lisa hated the silence that followed his question. Boy, how she wanted to be completely honest with him. How she wished she could confess. Maybe it was time to confess. Tell him everything, then admit she loved him. Here was an opportunity for him to put his money where his mouth was. Could he live up to all the promises and declarations he'd made over the past months? Would he still understand after she admitted everything? She wanted to know how far he'd go when all the facts were placed in his lap.

Fear bubbled up inside her and threatened to choke her.

Stephen had hurt her so badly. Not only had he rejected her, but he had humiliated her in front of her family and their colleagues. The gossip and snickering behind her back had nearly destroyed her. That incident made her stronger, and when her life settled into a different routine she had promised to steer clear of office entanglements. *And look at me now,* she thought derisively. Caution and logic had kept her heart safe and intact from emotional entanglement and love until Matthew barged into her life, running shorts and all.

While her colleagues saw only the professional side of her, Matthew had become part of her very soul. He'd seen the insecurities and fears that were eating her alive. Matthew had won the prize, her heart.

Oh, how she would love to have his baby. The very idea sent her heart racing, her pulse doubling. It would be wonderful to feel herself grow large with a baby inside her as she anticipated its arrival. She shook her head, rejecting the beautiful images. Reality took charge and her fantasies faded.

"It's not a problem. I used something," she kept her voice even, concentrating her energy on her answer. He didn't need to know what she used. That was her little secret.

Matthew studied her face, checked the myriad of emotions skirting across her face. "All right. I won't press the issue. But that doesn't answer any of my other questions. Lisa, tell me, what do I need to do to get you to give us a chance?"

Love me unconditionally, Lisa cried silently. *Accept my limitations and the things I have done,* quickly followed the first thought.

Lisa wished there was an easy solution to what Matthew wanted. She wanted desperately to be close to him and dream of the type of life he offered, giving and sharing their love, work, and aspirations.

God, why couldn't life be simple? Lisa questioned, chewing on her bottom lip. Matthew deserved an explanation, there was no doubt about that. His sincere encouragement had gone a long way to alleviate her feelings of inadequacy, had made her consider revealing the truth to him. But some lingering doubts still plagued her, and until all of her doubts were eliminated, she would never reveal the truth.

"Lisa," Matthew whispered, lifting her chin with the tip of his finger. "I've tiptoed around you for a while, giving you the space and time I believe you needed. Now, I think you owe me an explanation. Things were so good between us that night. I felt it was a beginning, not an end."

Her eyes skirted away from his penetrating gaze, instead concentrating on her hands twisting together in her lap. A tense, charged silence sizzled between them. Lisa shifted uncomfortably on the sofa, waiting for Matthew's concern to fade and anger to replace it.

"Sweetheart, look at me," he ordered. Matthew's voice was uncompromising, yet oddly gentle. He moved closer on the sofa and took one of her hands between both of his. There was a firmness in his eyes that commanded her attention, informing her that he had no intention of giving up until he received satisfactory answers.

"Your silence is killing me . . . us. Please talk to me," he pleaded. The slow stroking motion of his hand sent pleasure coursing up her spine.

"A relationship between us could only lead to new problems," she explained, in a tight forlorn voice. "What we had that night was special, but it was a mistake. It should never have happened. I shouldn't have let it happen."

"You couldn't have stopped it if you wanted. We needed that night. And I don't regret it at all. Just tell me what I can do to make things right. We have so much to build on—careers, community activities, desire for a family, and maybe even the beginning of love between us. Why won't you let me comfort you, keep you safe, and love you? Tell me what's causing you so much pain in your life. Let me slay all of your dragons. I can, you know."

"Don't push me," she stated, defiantly pushing him away. "You can't make me love you."

"No. I can't do that. But, I don't think it's something I have to make you do. You already do," he said with confidence in his voice. "You just haven't given me the words. I felt it when we made love that night and I feel it every time we're together. Why won't you admit it?"

"That was sex. Pure and simple," she answered bravely while a tear slid down her cheek. "Don't romanticize it."

"Brave words. When are you going to stop running and stand up for what you want? Stand up for us," he challenged. Slipping from the sofa, Matthew dropped to his knees before her, pulling her onto the floor in front of him. Framing her face with his hands, he leaned closer, licking the moisture away from her cheeks with his tongue.

"Shhh. I'm here," Matthew coaxed soothingly. His arms wrapped around her, pulling her close, gently rocking her back and forth. Stroking his hand down her hair, he guided her head to his chest, resting it there. Her head fitted perfectly in the hollow between his shoulder and neck. "We'll work it out."

He was wrong. There was no way to work things out, but no matter how much she tried to discourage him, he always came back.

Desire, hot and quick, coursed through her as his fingers slid sensuously over her back. Matthew's hands returned to cup her face, bringing it upward to receive his kiss. His kiss was tender and light, fluttering softly across her lips like the wings of a bird.

Without warning the kiss turned hot and demanding, shocking Lisa with the deluge of emotions that accompanied it. She found herself eagerly pressed against him, responding with total abandonment.

Stopping him was the last thing she wanted to do. Riding out the tidal wave of emotions, she enjoyed the taste, scent, and feel of Matthew. Everything he had to offer, she greedily accepted. They clung together, swept away by their long suppressed emotions.

Tensing suddenly, Matthew snatched his lips away, drawing deep, calming breaths into his lungs. A groan that was very close to pain escaped from him.

"Don't leave me," she begged, burning with desire. The aching need to be close to him made her forsake her pride. She needed his warmth, her body felt bereft without him. Impulsively, Lisa wound her arms around his neck, blindly searching for his lips, all the while forcing his head down to hers.

"Never," he promised, raining sweet, hot kisses over her face and throat, drawing her with him to her feet. Instantly he swept her, weightless, into his arms. Matthew took long strides to her bedroom door, pausing outside the room.

"Are you sure?" He asked, his features tight with passion. "I want you to be sure. There won't be any turning back after tonight."

"Love me," she pleaded, using her foot to push the slightly ajar door completely open.

"I plan to."

Twenty-five

Well after midnight, Matthew entered the offices of Games People Play. Shadows bounced off the walls creating odd-shaped images as Matthew strolled down the corridor to his office.

Making love with Lisa had rejuvenated him, but had made him take a hard look at his emotions. He couldn't deny it anymore. He loved Lisa. It tortured him to love Lisa and yet have so many secrets and doubts between them.

With each step he took Lisa's sweet scent rose from his clothing. His sure footsteps faltered and slowed as the image of them together focused in his memory and his mind's eye again saw them flesh against flesh, man loving woman.

"I shouldn't have left Lisa," Matthew muttered uneasily as waves of apprehension surged through him. He needed to be with her when she awakened, reassure her that he planned to be part of her life.

There had been a moment where he stood in her darkened bedroom fighting the urge to crawl back into bed and curve his body around the soft contours of her body and let the world do what it wanted. "Damn!" he muttered as his lower anatomy hardened as the memories flowed freely. "I should have stayed, talked the whole thing out, and demanded that she tell me everything."

First things first, Matthew decided, fighting unsuccessfully to remove Lisa's nude image from his mind. He needed to concentrate on Games and talk to Jacob. *I can't go on like this. I'm losing my mind.* They had to come up with a plan. Now! He needed answers and quick because his relationship with Lisa was teetering on the edge of destruction.

Uncertainty gnawed at his insides. Too much of their future still lay unresolved. Following his instincts, he had taken the afternoon off to care for Lisa. New and unexpected discoveries awaited him as he'd spent precious time with her. They'd broken down some of the barriers that had kept them separated, but in doing so Matthew had recognized something Lisa hadn't acknowledged herself. She cared for him, possibly loved him. A warm glow flowed through him. And that was the prize he'd pinned all his hopes on. Matthew couldn't restrain the smile of pure pleasure that spread across his face.

But the smile retreated rapidly when he remembered Lisa's repeated rejections. They cut deep, bringing him more frustration and pain than he'd thought possible.

Unlocking his office, Matthew strolled across the room, ignored the lights, and sank into his chair. Without the pressure of running the company, this was a perfect time to think, work out a plan. He watched the gold-and-red sunrise from his spacious office windows, elbows on his knees, hands cradled his chin. After spending the day with Lisa, he hoped he'd feel better. But he didn't. A big question still hung over her head.

I've got to know. And I've got have answers now! He swiveled the chair toward his desk, picked up the telephone, and punched in a number.

The phone rang eight times before Jacob answered. "Yeah," he rasped into the receiver in a tone that suggested he planned to hang up any second.

"Jay, it's me."

"Man, have you lost your mind?" He spit out. "It's after five. I just got to sleep after working on your crap, I might add." Through the phone lines Matthew heard the blend of anger and frustration in his friend's voice.

"I know. I know. I'm sorry," Matthew's tone was apologetic. "I need to talk."

"Mmm. Okay," Jacob sighed. "What do you need? What's goin' on?"

I need reassurances that Lisa isn't involved with this stuff at Games, Matthew shouted silently. *I need answers.* "It's time, man. I can't take it anymore. No more games." There was a possessive desperation in his voice that he couldn't hide. "I've got to have some answers. No. That's wrong. I've got to have all the answers."

"What are you talking about? Answers to what exactly? How much have you drunk tonight?"

Matthew ran a hand across his forehead as if it hurt, and in truth it was beginning to ache. "None. I haven't had a drop. It's time to find out who's stealing from me." His smooth, insistent voice rang clearly through the lines. "We need to figure out a way to flush them out. Bait them. You're the computer genius, come up with something."

"By that you mean, Ms. Daniels? Am I correct?"

"Yeah. That's part of it. I need it done yesterday."

"I've got an idea." Jacob paused, then added cautiously, "but I'm not sure how you're going to handle it."

"Don't worry about me." He straightened in his chair, drumming his fingers against the desk surface, braced for anything. "What is it?"

"Let's give them what they want."

Jacob's cryptic remark didn't help Matthew's headache. His forehead crinkled and he asked, "What? How?"

"Since your crook is using the Internet to steal from you, let's turn the tables on him."

"And we're going to do what?"

"Think, man. If he's using the Internet to steal software, what better way to sell it?" Jacob's deep voice simmered with barely checked excitement. "The net is the most anonymous place in the world. Anything you want, you can get there and no one will ever know. All you need is the right connection and the money. We're going to offer your crook the money."

Matthew shook his head, unable to keep a note of skeptism out of his tone. "Jay, how can we be sure he'll take the bait? I mean, there are zillions of people on the net trying to sell software."

"True." He agreed. "The difference is we can customize our request to something that only your company offers."

Nodding, Matthew agreed, "I can see that."

"The seller would have to know what's going on at Games to answer this particular query."

"That's how we'll know it's our guy. We'll make the seller pull from your stock and then sell it back to us."

Matthew rolled a pen between his fingers and nibbled on the edge of his mouth. "Okay. Say we do this, how much time do you think it'll take to get this guy?"

"Don't know," Jay answered tersely.

"No can do. I need more than that. You've got to give me some time frame here."

"Sorry, buddy. This is not an exact science. It could be a week. Or it can take months. What's in your favor is he doesn't know what we know. Or will he?"

A pregnant pause followed Jacob's query.

"Jacob, what are you saying?" Matthew demanded in a harsh tone.

"It's very simple. Are you going to let Ms. Daniels in on our plans? Speaking of which, how much have you told Ms. Daniels?"

"Nothing," he replied defensively.

"Mmm, hmm." A skeptical note filled those murmurings.

"I don't lie. I haven't told her. But I want to. I wish we could get this garbage out in the open." Matthew squeezed his eyes shut. "So the best thing we can do for Games and me is to find the bastard yesterday."

"I feel you, buddy. I feel you. Let me ask you a question."

"Go for it."

"What happens if we find Ms. Daniels on the other end of the Internet? What are you going to do then? Will you still prosecute? Can you do it, my friend?"

All of his excessive confidence was blown away by Jacob's question. "I—I don't know. I'll work it out when the time comes."

"Let me take this a step further. I'm not going through all this work to see you jerk off in the end."

"I said I'd prosecute and I will."

"Even if it turns out to be Ms. Daniels?"

"It's not Lisa," Matthew retorted with all the desperation of someone who truly wanted to believe but still possessed lingering doubts.

"Okay. I'll set things in motion. Expect an update from me later today. Now, can I go back to sleep?"

"No. I've got one more thing to ask you. What about the lease?"

"I checked into it. Brock and Ms. Daniels went into the lease together. They haven't done anything since. I saw the space. There's no furniture, phone, or anything. That's all I could find out. There isn't any additional info."

Matthew massaged his temple. "Another dead end."

"True," Jacob answered. "But it ain't over 'til it's over. I'm still digging for more info. Something could come up when and where we least expect it. Don't give up on things, okay?"

"Okay, Jay. Thanks for listening to me, man. I needed it."

"No problem. You're my bud."

Ending the call with Jacob, Matthew rose from his chair, removed his jacket, and dropped the garment on the conference room table on his way to the bar. Rubbing a hand across his chin, he muttered, filling the coffeepot with fresh water. "I need to wake up."

Spooning coffee into the filter, he checked the time and groaned. Damn. It was almost dawn. No wonder Jacob thought he was a madman when he picked up the phone. Thank God his bud understood his anxiety and the urgency that drove this particular nightime rant. The dilemma at

Games was eating away at his soul like maggots on a piece of beef.

Hands braced on the bar, he waited for the coffee to finish brewing. On one hand, there was a sense of relief attached to taking a stand and making a move to resolve the financial situation troubling Games. It was past time for Jacob and him to find this guy and put him behind bars.

Setting a trap for the thief made Matthew feel like he was in charge again. Why not use the little information they have to set a trap, make the thief come to them. After he got his brain unscrambled, he'd start work on a dummy program they could use as bait for this ass. Send out a memo to the staff detailing some of the intricate details so that the thief would know what was available. Put a query on the net and wait for the action to start. That idea brought a smile to Matthew's lips.

The coffeemaker spit out the last drops of coffee, filling the room with the reviving aroma. He grabbed a mug from the cupboard, filled it with coffee and headed back to his desk.

Jacob's questions replayed in his head, wreaking all manner of havoc to his internal organs. *What happens if we find Ms. Daniels on the other end of the Internet? What are you going to do then? Will you still prosecute? Can you do it, my friend?*

Could he prosecute Lisa? Send her to jail like any other common criminal? Ice ran down his spine. "I don't know," he muttered, fidgeting with his pen. "I don't know."

That wasn't the only bit of advice that Jacob had given him. *Don't fall,* he'd advised. Matthew chuckled without humor, shaking his head. *Too late.* He'd fallen and he hadn't hit bottom yet. But he would, and soon, if they caught Lisa with her hands in the cookie jar.

As the sun peeped through the darkness, Matthew still sat at his desk, no closer to a solution regarding Lisa. If it worked, the sting operation should put an end to all his questions and doubts. "That is, if Lisa's not involved," he said to himself. "Lisa is not a criminal." There were other suspects; Dale Smith, for example, Lisa's friend Cynthia Williams, and Stephen Brock topped Matthew's list. The evidence hadn't led back to Stephen Brock, but Matthew had a feeling that, given time, it would. There was something about that man that rubbed Matthew the wrong way. He was too smooth, too slick, and always cheezin'.

Swiveling away from the window, he picked up the telephone and dialcd Lisa's telephone number. He needed to hear her voice. Now. Before he started his day.

The answering matching clicked in after the fourth ring and her soft, sexy voice explained that she wasn't available at the moment, but please leave a message. Oh yeah, he'd forgotten that he'd turned off the telephone ringer when he left last night.

Matthew leaned back in his chair and allowed the sweet sound of her voice to soothe his soul. The images of her soft, velvety skin against his and the lingering scent of her White Diamonds perfume made him grow hard.

A series of beeps followed her "leave me a message," then he said, "Hi. I know you're asleep but I just wanted to check on you. Hear your voice." He paused, debating what he should say next. There were so many things in his heart that he needed to express, tell her. But not yet. Soon, after the problems at Games were resolved.

"Remember, we'll work everything out. Have a little faith in me. Feel better and I'll call you back later today."

Recradling the telephone, Matthew tented his fingers together and wondered if he was setting himself up for a fall. In his heart, he believed in Lisa. The woman he'd grown to love wouldn't steal from him. But the right side of his brain said there must be more, something Jacob and he missed. There must to be a logical explanation to clear up Lisa's involvement with Brock and this lease agreement stuff.

Maybe she was being manipulated into stealing. It could happen.

Stephen Brock popped into his head. Consciously or unconsciously, could she have been persuaded to do something like this against her principles? He didn't know.

Did Brock have some hold over her? His gut told him everything revolved around that damn lease agreement. What caused Lisa and Brock to argue over it? Could Brock have used that lease as leverage to make Lisa do what he wanted?

Jacob would find the answers and then everything would be cleared up. After that he could move toward the relationship he wanted with Lisa.

Twenty-six

The sharp odor of turpentine shot up Matthew's nose. "Man, I'm sick of this," he snarled, pulling his handkerchief from his pocket and rubbing his nose. Stuffing the white linen back into his pocket, he glanced around the cramped librarian's workroom and then at Jacob. This cubbyhole wasn't large enough to fill a glass with water, let alone offer enough space to accommodate Matthew, Jacob, and the library staff that swept in and out.

Jacob sat at the computer, typing away. Calm and unconcerned, his buddy glanced at him, then returned to his keyboard.

Frustrated, Matthew drove his fist into the palm of his hand and paced the floor. "We've been here for eleven days. That bastard's not going to show."

"Be patient," Jacob glanced in Matthew's direction before returning his attention to his laptop.

"No can do. If he gets away with this software, we've lost our edge."

"He won't."

The confident note in Jacob's voice raised a red flag in Matthew's mind. He studied his friend's calm expression. "How can you be so sure?"

"I embedded a little something to identify our software. Plus, I added a virus that will eat away at the files until they're gone. Either way, Games is safe."

"Whoa! Beautiful. That's my bud." A broad smile of approval spread across Matthew's face and he slapped Jacob on the back. "Now, you're talking. That makes me feel a little better." He patted his chest and sighed heavily.

Jacob glanced at Matthew and back to his keyboard.

"Why didn't you tell me before?"

"I was saving it for the moment when you really needed it." Jacob removed his hands from the keyboard and gave his friend his full attention.

"All we have to do is hope the thief shows up."

"So stop worrying. He'll show," Jacob answered with certainty. "This is going to happen."

Matthew shoved his hands into the back pockets of his jeans and asked, "How do you know?"

Typing away on his laptop, Jacob turned to his friend. "I know because this is about money. Pure and simple. He'll be here. If not today, soon."

Jacob kept repeating a variation on the same theme for days. Matthew had his doubts. Since they set the sting operation in motion their days consisted of waiting. Wait for the ghost in the computer to respond to their broadcast message. Wait for the bait to be taken. Now they sat waiting for whoever to show up and retrieve the data.

"I've got another question for you." Matthew stepped around the small room and stopped in front of Jacob. "How did you know this was where he e-mailed the software?"

"Trailed it. I wasn't able to get a name, but I was able to following the transfer. It led to this library."

"Cool." Matthew's forehead crinkled above his eyes. "Most libraries don't offer the kind of setup our thief needs to retrieve the data."

"This one does. Your thief can do just about anything on this Internet system. He has been pretty thorough stealing from you since the beginning," Jacob said. "I'm sure he made inquiries at the library before sending the software here."

"You're probably right."

"Let's change the subject. I've asked you a couple of times and you still haven't answered my question," Jacob reminded softly, nursing a cup of coffee. "What are you going to do if your Ms. Daniels walks through the door?"

"It's not Lisa," Matthew stated stubbornly. "She's has no part in this." Damn, he prayed he was right because it would just kill him if he had to eat those words.

"Humor me," Jacob suggested, a serious, noncompromising expression on his face. "Are we going to jump whoever walks through the door? Even if it is Ms. Daniels? Or does she get special treatment?"

"I told you before, if Lisa does show, we'll work it out."

"How?"

Fear for Lisa knotted his insides and Matthew shifted away from his friend, rubbing his sweaty palms together. He couldn't tell Jacob that he hadn't figured it out in his own head yet. Just thinking about it scared the crap out of him.

In his heart, Matthew knew he couldn't stand by and allow Lisa to go to jail. He loved her. But there was also the possibility that everything was already out of his hands. If Lisa walked through the library doors, it wouldn't be possible for him to protect her. The police would step in and take jurisdiction over the situation. It was the lack of control that frightened him the most.

"Whoa hoo!" Jacob sang. The lines of concentration deepened along his brows as he studied the computer screen. "We're getting some action. Someone just connected to the database."

A wave of apprehension swept through Matthew. Afraid he'd find Lisa sitting at one of the computers, he dragged himself across the room on legs that felt like lead and peered out the window. Searching the library, Matthew sagged against the door as relief washed over him when he didn't see her anywhere.

"There's some kid who just sat down. You should see him. The kid looks as if he jumped out of one of those VH1 videos. A diamond stud in his nose, du-rag tied around his head, and he's got on a pair of those big-leg jeans that wrap around his butt instead of his waist." Matthew chuckled and turned back to Jacob. "You know what. He's too obvious. I bet he's trying to get on the Internet to check out some porn."

Jacob glanced at his laptop screen and back at Matthew. "Well, there's definitely some activity going on. Is there anyone else out there?"

"Yeah. There's a little old black lady. She looks as if she might be in her late fifties, maybe sixties. She's been at the computer for a few minutes. Hey, wait a minute. What the hell!" He exclaimed, looking out the door. "You won't believe this. That old girl just connected a burner to the computer and pulled out a stack of CDs."

Jacob grinned and strummed a finger at him. "Now, that's obvious."

Matthew chuckled. "True. Okay, she pulled a white sheet of paper from her purse. And she's got it next to the computer and is typing away. Maybe it's instructions. What do you think?"

"Possibly," Jacob answered.

"I'm going out there."

"No. Wait." Jacob rose, clapped a hand around Matthew's upper arm. "You'll frighten her away. Let her start downloading the files, it'll take a while. Then we'll stroll out there and see what she's doing."

Matthew ran a finger back and forth across his chin. He stepped around Jacob, picked up a yellow writing pad, and started toward the door. "No. I've got a better idea. I'm going to sit next to her and work on the computer. Then I can check out what she's doing."

"I'm not sure about this idea." Jacob's brows drew downward in a frown. "I don't want you to do anything to cause us to lose her."

"Relax. I won't. At least this way, we can confirm if she's the person we're looking for." Matthew snatched a pencil from the clerk's desk and stuck it behind his ear. "After I've seen what she's doing, I'll send you an e-mail."

"Wait." Jacob's eyes narrowed to silver slits. "I've got a better idea. Log on to Games intranet and go into your private chat room. We can stay connected while you watch her, then it'll look as if you're really working on the computer."

"Good idea."

Jacob pointed at Matthew and warned, "Be careful. We've worked too hard to make this happen to screw up now. Don't scare her off."

"No can do." Matthew slipped through the door. Jacob was acting like a father hen.

Matthew drew in a deep breath and headed to the bank of computers. He glanced at the woman's computer monitor as he passed her on his way to the next computer, slipped into the chair, and tapped the mouse to bring up the monitor. His fingers drummed out a tone on the desktop while he waited for the computer to connect to the Internet.

"Hi," he greeted, breaking into an open appealing smile.

The old lady glanced at him, then back at her computer screen. "Hello," she answered, then returned her attention back to what she was doing.

"How're you doing?" Matthew asked, logging on to Games Intranet.

"Just fine," the old girl responded, popping a CD into the burner.

You there? Matthew typed.

I'm here, Jacob returned. *What is she doing?*

"It turned out to be a pretty day, didn't it?" Matthew asked.

"Sure did. You know, when I got up this morning, I thought it would rain all day. But the sun came out and it's beautiful," the lady said.

Good, he thought. *Finally, I've gotten more than a one- or two-word sentence from you.* "Yeah. I didn't want to get up this morning. Rain makes me want to stay put, dig deeper into my bed."

She laughed and nodded. "Ain't that the truth."

"My name is Matt James." He offered his hand and searched her face for a sign of recognition.

She took his hand in a firm grip and answered, "Hattie. Hattie Williams. It's nice to meet you."

What's going on? flashed across the screen.

I'm talking to her. Trying to get her to open up. Matthew hit the enter key to send his message.

For the next half hour they sat without speaking. Hattie concentrated on her data download, while Matthew worked on a way to restart their conversation.

"Mmmm." She searched through her bag. "Darn! I forgot my book. This is going to take a while, so I always bring something to keep me busy."

Matthew's heart pumped erratically. *Take it slow,* he thought, *don't appear too interested.* "You do this often?" He held his breath, waiting for her answer.

"Few times," Hattie answered evasively. "I know it takes awhile to finish this. I should have gone to the fiction section before I sat down."

This is too good an opportunity to pass up, he thought, "Go browse, I'll be happy to look out for your computer while you're gone."

"You sure you don't mind?"

He shooed her away with a wave of his hand. "Go."

"That's nice of you. I think I will." Hattie studied the computer screen, ran her wet tongue across her lips, and rose, hesitating for a moment. "Hmmm. You shouldn't have to do anything. It looks like it's going fine. If it stops, can you come and find me?"

"Will do." He waved her away. "Go. I'll be right here when you get back."

"Thanks."

She just walked away. Where's she going? Jacob wrote.

Her name is Hattie Williams and you won't believe this. She just asked me to watch her computer while she goes and finds something to read. Can you believe our luck?

No way! The gods must love you.

Something like that. I'm going to check out the files while Hattie's gone. See if I can figure out what she's downloading.

Cool. Remember, don't open any of the files. We don't want the virus to spread to the library computer system. Look at the index, check the URLs, and see how big a file it is. We might be able to match it up from the size of the download. Then get your butt back to your computer.

Yes sir, boss.

Looking around the library, he found Hattie at the far end of the room absorbed with the back cover of a book. Good. This was his chance.

Matthew scooted into her chair and studied the download. The file name didn't ring any bells for him. But he didn't expect that. *It's pretty big,* he thought, writing the name and size of the file on his yellow pad. Worried that she might appear without notice, he glanced around the library, searching for Hattie. He found her in the same location.

He studied her screen. Wait a minute. What was that? He focused on the top right-hand corner of the monitor. There it is again. A tiny surfboard appeared and disappeared with a blink of an eye.

They had her. Jacob had added a signature object to the file.

Hey, you still there? Matthew found printed across the screen when he returned to his computer.

Yeah, Matthew typed. *Did you add a little something that would appear while the files are being downloaded?*

Why? Jacob's question appeared on the screen. *What did you see?*

A little surfboard pops up in the right hand corner of the screen. It's your signature, isn't it?

You've got me.

Oh you're slick, man. Matthew wrote. *I'd tip my hat to you, if I wore a hat, that is.*

The surfboard is my trump card, my failsafe in case things got out of hand. Jacob explained.

Well, it's beautiful. All we need to do is question Hattie and find out what she knows.

I'm coming out so we can confront her together.

Cool.

At least we know it's not Lisa. Matthew typed.

We don't know anything. All we've learned is that your thief employs lackeys. Lisa could have sent this Hattie person into the library to take the heat.

Matthew linked his fingers and placed them behind his head. He frowned as he watched Hattie putter among the bookshelves and wondered about her role. He'd only talked with her for a few minutes, but he felt certain this woman wasn't the mastermind behind a major software ring. She was a flunky doing someone else's bidding. But who? Who?

"Hey, man," Jacob slapped Matthew across the back, leaned over Hattie's empty chair, and tapped in a few keystrokes. Within seconds the printer spit out a document summary page with statistical information on it. Removing the sheet from the printer, he glanced at Matthew and asked, "Where is she?"

Tipping his head toward the fiction section, Matthew said, "Over there."

Jacob's gaze followed Matthew's lead. "Good. We've got a little time. I want to check the file before she comes back."

Matthew turned to his friend. "Then what?"

"When she comes back we drill her for all the information we can get."

"Jay, she's not who we're looking for. Look at her. Does she look like the mastermind behind all of this? Besides, she's doesn't work at Games."

Jacob dropped into Hattie's vacant chair. "I know that. Someone sent her in here today to retrieve those files. We want to know who that is."

"The thing is," Matthew paused, choosing his next words very carefully, "Hattie's an old lady, we don't want to scare her into a heart attack."

"Are you trying to play hero or something?"

"No. No, I'm not," Matthew responded. "We know she's not behind all of this. I don't want to scare her, then we get nothing out of her. Do you see my point?"

"I do." Jacob nodded. "We'll take it slow. You have to understand that she's our first true lead and I'm not going to let her go without prying out some information. Understood?"

"Got it." He slapped Jacob on the back. "Thanks, man. I'll feel better if we do it slowly."

"Excuse me. What are you doing at my computer?" Hattie asked suspiciously. She stood over the two men, four books in her arms, with a scowl on her smooth sepia-brown skin.

Jacob rose slowly from her chair, stood over Hattie, and pointed a finger at Matthew. "Actually, I'm here with my buddy. I've just checked the file you're downloading."

"Why would you be checking my stuff?" Hattie placed her books on the table next to the computer and picked up her black tote bag. "What's goin' on?"

Jacob scratched his ear and answered, "I know a great deal about those files. Honestly, I created them."

Hattie's gaze slipped from one man to the other. "Who are you really? The police?"

Jacob shook his head. "No. We're from the company that owns those files you're stealing."

"I'm not stealing anything," she exclaimed, shifting her black bag from one arm to the other and backing up a foot or two.

"Oh? What do you call it?" Jacob asked.

Hattie turned on her heels and hurried along the aisle, heading for the door.

"Catch her," Jacob ordered, springing to action. He barreled down the aisle after her.

Matthew jumped to his feet and darted in the opposite direction, hoping to reach the door before Hattie hit the street. If she made it out of the building, all bets were off.

Twenty-seven

Adrenaline pumped through Matthew as he rushed after Hattie. He refused to let her get away. She represented the first solid lead since the beginning of their investigation.

Seconds before she slipped out the library's doors, Matthew lunged, clamped firm fingers around her upper arm, and held on, determined to keep her from getting away.

God, Hattie was strong! He thought, digging his heels into the carpeting. To hell with the weak, old lady routine, the old girl practically dragged him through the door.

"Hold on. I just want to talk with you." The sun's summer rays blinded Matthew, but he held his grip. He lifted a hand to shield his eyes and blinked repeatedly until his vision cleared.

Breasts heaving, Hattie halted. Her eyes narrowed to angry slits and shot daggers at him. Far from convinced, her militant expression and stance indicated she didn't believe a word that came from his lips.

Approaching the pair, Jacob added in a cool, professional tone, "Truthfully." He wedged himself against the opposite side of Hattie. "We're not the police. After we're done, you can go. I promise."

"Who are you? And why should I believe you?" Her brows bunched together as she studied one man than slid to the other, sizing them up.

Matthew moved closer, glared at her intensely. "I own

Games People Play. That's where you've been downloading software from," he explained matter-of-factly. "At the rate you're going, you'll put my company out of business within the year."

Shocked, Hattie's face fell. She opened her mouth and her lips moved, but nothing came out. After several minutes, she recovered. "I don't know anything about you or your business. As a matter of fact, I've never heard of you." She jerked against Matthew's restraining hand. "Let go of me."

"If you're so innocent, why did you run?" Disbelief oozed from each of Matthew's words.

"Why wouldn't I run? I'm an old lady. Criminals prey on old people," Hattie answered, a sullen expression on her face as she hooked her black bag on her shoulder. "You scared me."

Matthew's gaze was steady. He released his hold on her arm and got in her face. "I don't believe you. I'm no psycho and you know it. You talked with me for nearly an hour. Plus, you didn't have any problems with me when you asked me to watch your computer while you browsed the library."

Hattie snorted, folding her arms across her bosom. "I don't care what you believe. Besides, you weren't watching my stuff, you were snoopin'. Trying to get into my business."

"Damn right. That's my company you're destroying CD-by-CD. And I want it to stop. Now!" He stabbed a finger at her.

"Okay. Let's calm down." Jacob said in a soothing tone, steering Matthew away from the old woman with a hand at his shoulder. "Hattie, we're not accusing you of any wrongdoing. All we need from you is a little of your time. Answer a few questions for us and then you're on your way. Nothing more. There's no hidden agenda."

The tip of her tongue was lodged in the right corner of her mouth while she considered all that Jacob had stated. Her eyes darted suspiciously from one man to the other. "Answers? That's all you want, right?"

Jacob nodded, offering an encouraging smile. "Correct."

"I can leave after you've asked your questions?"

"Correct."

"What if I don't have the answers you're looking for? Will I still be able to leave?"

"Absolutely," Jacob answered.

Matthew frowned. "Wait a minute, how do we know she'll tell the truth? Why should we believe her?"

Jacob turned his body, so that Hattie couldn't see him and whispered, "You said earlier that you didn't believe she was the mastermind behind this. Are you changing your mind?"

"No. She can barely operate a computer. Plus, she was using instructions to download. And I don't believe she would have been so free with me if she had more to lose."

"Fine." Jacob slapped Matthew on the back. "We'll talk to her. Then I'll follow up everything she says. We'll know what's true and what's not."

"In the meantime, she could screw up royally. Have you thought of that possibility?" Matthew whispered back.

"Yes, I have. Unfortunately, Hattie is the only lead we have and I plan to make use of her. Like anything else, we'll have to weigh and check the info. But, we have to find out everything we can before we let her go. We are not the police. We can't hold her on any charges."

Matthew ran a hand back and forth across his chin, frowning. "I'm not liking this at all."

"Relax. I've got it covered." Jacob turned back to Hattie and smiled. "Sorry."

"What type of guarantees am I going to receive?" Hattie shifted her weight from one foot to the other, stalling, as she continued to try and gauge the truth of their words. "How do I know you won't sucker me into talking, then put me in jail?"

"We won't," Jacob answered.

"That's not good enough."

Matthew asked, "What do you want?"

"I want something in writing."

"I'm not giving you any—"

"Mattie," Jacob waved a halting hand in Matthew's direction. "When we go inside, we'll write something up."

Hattie nodded. "After you sign something, I'll talk."

Matthew loomed over her in a menacing fashion and said in his most ominous tone, "Don't get smart. You may not be our target, but you were stealing from a major corporation."

"Enough with the threats. We're here to try and figure things out." Again Jacob stepped in, pushing Matthew aside. "As long as you keep your word and answer our questions, things will be fine."

Matthew wiped the back of his hand across his sweat-beaded brow and opened the door to the library. A gush of cool temperature-controlled air made goose bumps rise on the surface of his skin.

"It's too hot out here. Let's go back inside. We'll sit down like civilized people and talk." With a hand at Hattie's elbow, he guided her through the stacks to the workroom. Jacob followed at a slower pace.

The cramped space provided privacy. Matthew pulled up a chair and offered it to Hattie. "Would you like anything? Maybe a glass of water, coffee, or soda?" he asked, wanting to make her feel comfortable.

Her eyes moved around the room, then met his multicolored gaze. "Soda. Coke, if you have it."

"We can do that. Jay?"

"I hear you." With long strides Jacob moved to the elevator and punched the button. "I'll get it. Don't do anything until I get back."

"I'm on it."

Her dark eyebrows rose inquiringly, watching Jacob step into the elevator and the doors shut behind him, she asked, "What is he? Your boss?"

Laughing, Matthew pulled up a chair facing Hattie and sat. "No. He works for me."

"Really." Heavy with sarcasm she muttered, "I would never have guessed."

Matthew shrugged. Hattie's dig missed its mark. "Doesn't matter. We work together. And that's what counts."

That remark ended their discussion until Jacob returned. The 'bing' from the elevator seemed loud in the quiet of the room. Matthew waited as the doors opened and Jacob returned with Hattie's drink.

He grabbed his bottled water on his way to the sink, washed off the top of the can, and dried it with a brown paper towel. Returning to where they sat, he handed the red can to her.

"Thanks," she muttered grudgingly.

"No problem." Jacob pulled up a chair so that he and Matthew were shoulder-to-shoulder, removed the cap from his bottled water, and drank. "Like I said before. We aren't the police. All we want to do is talk."

She popped the tab on the can and took a long, hard swallow. "I'm not answering any questions until I get a signed agreement."

Jacob turned on his laptop and began to type. Once he was done, he printed from his portable printer and handed the sheet to Matthew. "Will this work?"

Reading the page, Matthew nodded. "Yeah." He pulled a pen from his back pocket, signed his name, and handed it to Hattie.

She scanned the sheet, folded it, and dropped it into her bag.

Matthew retrieved it and placed the sheet on the table behind him.

Her eyes opened wide in surprise. "Hey! That's mine!"

"You'll get this back when we're done."

A duel of wills began. Matthew's gaze bored through Hattie, as he silently waited for her to make her move. He could feel her hostility reaching out to him as the room swelled with tension.

"Okay," she muttered after a few taut moments. "Ask your questions."

"Who sent you here to download those files?" Matthew inquired.

"I don't know," Hattie responded, holding the can in both hands as if it were a life preserver. "I've never met 'em. He, she, or them always sends me instructions through the mail."

Frowning, Jacob leaned closer. "You've never met them. How do you get paid?"

"Same way. Through the mail."

"And I suppose it's always in cash?" Jacob surmised.

Hattie nodded.

Rubbing a hand across his chin, Matthew asked, "Don't you find that the least bit strange?"

"Yeah. But I needed the money." She shrugged. "Besides, I never had a problem getting paid."

Jacob's brows drew together in a confused frown while his voice held a hint of disapproval. "You never talked to anybody? No one hired you? How did you get this job?"

"I found a note on one of the bulletin boards in a classroom at school. It said something about making quick cash with a few hours of work each month." Hattie swallowed more of her Coke. "So I sent a note to the guy."

Jacob demanded. "Guy? What guy?"

"He, she, whoever. It could be anybody."

"What school?" Matthew dropped his laced fingers between his legs and searched Hattie's face for lies.

"Wilbur Wright College," she responded.

Jacob rose from his chair and began to pace. He ran his hands through his blond hair, then turned to Hattie. "What did the ad say? Do you still have it? When did you get it?"

"Are you kidding?" She giggled, answering his last question first. "Still have the ad, no. That happened over a year ago. But I do remember a typed poster with a P.O. Box number for the address."

"What about the P.O. Box? Do you still get stuff from it?"

"No." She shook her head. "Somebody else has that box now."

"How do you know that?"

"I got scared after I did the first download. So I mailed a letter to that address, but it came back with no forwarding address."

"Mmmm. You started about a year ago. How many times have you downloaded info?" Jacob inquired.

"Seven."

Matthew sat back absorbing the info. When the time came he'd have a few questions of his own. For now, he felt content to let Jacob take the lead while he listened and digested Hattie's answers.

"Do you always come here?" Jacob tried a different approach.

She shook her head, playing with the soda can tab. "No. One time I went to one of those copying places that has computers. Another time I went to Northwestern's computer lab. That's part of the instructions. It includes where he wants me to go and do the downloads. Everything is always setup. I never have any trouble once I get to the place. The files are always there."

"Let's get back to your boss." Jacob drained his plastic bottle, recapped it, and tossed it in the trash. "Have you ever met anyone? Been contacted by phone? Anything?"

"I told you, no. Everything is done through the mail. There's no return address on the envelopes. Why do you keep asking me the same, stupid questions?"

"It's hard to believe you've done this seven times and never talked to a single soul." Jacob stopped pacing and stared hard at Hattie. A frown marred his suntanned features. "There's got to be more."

"Believe me, there isn't. I download the stuff, mail it, then wait for my money."

Matthew straightened in his chair latching on to that particular statement. "When you get your money, is there anything else in the envelope?"

"No. I hung on to the first instructions and the envelope like it was the Bible. I'll tell you I was scared I wouldn't get paid. But my money came about a week after I mailed that stuff. So, I tossed it. I didn't need it. And after that I never had a problem, so I tossed the letters when the money comes. See, I told you I didn't know anything. And I don't lie."

Matthew sat up in his chair. "Wait. You've said that a couple of times. Mail the CDs where?"

"To a P.O. box." She answered.

"Is it the same one you that was on the flyer?" Matthew continued.

"No." Hattie shook her head. "Some town bordering Indiana."

"Do you have the address with you?" Matthew probed.

"Sure." Hattie reached for her bag and dug inside, pushing things around. "I always mail them as soon as I'm done. Here it is." She waved the slip of paper in the air then drew it against her chest. "I'll be out of a job when I hand this over."

Matthew got the feeling that Hattie was ready to dig in her heels and cause major headaches for them. "Maybe."

"What do I get out of this?" Her head tilted to one side. A sly gleam entered her eyes.

"A get-out-of-jail-free card," Jacob answered. A warning note radiated from his comment.

A stricken look replaced her sly expression.

Matthew offered, "We'll pay you for your time."

Hattie's eyes clouded over. Matthew suspected she was counting dollar bills in her mind. "I can do that."

Jacob snatched the sheet from her hands and wrote down the number. "Thanks."

"Hattie," Matthew said in a low, desperate voice. "Are you sure you haven't had contact with anyone else?"

Shaking her head, Hattie answered, "I've done this seven

times and I've never met a soul. I told you before I don't know anything. I'm sorry."

Jacob studied his friend. "Clear your mind of everything. Concentrate on solving this problem."

Matthew nodded.

"What are you talking about?" Hattie asked, glancing from Jacob to Matthew.

"Nothing. Never mind." Matthew answered curtly.

"We'll get it straightened out. Believe me, I'm working on it. We're one step closer to finding out who's behind this." Jacob turned to Hattie. "You've said that after you download the CDs you mail them to the address on that piece of paper."

"Yeah. That's what I do."

"How long after you mail the disk do you get paid?" Matthew tossed in.

"If I mailed it today I can expect my money within ten days."

Jacob nodded.

"I've got an idea." Matthew stood, rubbed his hand over his face. "This is what you need to do. Let's go back into the library. I want you to finish your download and mail the CDs just like you normally would."

Frowning, Hattie stared at Matthew as if he'd suggested she strip and dance on the tabletop. "But you said giving this stuff to him will ruin your business. This doesn't make any sense."

"Don't worry. I've got a plan. Mail off the CDs. Then Jacob and I will take it from there. All I ask is that you do what you always do and keep that information to yourself."

"For the right amount of money, I'll do it."

"I can do that." Matthew answered, helping her from her chair. They strolled across the workroom back to the bank of computers.

Waiting as Hattie downloaded the rest of the software, disappointment gnawed at Matthew's insides. Instead of having all the answers, he and Jacob were embarking on another wild goose chase.

When he saw that flashing icon in the corner of Hattie's computer screen, he believed they had finally found their thief. Unfortunately, their thief had made a victim of Hattie. And that person continued to evade him and Jacob.

Whether she realized it or not Hattie had provided another piece of the puzzle. The mailing address to where she mailed the CDs and the amount of time it took to get her money narrowed the time they may have to spend waiting for whoever is behind this to show up.

When he'd sat down next to Hattie, he had been confident that they were finally going to resolve everything. That didn't happen. They were a step closer to finding the thief, but not yet.

Twenty-eight

"Is this how we're going to spend the rest of our lives?" Matthew snarled at Jacob, slamming his fist into the palm of the opposite hand. Mail dominated the tiny room. Sorting machines, mail bins, and envelopes of every color in a box of Crayola crayons took up most of the space.

Disgusted, Matthew frowned as he glanced around the back room of Office Extensions, shoved his hands inside the back pockets of his jeans, and said, "After eleven days at the library, all we've done is exchanged one cubbyhole for a smaller one."

"I told you before, this part is tedious." Jacob swallowed a mouthful of bottled water and peered out the small porthole in the door. A bored expression covered his face, yet he seemed to be content to wait. "That's why I always bring my laptop. It gives me something to do during the long hours. If you can't handle it, go back to the office and I'll call you when there's something to tell."

"No can do," Matthew folded his arms across his chest and answered with cool authority. "I'm not going anywhere. You're not getting rid of me that easily. I'm here for the duration. I've come this far; I plan to finish this. Find out who's behind this elaborate scheme."

Whoever walked through those doors and opened mailbox 1564, Matthew planned to be the one that nabbed him. *And what then?* Matthew wondered. At this point, the thief could have picked someone off the street to come and empty the box. Hell, Hattie had been a lackey. Why not send another one to pick up the CDs?

Like a caged bird, Matthew paced the confined space. Worry made his head throb. What would he do if it were Lisa? He loved her, although he'd never said the words to her. And he couldn't imagine his life without her.

Jacob moved across the brown-and-beige tile floor with the bottled water in his hand and sank into a molded plastic chair. "Hattie said that she got paid between five and ten days after she mailed the CDs. We're right on target. It's been a little over a week and the stuff is still here. It's going to happen and soon. Be patient."

"I know you're right. Bear with me. It's been a tough couple of weeks." Matthew picked up a pen from one of the tables and twirled it between his fingers. All the frustration and fear were evident in his evenly spaced words. "I want this done."

"It's going to happen." Jacob took a long swig of bottled water. "Have a little faith." He rose, returned to the door, and glanced through the small, round window. "Whoa!"

"What?" Matthew shot across the room.

"We've got some action." A half-smile touched his lips while he nodded. "I see a familiar face."

"Who?" He stood behind Jacob, shifting from one side to the other, trying to get a glimpse out the porthole. "Who is it? Is—is—is it Lisa?" The words tumbled from his lips as his blood pressure shot through the roof. *Please don't let it be Lisa. Please.*

"No." Jacob chuckled, glanced at Matthew, an I-thought-so expression on his face. "Although it's someone she almost married."

"Brock?"

"You've got it in one." Jacob grinned. "I started checking him out a few days ago."

"Why? What made you suspect Brock?" Matthew ran a hand back and forth across his chin. "Did it have anything to do with the lease that I found in Lisa's apartment?"

"Nope. That produced nothing. His finances were a different story. Something smelled off, weird. The numbers didn't add up." Jacob took another swallow of bottled water.

Pacing around Jacob, Matthew asked in a bone-tired voice, "Is Lisa with him?"

"No." Jacob put a comforting hand on Matthew's shoulder. "He's alone. Don't get too thrilled. Brock could be a gofer just like Hattie. We've got to find out how much he knows and who's involved." He twisted the cap on the half-filled bottled water and placed it on the desk. "Get ready. He's got a key. As soon as he pulls the CDs from the box, we're out the door. I don't want him to slip away."

"I hear you."

"Remember"—Jacob pointed a finger at his friend, warning—"we don't know anything yet. Let's get as many facts as we can."

Slapping Matthew on the back, Jacob said, "Let's go and get this done." He pushed the door open and started for the mailboxes, Matthew followed. "Don't forget, be calm. We need answers."

They strolled out of the back room to where Brock stood sifting through his mail. Matthew saw the bulky package that contained the CDs and his hopes soared that he and Jacob would indeed remedy this problem today.

Matthew greeted in a neutral tone, "Brock."

Stephen turned, a look of total surprise on his face. "James. Summers. What brings you here?"

"You." Jacob moved to the left side of Brock while Matthew took a position to the right.

"Me?" Brock's brows rose questioningly. "You know there are easier ways to contact me. If there's some bit of business that you need my input, I have a telephone."

"That I know, but we wanted to catch you here," Jacob said.

Brock stood perfectly still for a moment. "Why?"

"What've you got there?" Jacob pointed at the pile in Brock's hands.

"This?" Brock lifted the bundle. "Mail, advertisements. Nothing important. At least, not to you or me."

"What do you mean, not to you?"

"While I'm out and about, I'm doing a favor for a friend."

"Oh?"

Brock nodded. "You know Lisa Daniels. This is mail from her box."

Matthew staggered on suddenly weak legs. His heart hammered in his chest and he stumbled back a step before catching him. Although Brock's words had shocked him, his heart didn't believe it.

No! Matthew's mind screamed as he fought down his feeling of despair. Losing Lisa was too high a price to pay. Recovering from the shock, Matthew reevaluated what he'd just heard. No. Lisa wasn't behind this. He believed that with everything in him. Somehow, he had to prove it.

Brock smiled in condescension. Matthew's breath caught in his throat. Brock was a little too smug.

"Lisa opened this box about two years ago. She said she wanted to have it for her business." He shrugged his shoulders and continued, "Yeah. I'm not sure what she's got going, but I know she signed a lease for some office space downtown."

"Lease?" Matthew asked quietly.

"Mmm, hmm." Brock placed the mail on top of his briefcase. "She's definitely an ambitious girl."

That's right, Brock. Keep talking, old boy. Keep talking, Matthew said silently. *You're going to talk yourself into a hole that you can't climb out of.*

"I was hoping to keep her at Games for a few more years. Do you know if she is going into business with anyone else? Soon? Or have a silent business partner, or something? Plan to share her office space with a friend?"

"Not that I know of. But, then again, I'm not in her pocket," he answered flippantly. "My girl has it going on."

That was a blatant lie. When Matthew found the lease in Lisa's apartment, Brock's signature was on the line right above Lisa's. If Brock would lie about something so trivial, what else was he hiding? Why would he lie about such a small thing to begin with?

Jacob had said he felt Brock might be involved. Was this a ploy to throw them off Brock's trail? Maybe redirect the suspicions away from him and toward Lisa? That would explain the quick reference to Lisa.

Matthew believed if the staff would let him check their records, he'd find Lisa's name on the box, just like it was on the lease. But Brock's slick comment made him question if that signature was hers.

With new determination, Matthew realized the woman he loved would never do anything like this. So that left Brock, and Matthew had a feeling that Brock was calling the shots on a lot of things.

He had access to the same information that Lisa had. As a top-level manager of Games, he could request any information and the staff would deliver it without question. At one point, he had been her fiancé. The chances were he knew her password, or knew how her mind worked when she created passwords.

Jacob had learned that Brock's finances were shady, didn't add up. And the dirt kept adding up against him. There was more to the story.

"Mattie?" Jacob touched his shoulder. "You okay?"

He nodded and turned to Brock. "I didn't know you and Lisa were such good friends."

"We've always been friends."

"I'm going by her place on my way home, I'll save you a trip." Matthew held out his hand. "I'll be your delivery boy."

"Thanks for the offer, but I'll take care of it." Brock smiled broadly, but his eyes were watchful. "Besides, I want to see my girl. Don't you guys have anything better to do?"

Lisa's not your girl, Matthew thought. *She's never been your girl.*

"Is Lisa sick?" Jacob picked up the string of Matthew's questions. "Is that why you're retrieving her mail?"

Brock's pleasant demeanor dropped. He took a step away from the pair. "What does it have to do with you? But since there's this big need to know, when I'm on this end of town I stop by her box. No big."

Matthew lifted the mail from Brock's briefcase and sifted through it.

"Hey!" Brock cried. "What is your deal?"

"I don't see Lisa's name on anything, only yours. Is this your box, too?" Matthew answered, turning away from Brock.

"Damn it, man. That's none of your business." He reached for the mail, but Matthew shifted away, blocking his hand.

"Whoa! What it this?" Matthew turned the bulky package with the CDs over in his hand. "It doesn't have Lisa's name on it. Is it yours?"

"Of course not," Brock snatched the package back.

"If not you, who does it belong to?" Matthew ran his hand across his chin.

Brock's head snapped back as if he had been punched. "How would I know?"

"You know what I think?"

"Probably not. But, I don't think that will stop you."

"I think you're trying to pass the buck. Put Lisa on front street to cover your own sorry ass. You're not going to get away with it. I'm not going to let you," Matthew stated.

"Believe whatever you like." Brock opened his briefcase, dropped the bundle of mail inside, and snapped it shut. "As long as you leave me the hell alone."

"You're not going anywhere. I'm not done with you. You know, I would have bought your excuse except you threw Lisa's name into this. All the facts pointed to her and you must have known that. So this was an additional way to stick it to her. I think we're going to change the focus of our investigation from Lisa to you."

"Because I have mail? You're crazy."

Ignoring his comment, Matthew continued, "And then,

you, me, and the police are going to hash out all the lies you've been telling."

"Police? Fellas, listen, I don't know what's going on, but don't involve me in your police mess."

"You know. Pretend all you want. But I'm beginning to understand how your mind works. I would like to know why you're doing this. What's motivating you to throw your career away?"

Chuckling, Brock glanced from Jacob to Matthew and picked up his briefcase. "Obviously, you are suffering from some form of delusion. I don't know what you're talking about. I'm on my time and taking care of personal business. If you gentlemen will excuse me, I'll see you at work."

Matthew stepped in Brock's path. "We're not done."

"Fellas, come on. Can I buy a vowel here, because I haven't got a clue what you are talking about."

"You know exactly what I'm talking about."

Brock took an additional step away from the men. There were only a few feet between him and the door. "I told you, I don't know what you're talking about."

Jacob slipped behind Brock, blocking the door with his body.

Matthew dipped his head toward Brock's briefcase, adding triumphantly, "We know about the CDs."

Brock took another step away from Matthew, creating several feet of space for himself. He smirked at Matthew. "I still don't know what you're talking about." His eyes had that trapped-like-a-rat expression.

"We've followed the trail this far and now we know you're somehow involved."

Brock placed a finger to his lips, than said, "Okay, I'll play along. What do you think I'm involved in? I told you, I'm picking up mail for a friend."

Using the briefcase like a battering ram, Brock bashed Jacob in the gut, sending him crashing through the door's glass. Jacob lay motionless on the hot concrete.

"Jay!"

Turning, Brock swung the briefcase high in the air, smashed it into Matthew's head, sending him flying against the wall. Matthew hit the floor hard.

Dazed, Matthew saw a fuzzy Brock speed out the door, cross the street, and disappear in the crowd. Both men stumbled to their feet on unsteady legs. Blood trickled down Matthew's face from a gash over his eye. Jay's clothes were covered in glass.

After giving the police a report and allowing the EMS crew to treat their cuts and bruises, Matthew and Jacob sat in the back room of Office Extensions.

Matthew watched Jacob pick glass from his clothes. "I take it you didn't find a clue about where Brock was headed."

"No. I looked up and down the street but Brock had disappeared in the crowd." Jacob's hand sliced through the air. "Found nothing."

"I checked the opposite way. Didn't see a thing. I even called his place." Matthew shrugged. "No Brock."

"Brock won't go home. He'll find some place to hang out until he's sure he has a way to get out of town."

"What about Lisa?"

"What about her?" Jacob asked.

"If Brock was willing to throw her name out and use her, is he above hurting her to get what he wants? Is she safe?"

"I don't know. Possibly."

"That's not good enough. We've got to get to her right now."

"Mattie, let the police take it from here. We've found your crook and now that we know it's Brock I can track his sales and get your buyers. You'll get your money back. Or at least be able to prosecute." Jacob waved his hand in a gesture of dismissal. "It's done. After all our hard work, it's time for the police. They have more resources and better ability to form a net to catch Brock."

"That's not the most important thing anymore. I don't think it ever truly was."

Turning to Matthew, a curious expression in his eyes, Jacob asked, "What more is there?"

"Lisa."

"We're back to her," Jacob drew in a deep breath. "Let it go, Buddy. You heard Brock. She's the one who sent him here."

"No. I don't believe that."

"And I don't either. That's why you followed my lead when I questioned Brock about his relationship with Lisa. Something felt wrong."

Breathing hard, Matthew reminded, "It's not fair to leave her out to fry with Brock. Look what he did to us. He might hurt her."

"I'm sorry. This is out of my hands."

"No, it's not. And we're not giving up."

"It's pure and simple. If she's in this with Brock, she's toast."

"Hell, no!" Matthew yelled, unable to control himself and sick of the whole mess. "I'm not going to let that happen. We have to protect her. Brock could show up on her doorstep and hurt her."

Tossing the book bag on the table, Jacob turned to his friend. "Matthew, let it go."

"No can do." His cell phone began to ring. He fished it out of his pocket and glanced at the screen, recognizing the number. "Wait," he said to Jacob. "Let me answer this. It's Lisa." They talked for several minutes, and then he disconnected the call.

"Something's wrong, man. I'm going to her place and make sure she's okay. Are you coming with me?"

"No. I'm going home," Jacob grabbed Matthew's shoulder with one hand and shook him. "Move on."

"I can't," Matthew admitted in a desperate whisper. "I won't," he added in a firm, determined tone. "I love her."

"Shit. Matthew, what are you doing? I told you not to fall. You should have protected yourself better."

"Too late. It happened. And there wasn't a thing I could do about it. You're my friend, right? Then come with me." He jerked a thumb to the door. "Help me. Help her."

Twenty-nine

"Hold on a minute," Lisa responded to the soft tapping on her apartment door, as she hummed along with Phyllis Hyman's, "You Know How to Love Me."

She hoped it was Matthew because she really wanted to talk with him. Discuss their future and feelings. After the night they made love in her apartment Lisa couldn't deny her feelings anymore and needed to tell him everything.

Hurrying down the hallway, she unlocked the door and turned the knob. The door swung open and her warm smile of greeting turned sour.

Momentarily stunned, the pleasant feelings she had been experiencing were immediately wiped away when her brown gaze clashed with cinnamon-brown eyes. What brought Stephen Brock to her door?

Lisa stretched an arm across the doorway, barring his way into her apartment. Whatever he wanted, he knocked on the wrong door. "Stephen? Why are you here?" She asked in a tone that lacked warmth.

Staring pointedly at her arm, he answered in an emotionless voice that chilled her. "Welcome to you, too."

"What do you want?"

Ignoring Lisa's question, Stephen pushed his way past her. He knocked her arm from the door frame and disappeared into the living room.

Lisa stormed after Stephen, ready to kick him out. Her footsteps slowed as she pondered the subtle differences in him. Shocked by the rumpled and wrinkled state of his tailored suit, her steps slowed. Stephen paid particular attention to his appearance and would not leave his house unkempt.

From her living room doorway, she stopped and her fingers played with the gold chain at her neck. They weren't friends and she had no loyalties to him. Something was very wrong. Stephen lounged casually on her sofa, waiting for her to join him.

The tension grew stronger and tighter with each moment. Although Lisa preferred to not get involved, she felt certain Stephen planned to educate her on all the intimate details of what brought him to her door.

"I've got to talk with you," Stephen explained in a desperate tone that couldn't be masked. "And it's got to be now."

A knot formed in her stomach as fear grew hot and quick within her. *Be careful,* she warned silently. This could be another one of his schemes. Reluctantly, she entered the room and made her way to the stereo. Her movements were stiff and awkward as she switched off the music. Warily, she scooted across the room.

Watching her approach, he quite openly studied her. "You seemed awfully eager to answer the door until you found me on the other side. Expecting company, are we?" he mocked. Icy contempt flashed in his eyes, simultaneously a muscle jerked at the corner of his mouth. "As if I need to ask?"

Anger seized her, but common sense whispered a gentle warning in her head. Whatever her plans, they didn't involve him. "Say what you have to say, then go."

Eyes, flat and dead as a stone, stared back at her from Stephen's face. Sweat beaded on his forehead and his hands shook. The well-groomed man she knew would never allow his appearance to get this shabby. *What could possibly have happened?* she wondered.

"What's going on?" Putting a bit of distance between them, Lisa perched on the arm of the chair at her desk. "You look as if you've been running from the police."

He chuckled. But no warmth reflected from his eyes. "It's interesting that you used that phrase."

Her eyebrows flew up. "Oh?" This sounded pretty bad.

"Mmm, hmm." Flashing his pearly whites at her, he said, "There's a problem that I believe you can help me with."

Don't try to charm me, she thought. *Those days are long gone.*

"I'm not going to help you with anything. You haven't been very cooperative on that lease situation. Why should I help you?" Lisa stood. "This conversation is over. We'll talk after you keep your promise."

"Forget that damn lease," he hissed between clenched teeth. "Right now, that's the least of my concerns. I want you to focus on Games."

She frowned, parroting, "Games?"

"Yeah. On Matthew, if you need me to be more specific."

A dozen questions filled her head and she couldn't hold them in. "About what? How is Matthew involved and what is he involved in? What did you do, Stephen?" She stood and moved close to the sofa, examining him with suspicious eyes. "What's going on?"

"There's some stuff going on and Matthew thinks I'm behind it."

Her pulse beat erratically as more questions raced through her brain. "What kind of stuff? What did you do?"

"Nothing you need to concern yourself with." He skated over her first question and ignored the second. "I can't go into details right now. But, I can assure you it'll be fine. You won't get into any trouble."

Spoken like a true con artist. She laughed and shrugged. "I won't get into any trouble. Those are your famous last words. Let me add my own to them. No can do. I won't help you. I don't trust you. This is your mess and you better find another way to clean it up."

Moving to the edge of the couch, Stephen reached for her hand. Lisa shook him off.

"Look, you won't be involved in anything illegal. James

misunderstood my actions and I need a go-between to calm him down, until I can prove my case."

"Prove your case?"

"Yeah. Just listen. Right now he's too angry to listen to me. But I know you've got the clout to make him understand."

Shaking her head, Lisa answered, "I'm not involved in this and it's going to stay that way. You're talking to the wrong girl. I can't help you. I don't have any superpowers with Matthew."

"That's where you're wrong." His brown eyes hardened. She felt his hot breath on her face when he leaned close to her. "I don't have time to debate or persuade you. You are going to help me. That's it."

Lisa heard the desperation in Stephen's voice and wondered at its origin. Standing, she said, "It's time for you to leave."

Stephen grabbed her arm as she passed the sofa. "Not yet." He softened his voice. "Look, I'm not asking for much. Just a little cooperation."

She tried to shake off his hand, but he held firm. "There's no reason for me to help you. You deserve nothing. And nothing is what you're going to get. We're done here. Go."

"We're far from done. I'm not leaving until you've agreed to help me," he stated, jumping to his feet and following her down the hallway to her door. "You must have some influence with the man. Hell, you're sleeping with him."

She gasped. Her sleeping partners were none of his business. "Leave! Now!" Lisa demanded, pointing toward the door. "I've said it before and I'll say it for the last time, if I did have any influence with Matthew, I wouldn't use it. I'm not getting in the middle of your mess. It's time you handle your business."

Stephen snatched her hand away from the doorknob and swung her around to face him. Like a cornered rat, the fear in his eyes shocked her, rendering her speechless for several seconds. "Listen to me. I can't go to prison."

"Prison?" she echoed. "Prison? For what? What have you done, Stephen? Come on, tell me all of it."

"You want all of it. Here you go. Matthew found out that I'm the one stealing software from the company and selling it on the market."

Surprised by his admission, her lips parted. Recovering, she demanded, "Stealing! Have you lost your mind?"

"That's beside the point." The lines of worry deepened between his eyes. "You've got to help me. I'm not going to prison."

Warding him off with a raised hand, she stepped away from him. "You should have thought of that before you got yourself into this situation. I can't help you. You're on your own."

He pointed a finger in her direction. "You're going to talk to him and convince him that it would be in his best interest to let me walk."

"No."

Smiling, Stephen returned to the living room, sat on the sofa, and waited for her to follow. "Come on, Lisa." He patted the cushion next to him, a smug glint in his eyes. "Have a seat. We've got to work out our strategy before Matthew gets here."

"No." She answered from the doorway. "You can sit here as long as you like, but I'm not going to help you."

The tip of his tongue swept across his bottom lip. "Remember that P.O. box you opened down in Fairfield?" His voice, though quiet, had an ominous quality.

The sudden shift in conversation caught her off guard. Wary eyes searched Stephen's face for some hint to his true meaning. "Yeah. What's that got to do with me?"

"Well, I never closed it." Stephen placed his elbows on his knees and rubbed his hands together. He reminded her of a cat playing with a mouse before he pounced. "Today when I went to pick up my mail, Matthew was there waiting for me."

"Why would Matthew care about a mailbox we set up over a year ago? Come on, Stephen. There's more to this story. You might as well tell me now."

"I didn't know it at the time, but Matthew was on to me."

"Good."

"Not really. I made sure he knew you were involved. That you were working with me from the beginning."

Words formed in her mind, but refused to come out. "You liar."

"Yeah, and? Your name is on the mailbox. We were going into business together. Plus, we signed a lease together." He rubbed his hands together and grinned at her. "Connect the dots."

"I don't care what lies you told him. I'll tell Matthew the truth and he'll understand."

He laughed out loud. "Have you always been this naïve? When I get through with you, Matthew will call me the hero and you the villain. That is, unless you help me."

She should have closed that damn box. When they split, she should have put an end to any past links with Stephen. As well as being a crook, he was a blackmailer. And this was payment time. If she let Stephen suck her into his scheme, she'd end up in jail. And he'd probably walk away without a problem.

Lisa caught her bottom lip between her teeth. "What's your point?"

"I'll make it simple." He shrugged. "If you don't help me, he'll learn that you were in on this with me."

She loved Matthew and he meant the world to her, but she refused to let her life be ruled by a threat. It was time to call Stephen's bluff. Either Matthew cared enough about her to believe her, or not. But she needed to stand tall.

Studying Stephen's smug face, a sliver of apprehension made her resolve waiver for a moment. "Go ahead." Lisa challenged with a shrug. Underneath the calm words, her insides were doing the tango. "Matthew won't believe you." *I hope.*

"That's were you're wrong." Stephen spoke softly, but alarmingly. "I've already planted the seeds of doubt. It's just a matter of watering my crops, then watching them grow."

Shutting her eyes, Lisa counted down from ten trying to relieve the tight sensation squeezing her heart. Exhausted by Stephen and his games, she drew a deep breath and let it out slowly before plunging ahead.

"I won't help you. You can do whatever you please. My days of being under your thumb are over. I'm not going to let you use me anymore."

He stared at her and then burst out laughing. "Brave words. Can you back them up?"

"Try me," Lisa answered with supreme confidence, feeling the tightness in her chest begin to recede. She checked her watch, picked up the telephone and punched in a number. "Let's see who comes out on top, shall we?"

"Who are you calling?" he asked in a tense, clipped voice.

Lisa put her hand over the receiver and answered, "Matthew."

Stephen frowned. His expression grew hard and resentful. But, for once he kept his mouth shut.

"Hi. It's Lisa. Are you busy? Good. Can you drop by for a few minutes?"

"Is everything okay," Matthew asked.

"I think so. But, I need to see you, right now."

"Lee, what's going on?"

"Mmmm. I can't go into it over the telephone. But I need you here as soon as you can make it."

"I'm on my way."

"Good."

Switching off the phone, she slid it onto the cocktail table, leaned comfortably into the soft leather, and muttered in a pleased voice, "He's on his way."

"You're bluffing."

"No need," Lisa answered, crossing her legs.

"You're making a big mistake."

"Maybe so. Maybe no." Lisa tilted her head from side to side. "We're about to find out, aren't we?"

"So, you like the idea of going to jail."

"Not at all. But I dislike being under your thumb even more. It's time to put an end to your threats and you."

"You can't win against me." He smiled, as if dealing with a temperamental child.

"I wouldn't take bets on that if I were you. One way or another, this ends today."

Stephen's gall amazed her. Barging into her home uninvited, demanding her help, then threatening retaliation when she refused. He could be a real pain when he felt like it.

Her days of playing the worm on Stephen's fishing hook were over. He could do what he wanted. It was time to start living again. This was the best way to start fresh.

She hadn't lied; Matthew was on his way. How he'd react to Stephen's visit was a mystery.

There was the possibility that she might end up in jail, but she didn't believe this. Matthew knew her. He couldn't possibly believe Stephen's lies.

Watching him, her confidence soared. She'd grown stronger, more self-assured, and she believed things would be different for her this time. Although it broke her heart to think of losing Matthew, she refused to live her life under a cloud of threats.

Finally and truly, she would be rid of Stephen. Regardless of how events ended, her life would be hers once more. And if necessary, Matthew and everything associated with him would also be placed firmly in the past.

Thirty

The doorbell chimed. With a pang, Lisa realized the time had come. Standing, she squared her shoulders, linked her fingers together to stop them from shaking, and started across the living room.

Stephen caught her arm as she passed the couch. "This is your last chance."

Lisa flinched at the threatening tone in his voice. *No,* she corrected silently. *This is my opportunity to get rid of you for good.* For his benefit, she planted a brave smile on her face, and shook off his hand before continuing through the living room, down the hallway to the front door.

With a hand on the doorknob, Lisa drew a deep breath and tried to relax. "Everything will be fine," she chanted softly. "Everything will be just fine." She smiled, opened the door.

When Matthew stepped through the door her first emotion was relief. He was here, at least.

He rushed through the door, running a critical gaze over her before asking in an anxious whisper, "You all right?"

"I'm fine," she muttered, looking in his face. Her lashes flew up. "Ohmigosh! Matthew," Lisa cried, touching the bandage at his brow. "What happened?"

He captured her hand between his and kissed the palm. "It's okay. I'm fine. We'll talk about it later." His arm snaked around her waist and drew her against him. She leaned into his body, drinking in the comfort of his nearness as the familiar sense of longing filled her. Heat penetrated her cold limbs at the same time his unique scent mixed with his tangy cologne filled her nostrils.

They parted, reluctantly. He kicked the door shut with his foot as a worried expression clouded his multicolored gaze. "Are you sure you're okay? Your call scared me. I had visions of all types of mayhem," Matthew probed, rubbing his hands up and down her arms.

"I'm fine." Lisa whispered back. Her thoughts returned to the man in her living room. Before anything else, the issue of Stephen needed their attention. "But we've got company," she explained, pointing to her living room.

He glanced past her to the living room and spied Stephen. His eyes narrowed slightly. "That's what I was afraid of. I figured he'd make a stop here."

"Mmm, hmm." Lisa led him down the hallway.

The moment they entered the room Matthew's hands clenched into fists at his sides. "We've got some unfinished business. I still have more questions for you."

"Relax," Stephen responded, and rose from the sofa in one fluid motion to move within feet of where they stood. "Lisa and I needed to talk privately for a bit. I figured you'd show up here eventually." Halting in front of the pair, Stephen stretched out his hand, silently offering it to Matthew. Ignoring the offending appendage, Matthew turned away, moving Lisa behind him.

"Stephen came to ask me for a favor," Lisa explained simply, resting a hand on Matthew's shoulder.

He ran a hand back and forth across his chin. "What in the hell does he want from you?"

"He wants me to convince you to forget about whatever he's done."

"No can do." Matthew impaled Stephen with a hard, uncompromising glare and added, "The police are involved and it's out of my hands. There's only one thing you can do to help yourself."

"Actually, I think there's plenty I can do to help myself."

"Which means what exactly?" Matthew asked softly.

"I can give you everyone involved, the gofers and buyers," he stated smugly, looking at Lisa. "Don't you want all of it in a neat little package? I'm offering you the mastermind behind this operation gift wrapped with a beautiful bow."

Matthew touched the bandage on his forehead and said, "You weren't so agreeable a couple of hours ago. What changed your mind?"

"Prison doesn't suit my personality or lifestyle. I'm ready to make a deal."

Lisa glanced from one man to the other. "Then, it's true? Stephen stole from you?"

"Yes," Matthew confirmed. "I'm fighting to keep my company out of the financial fire."

She gasped, staring at Stephen. "Financial fire! How could you do something that could hurt so many people?"

"Easily! After the crap I took." Stephen exploded. "You don't know anything. This had nothing to do with money."

"Then what was it about?" Matthew prompted. "Why would you throw away your career and reputation?"

"Career? Career!" Stephen's lips twisted into a cynical smile. "Shit, I don't have a career. At least, not at Games. John Mitchell made sure of that."

"Mitchell?" Matthew stared at Stephen as if he'd jumped out a window.

"How?" Lisa queried. "Mr. Mitchell gave you your start. What could he have possibly done to cause you to treat him this way?"

Stephen's eyes glowed with impotent rage as angry words spilled from his lips, "Let me tell you about your John Mitchell. That old fraud lied and cheated everyone. He used me to get this pitiful company back on track, make it appear profitable so somebody would buy it. All the while he promised to give me first crack at buying it when he retired."

Lisa stood frozen, watching the play of emotions on

Stephen's face. How could she have loved someone with so much hate in his heart?

"Mitchell knew I'd do just about anything to own the business. So he dangled that particular carrot just out of my reach for damn near a year. He kept telling me if I'd help him get things back on track I'd be in line for a piece of the company. I worked my butt off, went the extra mile to have the first chance to buy it, saved every penny to make an offer. My future looked pretty good. At least I thought it did. Then I found out what a bastard Mitchell truly was when he sold everything to him," he snarled, thrusting an angry thumb at Matthew. "The great Matthew James. Mr. Big Man. Someone he didn't even know. I earned the right to make a bid. I paid my dues." Stephen's eyes seethed with hatred and he slammed his fist against the palm of his other hand. "And all the time he refused to listen to my offer."

Lisa shook her head. "There's more to this. You must have misunderstood. I'm sure Mr. Mitchell had his reasons. He doesn't use people," she insisted, not bothering to hide her disbelief. "Have you ever considered the possibility that he might have been trying to protect his employees? Being certain that their interests were secure."

"Mitchell cheated me out of my chance," he answered in a voice heavy with sarcasm. "The only person John worried about was himself. I'll give him credit. He was no fool. Mitchell put all of his eggs in a row in case his deal fell through with Mr. Big Man."

Stephen turned to Matthew, allowing all the loathing he'd hidden for months to blaze from his eyes. "Once you took control things got worse. Your condescending attitude made me want to strip you of everything. I hated you then and I wanted you to fail. You didn't deserve this company. So each time I made a sale, it put me one step closer to getting what I wanted and getting rid of you. When you got tired of fighting a losing battle and it was all over I could pick up the pieces and buy it for little or nothing."

Matthew stepped forward. "That won't happen because

I'm on to you. Jacob and I have tracked you and have the evidence we need to put you away."

"How could you even think of doing something like that?" Lisa cried. "It's so cruel. What were you thinking? There are people with responsibilities, homes, and children. You planned to ruin their lives for your personal vendetta? What kind of man are you?"

"A businessman."

"No. A businessman cares about his company and the people who work for him. You don't care about anything but yourself. You're nothing. A loser." Shaking her head in disgust, she stared at him sadly. "I never knew you, did I?"

"You knew enough." Stephen smiled nastily, glaring at Lisa with such contempt it sent her pulse racing. "Just as I know the intimate details about you."

Lisa's heart galloped, as she took a step away from the cruel expression in Stephen's eyes. The time had come. He was going to implicate her in the thefts.

"I think I'll start with Matthew." Stephen turned to the other man, a smug grin on his lips. "Did you know your boy here was on to me?"

Lisa's expression remained watchful.

"When I picked up my disks he was there. Matthew and his buddy, Jacob." Stephen laughed with malicious intent. "Good old Matt expected to see you right there with me. He believed you and I were in this together."

Lisa turned to Matthew, expecting him to deny Stephen's accusation. "Matthew?" Taking a step closer to him, she touched his arm. He flinched away, maintaining his silence.

"Go on, tell her, Mr. Big Man. Tell her how you and your computer nerd thought she was involved. I bet that's why you started romancing her, while you were trying to figure out what was going on. Don't forget the lease agreement?"

"The lease." There was a confused note in her voice. "How do you know about that?"

Matthew's eyes darted away. "I-um-um. I saw it in your desk drawer and I read it."

"Ohmigosh!"

"I'm sorry." Matthew reached for her. She dodged his hands, wrapping her own arms around herself as if she were cold. Indeed, she was.

"Now, it's your turn." Stephen stared hard at Lisa. "You think you know her? The one who's been keeping a very important secret from you for months." He chuckled maliciously. "I wonder how much respect you'll have after this. I dumped her because—"

"No," she cried, stepping in Stephen's path. The idea of Matthew learning this particular secret from anyone but her ripped her insides apart.

"Get out of my way!" Stephen demanded, pushing Lisa aside. She landed hard against the wall, winded.

"Don't touch her, you bastard!" Matthew yelled, grabbing Stephen by the collar. Matthew slapped the other man back and forth across his face until he bled.

Grabbing Matthew's arm, Lisa held tight until his black rage subsided. "Stop! Stop!" She chanted. "You'll kill him!"

Stunned, Matthew dropped Stephen to the floor like yesterday's underwear. "What does he know? You tell me. I don't want to hear any deep, dark secrets from him."

Matthew was right. This should come from her. This was her opportunity and she planned to use it. "I can't have babies."

"What?"

Cold hands gripped her spine, as her fears became reality before her eyes. *Ohmigosh!* She thought, tears pooled in her eyes. *I'm not going to be able to pull this off. I've lost him.*

From the corner of the room, Stephen let out a hoot of laughter. "I didn't think she had the balls. Told you, you didn't know her. I guess neither did I."

Matthew dug in his pocket and pulled out his cell phone. "Jacob, he's here. Come up and get him." Returning the phone to his pocket, he turned to Lisa and said, "After Brock's gone. We're going to talk."

Thirty-one

Confused, Lisa wandered aimlessly around her living room, experiencing a gamut of emotions. "Is it true?" she asked in a chilly tone. "Did you come on to me, ask me out so that you could check me out? Spy on me? Because you believed I stole from you?"

"Lisa, you've got to listen to me. I didn't want to do this—"

"Why didn't you ask me about the lease? How did you find out about it? About any of it?" Lisa asked in a dead calm voice, watching him from across the room. Although she gave the appearance of having everything under control, in truth she felt as if she'd been gutted with a knife. All of her feelings were spilling out in front of her.

Matthew shoved his hands inside his pockets and stared at the floor. "Remember the day I came to your office for a demo?"

She nodded.

"I noticed how protective you were of that blue folder. When my car got smashed up in your parking lot, I went in your desk for a pen and saw it."

"Who gave you permission to look at my private property?"

"Please understand, I was trying to clear your name."

Hands spread wide, she asked, "Did it ever cross your mind to ask me? Give me the benefit of the doubt because of my years of service?"

"Lisa, please," he moved around the room to stand near

her. "I wanted to tell you. Ask you about everything. Believe me, I never wanted to keep something this important from you. But Jacob said we had to be careful. He didn't want to tip off the ones involved."

"And that included me."

Matthew's face became somber. He lowered his head, stared hard at the carpet, and answered, "Yes."

"I see," Lisa mumbled, unconsciously twisting her hands together. Truly, she didn't see a damn thing. Her head ached with questions and doubts, but no answers.

"Trust me—"

Her voice rose to a shriek, "Trust you? Why should I?" Not after what she'd just learned.

"My hands were tied. I couldn't say anything to anyone. It was killing me," he explained in a dead voice.

"You didn't trust me. You believed I was capable of stealing from your company. I opened my life to you. My home, my body," Lisa cried over her choking, beating heart. "While all the time you were searching for a crook."

"I'm sorry," he reached for her. She dodged him, hurrying to the opposite side of the room. "I know it wasn't the best thing to do. I'm responsible for over a hundred employees. And their future depended on how well I handled this situation. It was wrong of me to not trust you. It tore me up to have to do the things I did. But I had to protect everyone. They had to be my first priority. My feelings played a poor second. There was no other way."

"Protect them from me," she squeezed her eyes shut and whispered.

"Protect them from whomever was stealing," he corrected. "And I didn't know who that was."

Opening her eyes, she saw a hard, calculating man and the man she'd learned to love. "Why was I a suspect?"

"You had the security level to go anywhere in the system."

Torn by conflicting emotions, she hesitated. "Then why didn't you just move me? Or arrest me? Games is your company. You had the authority to do anything you wanted. Why keep me in that position?"

"It wasn't that simple. We needed to know the buyers, who they sold to. Jacob's still working on that end of the deal. That's the only way we'll be able to prosecute."

Shaking her head, Lisa folded her arms across her chest and paced the room.

"Lisa, we were investigating other people." Stopping her in her tracks, he explained. "Dale Smith, a couple of guys from the IS, and Human Resources were investigated. Even your friend Cynthia became a suspect. But your password and security code came up a couple of times as part of the path. The way the software was funneled through the company's e-mail and Internet pointed to you."

"You believed this? After everything we did together." She raised her eyes to the ceiling and shook her head, searching for some way to understand how he could think this way about her and still make love with such emotional intensity. "I never thought that when I let you into my life you were investigating me, using me. Obviously, it was all a lie."

"I never used you. My feelings for you were getting in the way of my doing my job. I was walking a tightrope of hell. Do you understand me, it was pure hell."

"That's why you always had so many questions for me. That invitation for lunch at the hospital and the day at the museum, that was part of your plan, wasn't it? You wanted to get close." Then very quietly she mumbled, "Boy, was I stupid."

"You're not stupid. You know me. I'm the man who loves you. Whatever your secrets, I love you."

There was a time when his declaration would have brought her such joy, peace. But not now. Not after the way he'd deceived her.

"My life is an open book," she reminded him. "I didn't hide anything from you."

"Didn't you? What did Brock say? Secrets," Matthew reminded. "I'm not the only one with secrets."

"What are you talking about?"

"The question is, what was Brock talking about?"

All the fight went out of her. Matthew was right. She hadn't been completely honest. There were doors she kept locked against his prying eyes. They both had secrets that they had kept from the other. But she refused to apologize just yet.

"It's time," he said, placing his hands on her shoulders. "Come on," he steered her to the couch. "No more secrets. Talk to me. I want to know everything. And I'll do the same."

Lisa promised herself that she would tell him and now that the time had arrived, it was damn hard to do. "Just before Stephen and I were supposed to get married I went to my gynecologist because I was having some unusual bleeding. The doctor found endometriosis and told me I would have difficulty getting pregnant," she added in a small, miserable voice. "If I ever conceived."

"What else?" Matthew prompted.

"When I told Stephen, he broke our engagement." She turned away from Matthew before the light of pity filled his eyes. "He said he didn't want half a woman."

Warm fingers drew hers away from her face and linked them with his. Lisa looked at this man she loved with all her heart and felt fear. Matthew's expression gave nothing away. His eyes were dark and unfathomable. Did he understand or even care about what she's just told him?

"Is that why you kept pushing me away?"

"Partly. I was trying to protect myself. Stephen hurt me in ways I can't express. And I was afraid you'd do the same if I let my guard down."

"Lisa, I'd never do that to you." His voice cracked. "I love you. Trust in that, if nothing else."

She shrugged and looked away. "When we first met, you always talked about friends and family. One thing was clear to me: you wanted a family of your own."

"Things weren't easy between us back then." He stroked a

finger across her cheek. "I was so afraid that I would lose you because of the stuff at Games. I should have made it easier for you to come to me."

"It wasn't your fault. I was afraid after the way Stephen had treated me. I was afraid."

"Look at me." Placing a hand under her chin, Matthew forced her to look at him. "I'm not Brock. You should have known that."

"I did. But I was still afraid. I didn't know how to tell you. What could I say to you to make you understand? Don't get too involved with me because I can't have babies?"

"How was I supposed to understand when you never gave me the opportunity?" Shaking his head, he looked at her with sad eyes. His usually warm gaze was as hard as stone. "You arbitrarily made decisions about my feelings without knowing what I wanted. Whether or not you can have children is important. I'm not going to lie about that. I'm not taking it lightly. But this is something we should have done together, shared, worked at together."

"I could say the same things about you. You kept important things from me. Made decisions. You believed I was a thief, but you never gave me a chance to defend myself."

"True."

Frustrated, he turned away and ran a hand over his hair. "This has got to end. Now. I'm sorry I didn't talk to you and let you know the truth. I can promise that it will never happen again. Forgive me and let's move on. If you can't do that, then I'll leave now and I won't bother you again. The only way we're going to move on is to forgive."

With everything she'd learned today, it hadn't changed the way she felt about him. She still loved him and didn't want him to go out of her life. Maybe it was time for her to take a chance, bury all the pain and sadness Stephen caused, and reach out for this new life that seemed so frightening, yet enticing. To do like Matthew suggested, forgive and move on.

"I don't want to lose you," Lisa admitted. "Please be part of my life."

"Thank you," he muttered, drawing her into his arms. "I love you, period. And I want you with me, always." He held her so close she could feel the erratic pounding of his heart against her chest, then she thought of nothing more than the erotic sensations he stirred as he kissed her dizzy.

Lisa's heart leaped with joy. She felt almost embarrassed at how happy his words made her. Then immediately her doubts rushed back flooding her with old uncertainties.

She moved out of his embrace and asked hesitantly, "You . . . love . . . me?"

"I love you!" he repeated, pulling her back into his arms and sealing her lips with his. The taste of Matthew chased away all the shadows. The lingering doubts fled in the face of his declaration. "Now, it's your turn."

"For what?"

"Do you love me?" he asked, a trace of anxiety hidden within the texture of his words.

"Yes, I've already admitted that," she answered simply, unable to deny him the truth.

"Not since we've opened up to each other. Say the words. I want to hear them again."

"I love you."

"Thank God," he sighed. "That's all that matters. We'll work out the rest."

"Are you saying you don't want kids?"

"Oh, I want them," he answered. "But I want you more."

Her breath caught in her throat as she heard the sincerity in his words.

"As far as I'm concerned there's still a big question mark hanging over your inability to have babies. The verdict is still out on you."

"I don't understand."

"Did you get a second opinion?"

Lisa gave a sheepish negative shake of her head.

He smiled, hugging her. "That's what I thought. You allowed one doctor's opinion to shape your future. I won't accept that. We're going to find the best fertility specialist in

Chicago and let the doc determine the best course to take. Then we're going to get married and do whatever it takes to have our family, and we're not going to exclude adoption."

His optimism was contagious. But Lisa had to give it one more try. "Are you sure this is what you want? Be absolutely sure."

"I don't even want to think about living without you, sweetheart. As long as you love me, that love will help build our family. I love you, Lisa," his voice was husky with emotion. "Now, tell me again."

"I love you, Matthew."

Secure in the warmth of Matthew's embrace, Lisa decided she wouldn't tell him. She would enjoy this special time with him and wait until they consulted the specialist. She loved Matthew too much to commit him to a life without children. If the doctor couldn't help her, then she planned to take the decision from Matthew's hands and leave him.

Thirty-two

Today was D-Day! Lisa thought, sighing heavily. After three weeks of medical histories, blood work, and examinations, they were finally going to learn the results of the tests. All would finally be revealed.

Lisa hadn't slept well last night. The fragile calm that she held on to like a lifeline had been shattered by Stephen's call from the federal prison. Unlike the last time she'd spoken with him, he wasn't threatening her. He was begging.

Matthew had kept his promise and had Stephen prosecuted. She couldn't do anything. He'd chosen this path, now he had to live with it. Greed and power had brought him to this end.

Forget him, Lisa advised herself. *You have more important things to worry about.* Gazing around the tastefully decorated, pale blue walls of Dr. Schuler's consulting office, she frowned. *I hate doctors' offices.* Despite reassuring photographs of babies held in the arms of their proud parents and the cheerful attention of the nursing and office staff, it was still a doctor's office with all of its accoutrements. They all contained the same elements: illness and high-voltage worry.

Her stomach muscles quivered like Jell-O each time her thoughts focused on the worst possible scenario. Dr. Schuler's credentials as a fertility specialist meant nothing. Her and Matthew's dreams for the future could be smashed by a few well-chosen words from the doctor.

Her eyes drifted to Matthew. As promised, he sat right next to her looking relaxed and handsome in a pair of black denim jeans, a Tommy Hilfilger T-shirt, and dark leather sandals minus socks. His quiet strength had been the saving grace in a day that threatened to suck the life out of her. Without a word, he stretched an arm across the back of her chair and began to massage the taut cords at the back of her neck.

I'll lose my mind if I sit here much longer, Lisa thought. With a sudden burst of nervous energy she sprang from the chair and prowled back and forth across the carpeted floor.

She stepped around the desk and her eyes fell upon a photograph. Pensive, she picked up the silver frame, recognizing the beautiful face of Dr. Schuler. Lisa still couldn't believe the beautiful blonde woman in the photo with the face and figure of a model was her doctor.

How interesting, she thought. In addition, a red-haired man of about forty-five sat close to her. Two giggling kids flanked the couple, and Dr. Schuler's expression of loving indulgence completed the scene. Returning the photograph to the desk, Lisa continued prowling the office.

Before sleep overtook her last night, Lisa offered one final, desperate prayer to God. She'd pleaded for a rational explanation to her problem, a simple clerical error or mix-up of files that would put an end to this torture. But deep in her heart, she knew better and if she didn't come to grips with it soon, she'd fall apart before the doctor came through the office door.

"Lee, come sit down." Matthew patted the chair next to him. "You're making me crazy."

She moved away from the desk and resumed the seat she'd vacated only minutes before. Her fingers drummed on the arm of her chair as her eyes moved over the walls, pausing here and there to read the numerous degrees and awards.

Matthew leaned closer. The hint of a smile played across his full sensual lips. His toffee and hazel eyes glowed with admiration and love as they slid from the cap of her auburn hair to her cream-colored leather sandals. His gaze lingered on her fidgeting fingers. "Relax, sweetheart," he whispered close to her ear. Slowly, he reached out and took her hand in his.

His lips touched her cheek, his tongue stroking the soft, supersensitive skin near her ear before moving to the lobe. When he took the flesh between his teeth, she gasped, fighting the multiple sensations he so blatantly created. *Oh, what a clever man.* She knew exactly what he was trying to do. *Keep me otherwise occupied so I won't have time to worry.*

"Just remember, no matter what the doctor says, I love you," Matthew promised. His velvety, husky voice made her insides quiver in response to those magical words. "If kids aren't on the menu for us, we'll adopt. There's always a way if you believe. I believe in us."

He looked so calm, as if everything had already been settled. "Matt—" she began, fumbling over what she wanted to say. Instead, Lisa caressed his cheek with her finger and smiled into his eyes. How she loved this beautiful man. God wouldn't be so cruel to take him from her, would he?

The door opened and Dr. Schuler stepped into the room. Lisa's hand dropped away from his face and returned to her lap. Matthew pulled her hand from her lap and laced their fingers.

"I'm sorry I'm late." Dr. Schuler shook her blonde head. "We're running behind schedule today. I had a delivery," she explained, moving around the room with a stuffed manila folder under her arm. Dr. Schuler stood behind her desk as the faint scent of soap and rubbing alcohol lingered in her wake. A white laboratory coat with her name embroidered above the left breast pocket covered much of her frame.

Her blue eyes rested on Lisa, assessing her with eyes that seemed to see right into her soul. Her soothing, unassuming manner had won Lisa's confidence while they pressed ahead for an answer to her problem.

"So, how are you today?" Dr. Schuler asked, smiling at Matthew and Lisa.

"Great," Matthew answered promptly.

Lisa responded a tad slower, "Okay."

"Good. As you already know, all of the test results have come back and we're ready to discuss how to proceed." Sliding into her chair, Dr. Schuler pulled a pair of black-rimmed reading glasses from her desk drawer and perched them on her nose before opening the folder.

Lisa's heart thumped loudly in her chest. She felt a fine layer of perspiration settling on her forehead. *Breathe,* she instructed. *Breathe.*

"Ms. Daniels," Dr. Schuler began. Her pleasant features turned somber. "I've reviewed your primary physician's medical records and compared them with my own studies. Unfortunately, your previous physician's diagnosis was correct," she stated remorsefully. "You do have endometriosis."

Lisa shut her eyes against the full impact of the doctor's words. She began to shake as ice spread through her veins. Matthew's grip on her hand tightened, willing her to look at him. Refusing, she tugged her fingers free and shifted away, feeling the tears pooling in her eyes. *I won't cry in front of him,* she promised silently.

"But there's good news. Mr. James, your test results were fine," she continued. "Now that we have an idea of what the problem is we can discuss options."

"Wait," Matthew demanded, holding up his hand in a halting manner. As he began to speak, his voice quivered. "Before we discuss anything else, is Lisa in any danger? What is endometriosis?"

"Those are important questions," she stated, sorting through a pile of folders on her desk until she located a black, leather-covered binder. "I have a picture board that illustrates the process," she replied, then manipulated the binder on her desk until it presented a drawing of a woman's reproductive anatomy. She turned the sketch toward them.

"Now, Lisa's condition will cause her some discomfort and

menstrual pain each month. But nothing more severe than that. She can take something as simple as an aspirin to alleviate the discomfort," Dr. Schuler assured him. "But I have to warn you, some patients need much more."

Matthew sighed heavily. "Good. She's always my first concern. Now tell me everything about endometriosis."

"Particles from the endometrial lining of the uterus flow backward through the fallopian tubes into the peritoneal cavity, where they attach and grow," Dr. Schuler explained, using the tip of her black fountain pen to circle the different organs as she spoke. "In Ms. Daniels case, this growth has attached itself to her uterus, making it difficult to conceive."

"So what's next?" Matthew said.

"Well, there are several approaches we can follow," she explained, cautiously. "There's one particular procedure I'd like to recommend. It might be the answer for you. Do either of you know anything about in vitro fertilization?" Turning to Lisa, Dr. Schuler grinned broadly. "I think you're a perfect candidate."

"Excuse me," Lisa stood. "I need to go to the rest room."

Matthew gripped her hand and brought her attention back to him. "You okay?"

Lisa forced a smile on her stiff lips and said, "Fine. Be right back."

"I've got to clear up my face," Lisa muttered, pulling a paper towel from the dispenser. "I don't want Matthew to see me this way."

She should have realized this day would end this way. The morning had turned out so beautiful. Everything Matthew had said had been perfect for this situation and her fears. And yet, all of her fears had come true.

Turning on the cold water, she saturated the paper towel, then placed the cool towel on her cheeks. Even though she'd never allowed herself to hope, hearing the diagnosis out loud and in such a final way had put her over the top. It had taken everything in her to keep from crying before the specialist and Matthew.

Candidate for in vitro, that was a laugh. Who did Dr. Schuler think she was fooling? That was another way of letting them down easy. The only thing she was a candidate for was the useless women farm.

Trying to clear the redness from her eyes, she placed the wet towel over her lids. *Oh Matthew, I can't marry you. It would be cruel and selfish. I'm going to miss you and that optimism that never seemed to die.*

After removing the towel, she inspected her face, searching for any signs of tears. She didn't want Matthew or Dr. Schuler to see that. *Deep breath, Lisa. Deep breath. You know what you have to do, no getting around it.* After they finished with Dr. Schuler, she would ask Matthew to come up to her apartment and they would discuss the doctor's findings. Then she'd tell him she couldn't marry him and send him on his way. It was time to put an end to all these fantasies about marriage and a family.

The only way Matthew would get that family he wanted would be with another woman. It was time for her to step aside and let him have what he needed and wanted. And she wouldn't subject him to a life with her.

Thirty-three

Nine years later . . .

"Really, it's no problem," Mrs. James continued persuasively between sips of coffee while sitting at Matthew's kitchen table. "I'll just run home and pick up a few things. It'll take me about an hour and I'll be back before two."

Slipping the last dish into the dishwasher, Matthew replied, "Mother, it's not necessary. I've got it covered. Besides, I'm a pro at handling my crew. All I have to do is keep them happy and fed until Lisa gets home tomorrow. I'm a professional. I can do it."

That knowing smile spreading across his mother's lips didn't fool him for a minute. "What's so funny?" he asked, wiping off the kitchen counter.

Her eyes sparkled with merriment. "Nothing," Mother's one-word answer carried a wealth of information.

"Okay. If you really want to help us, baby-sit for me tomorrow when I go to the airport to pick up my wife."

"Sure. What time?"

"Her plane gets in at two-forty. I'd like to leave here around one." He removed a football, Harry Potter toy, and a doll from the white-and-black ceramic tile kitchen floor and deposited the toys together in a heap on the breakfast nook floor.

"I'll be here," Mrs. James confirmed.

"Thanks, Ma. That will make life a little easier."

He picked up the scraps of a peanut butter and jelly sandwich from the table and tossed it down the disposal. Grimacing, he shoved his hands under the faucet and rinsed off the sticky peanut paste. "My meeting's been changed to Friday afternoon. By that time, I can turn the kids over to Lisa." He brought his coffee mug to the table and slid into a chair across from his mother.

"I applaud your ingenuity, Mattie. You always seem to find ways to make things work. And that wife of yours has been making quite a name for herself. I plan to talk to her about investing in her company," Mother confessed, nibbling on a cookie. Pride shone through her words. "I couldn't be prouder if she were my own daughter."

"You're proud? How do you think I feel?" He chortled. "At this rate, I may retire and become a full-time house husband and let her take care of me."

"Dad!" cried the little tyrant of the James household.

"And then again, maybe not," he added. Seconds later a curly haired two-year-old moppet flew into the kitchen, followed by a dark haired, green-eyed boy of seven, clutching a plastic soda bottle. "Junior hit me," the moppet accused.

"Junior, did you hit your sister?" Matthew rose from the table and spoke to his son in his best parental tone.

"Yeah," Junior swung the bottle like a sword. "This is my light saber," he explained. Matthew sent a reproachful glare in his son's direction, removed the container from Junior's fingers, and placed the object on the table. He dropped to his knees, eye level with his daughter, and caught her as she threw herself into his arms. Erika's shrieks of outrage swelled to earthshaking proportions along with her huge crocodile tears. *The little fraud,* Matthew's mouth twitched with amusement. *We really must do something about this child,* he decided fondly. She'd give Halle Berry a run for her money.

Pointing a finger in Junior's direction, he said sternly, "You don't hit your sister. She's too little. And definitely not with a bottle."

"But it was plastic," Junior explained rationally.

"Plastic or glass, it hurts. Don't do it again." He swung the toddler into his arms, cuddling her close. The combined scents of baby powder, lotion, and salty tears on her plump cheeks filled him with wonder and love at this amazing little person he and Lisa had created.

"Shh, honey. Daddy's here." He rubbed her back and muttered soothing nonsense into her ear. "Do you want Daddy to rub your brains?" His mouth quirked with humor while his eyes met his mother's over Erika's head. *My child belongs on the stage.* He moved to the counter and ripped a sheet of paper towel from the roll.

Matthew ran his fingers through her hair, searching for injuries. "You'll live," he proclaimed, mopping up her dirty tears. "How about a cookie to make your brain feel better?" He opened the brown ceramic teddy bear-shaped cookie jar.

"Two?" the tiny voice quizzed, obviously expecting to be paid for her performance.

"No. Just one." He answered, offering his daughter a chocolate chip cookie. Determined to instill good manners into his child, he asked, "What do you say?"

"Thank you." She took the cookie from his hand and wriggled in his arms until he allowed her to slip to the floor.

Turning back to Junior, Matthew placed his hand on his son's head. "Son, soda bottles are not for you to play with. They're dangerous. Stick to your toys. There are plenty of them around here." He used the no-nonsense tone he'd mastered over the years. Several seconds passed before Matthew asked, "Okay?"

Head hung low, Junior nodded.

Placing a finger under Junior's chin, Matthew lifted the boy's head, smiled reassuringly into his son's eyes. "Good. Give Dad a kiss and you've got a cookie." Grinning, Junior wrapped his arms around his father's legs, wrestling him to his knees. He landed on top of Matthew's chest, knocking the wind out of him. Junior's small hands crawled up Matthew's chest and neck, tickling each spot along the way. They laughed and tussled for several minutes, before Matthew stretched full length on the floor, feigning defeat.

"Enough. You win," he shouted, throwing his arms wide on the kitchen floor. "Now about that kiss," he demanded, receiving a big juicy kiss in response to his request. Spying Erika on the sideline, he crooked his finger and beckoned her. "You, too," he ordered. Grinning, she ran to him, and gave him a smack on the cheek that left a trail of cookie crumbs on his face.

Getting to his feet, Matthew looked around the room. "Where's Michael and Eric?"

"Watching Pokemon."

"Eww. Don't let your mother know I let you guys watch that stuff, okay?"

"Okay. Can I play on the computer?"

"Yes. And it's 'may I play on the computer,' " Matthew corrected absently. "And take your sister with you. Turn on the other computer so Erika can play. Remember what I told you: no more bottles."

"Okay, Dad."

"Junior, wait a minute before you go. You and your sister pick up those toys in the breakfast nook and take them to your rooms."

"They're not all mine," Junior protested.

"Doesn't matter. Take them upstairs anyway."

Sighing as if he'd been asked to reduce the federal deficit, he picked up an armful of toys. "Let's go, girl."

"I need to check on your brothers," Matthew decided, following the kids from the room. "Mother, I'll be right back."

Returning ten minutes later, he found his mother brewing a second pot of coffee. The scent filled the room, making his mouth water. Expelling a deep breath, he refilled his coffee mug before collapsing back in his chair and gazing at his mother's profile. "So, what's the joke? Why have I become a source of amusement for you?"

"I don't know how to say this."

"Spit it out," he suggested, resting his hand under his chin and watching her semi-hidden smile turn into a full grin.

"You really do have everything under control. I'm sorry for doubting you. I never thought I'd see you this way, so comfortable in your role as a parent. It's endearing."

"Yeah, well, neither did I. Lee and I went through four rounds of in vitro before we got the twins and I promised to enjoy every minute of the time I have with my kids."

Suddenly, the voices of all his children rang out at once. Immediately standing, Matthew hurried to the door.

"Mom, guess what?" One excited voice yelled.

"Hi, Mummy, pick me up," demanded another child. Each excited voice rose above the last, trying to get their mother's attention.

"Ahh, Mom, can't we at least see the end? It's almost time for the commercial." Matthew heard Michael whine.

"Yeah, couldn't we see it, just this one time?" Eric questioned.

Uh-oh. Matthew thought. *I'm in trouble.*

Together, seven-year-old Michael and five-year-old Eric burst through the kitchen door with sullen expressions on their faces. Their mother closely followed them. Matt and Erika brought up the rear of the James family train.

Lisa stood in the doorway. *God, she looked good.* After almost nine years of marriage, she still had the power to take him from soft to hard in thirty seconds flat. Her rust-colored business suit accentuated the brown of her eyes and emphasized her curves, making him want to get her alone as quickly as possible. The familiar fragrance of White Diamonds perfume mixed with Lisa's unique scent drifted through the air and drew him to her like a magnet.

"Mr. James," she smiled sweetly, her eyes flashing with a hint of anger. "Do you know what your children were watching on television when I came in the door? Pokemon." She answered her own question, her voice held a note of reproach.

"I thought you monitored what they watched when I'm away?"

Acting quickly, he took her into his arms settling his lips on hers for a deeply satisfying welcome home kiss. Lifting his head, he whispered. "Hello sweetheart," his voice was husky and deep. "I've missed you."

She smiled at him. "I missed you, too. I took an earlier flight so that I could be home sooner. But that's not going to get you off the hook." Lisa looked around the room at her four little darlings.

"Hi, Carolyn," she greeted, spying the other woman over Matthew's shoulder and wiggling her fingers at her. "Don't tell me Matthew suckered you into watching the kids."

"Actually, no," Carolyn started to explain. "I came by to offer my assistance. But he had it all under control."

One eyebrow quirked, "Did you?" Cocking her head to one side, she flirted openly with her handsome husband.

"Pretty much," he answered smugly. His toffee and hazel eyes twinkled, promising retribution for her teasing.

"Mummy," Erika called, patting her mother's thigh. "Mummy," she cried a second time. "Mummy, I was crying for you."

"Why were you crying, baby?" Lisa asked in her soothing mother tone.

"Matt hit me with a bottle."

"What?" Lisa cried. Her eyes swung to her baby, lifting the toddler into her arms, examining her for cuts or bruises. Now that Erika had her mother's full attention, she was happy. The child snuggled into the crook of Lisa's arm, laying her head on her shoulder, sighing contentedly.

That baby smell always gets me, Lisa thought, rocking Erika to and fro, brushing her daughter's wild mane of hair from her face and kissing her.

Wrapping his arm around his wife's waist, Matthew pulled her against him. The heat from her body penetrated his clothing. He rubbed his cheek in her silky hair. *God, how I've missed you over the last few days.* Looking down at Erika affectionately, he tweaked her nose. "You little snitch," he accused, directing his next comment to his wife. "As you can see, she's fine."

"Did you talk to Matt?"

"Yes, and he understands," he assured her, removing the child from her arms and placing her on the floor.

"Go play," he told Erika, patting her on her bottom.

"I have an idea," Carolyn James announced, gathering her purse. "Why don't you let me take the kids home with me tonight so you two can have a little time together."

"Oh, Carolyn, we can't let you do that," Lisa cried, secretly wishing she could indeed pack them off so she could have Matthew all to herself.

"I insist. They're no trouble and I haven't had them with me in a while. Besides, when was the last time you and Matthew had time alone?".

"I don't know," Lisa hesitated, looking at Matthew for help. "I just got home. I haven't spent any time with my babies. I'm feeling a tad guilty, like a neglectful mother."

Pulling her close, Matthew whispered. "Don't feel guilty, sweetheart. There's plenty of time for them to terrorize you. One night without our monster babies won't harm them or us."

"Well," she muttered, wanting to be convinced.

"If we get rid of the kids, I'll give you a full body massage and I promise I won't miss a spot. I'll follow that by making slow, uninterrupted love to you until morning," he whispered into her ear.

"Mmm, it sounds very promising." Lisa smiled.

"I'm with you on this. Let's see if you can go the distance," he challenged. "Okay, kids, you're going to Granny's tonight. We'll pick you guys up around noon tomorrow."

"Carolyn, thanks." Lisa hugged the older woman. "I don't know what I'd do without your help, juggling family and business isn't easy and you're a lifesaver."

"You're welcome, and you'd do just fine if you didn't have my help." Carolyn rose and picked up her purse.

"Of course, without my cocky husband here, none of this would be possible," she remarked, turning to give Matthew a very special thank-you kiss. "I love you, darling. I don't know if I'll be able to show you how much."